Cedarwood Pride

DOC CEDARWOOD

MEGAN SLAYER

Doc Cedarwood
ISBN # 978-1-83943-892-9
©Copyright Megan Slayer 2020
Cover Art by Cherith Vaughan ©Copyright May 2020
Interior text design by Claire Siemaszkiewicz
Pride Publishing

DOC
CEDARWOOD

Dedication

For JPZ, my editor and my lucky ducks.
You all rock.

Chapter One

"My name is Aiden and I'm not a parent." Aiden stood in front of the support group and laced his fingers together. "I'm the not-so-rare breed called the child of gay parents. I grew up well-adjusted and happy. If my father, Keye, hadn't died, we'd still be a happy family. My other father, Len, decided not to seek out another partner after Keye's passing five years ago. Last year, he decided to try again with a man named Ross. Anyway, I knew I was loved, cared for, I had boundaries, and if I screwed up, my dads and Keye loved me enough to punish me." He swept his gaze around the room. Meeting at the hospital wasn't the norm for the group, but he couldn't complain. They'd been able to come to him and he appreciated the gesture.

Colin Baker stepped up beside Aiden. "He's leaving out the best part." He grinned. "Aiden grew up big, strong and to become a doctor."

"Well, there is that." The tips of his ears burned. He wasn't embarrassed to admit his profession. Being a doctor was in his blood. Sure, he had a good job, but he wasn't much different from anyone else. "I'm here at the hospital and I've put my work number on the business cards in case you or your children have questions. I've been in their shoes and know a lot of how they feel."

He flexed his fingers and waited for questions, but none came. Some of the group members left their chairs and others turned to chat with those around them. He eased away from the people and made his way to the door. His phone hadn't buzzed—good thing. According to the schedule, he was off for the next twenty-four hours, but that didn't mean much. If the emergency room staff numbers weren't up to regulations, he'd be called in until he maxed out his allowed hours. He'd racked up so much overtime that if he were hourly, not salary, the hospital would go broke.

"Good turnout tonight, especially since we scheduled it for a Thursday." Colin straightened the pamphlets on the table, then arranged the various cards. "It's not one of our usual chatty meetings, but the others will be happy to have another resource in you. The kids need to know they aren't alone and can succeed."

"Gage is doing just fine and I guarantee he knows he's not alone," Aiden said. "I've seen his artwork in the children's ward. I'm glad the school teamed up with the hospital to do that for the pediatrics. It's awesome and boosts our morale, too."

"He'll be thrilled." Colin stuffed his hands into his pockets. "You're going to be at the wedding, right?"

"I am." How could he forget the wedding of Farin Baker and Steve Moore? He'd only known Farin since the seventh grade. Everyone in the gay community seemed to be invited to the ceremony. He wished he had a date. Going alone would suck and he despised hook-ups at such events.

"I'm ready to rip out my hair. I never realized how picky my baby brother can be," Colin said. "If it's not the flowers or lack thereof, it's the music or the events at the reception. He's got the whole damn thing organized. There's a time for dancing and one for sitting and being quiet. Who's quiet at a wedding reception?"

"The brother of the groom. It's Farin's day — well, his and Steve's. Let them do it how they want." Not that he knew anything about weddings. He'd never been married and his last relationship had lasted a whole three years. Other guys loved being with a doctor and the paycheck he received, but hated his hours and how much time he was expected to spend away from them. *Maybe I'm dating the wrong men.*

"I keep telling myself that. Jordan tells me the same thing, but I still want to clobber Farin when he goes Groomzilla on us. I wasn't this bad when I married Jordan — at least I don't think so. We walked, we stood, we said I do, then had one hell of a party at the house." Colin shook his head. "I just wouldn't have thought he'd be…like this."

"It'll be over in two days. You'll live." Aiden clapped Colin on the shoulder. "Speaking of days, I have exactly one day off before I'm expected back at the hospital. I'm on for an eight-hour shift on Saturday, so if I'm running late, that's why."

"We'll keep an eye out. Thanks for the heads-up and thanks for talking to the group. Have a good night." Colin winked, then strode away.

Aiden grabbed his jacket from the coat rack. The weight of a twenty-four-hour shift had gotten to him. He wanted to go home but wondered if he'd make it. As he navigated through the halls of the hospital, he waved at a couple of the nurses and, in the foyer, nodded to the elderly woman behind the main counter. The moment he stepped into the chilly October air, he blinked and dragged a long breath into his lungs. Nothing worked to wake him up like crisp fall evenings. Well, nothing like those and a good blow job in the morning, but he wasn't likely to get one. He'd need a boyfriend first. He'd worry about his lack of a partner later. Right now, he wanted to go home, slip into a warm bath or hot shower and collapse for twelve hours straight. Maybe he would meet someone at the wedding or reception.

Maybe hell will freeze over first.

* * * *

Thirty-two hours later, Aiden strode out of the hospital again. Just as he'd guessed, the ER had been short-staffed and had called him in four hours before his eight-hour shift should've started. He rolled his shoulders. His joints cracked and popped. A long groan escaped his lips. *Why can't I meet a good massage therapist right about now?*

He made his way across the staff lot to his car. At least he'd had time to change into his suit before his shift had ended or he'd be beyond late. He checked his reflection in the driver's-side glass. The lines around his eyes were deeper than normal and the crinkles across his forehead were more visible. Christ, he resembled an ogre, not a thirty-five-year-old doctor. *Fuck it.* He had to get going.

Aiden slipped behind the wheel of the car, then sped out of the lot. According to the clock, he had exactly twenty minutes to drive across town to the church before the ceremony started. *Easy. Right?* He turned onto the main road leading away from the hospital. Unlike most hours of the day, few cars were on the thoroughfare. He increased his speed and headed north. A set of headlights blinded him.

"What the hell?" he groused. "Turn the brights down." He swerved to the right, but the vehicle with the LED lights kept coming at him. The closest street lamp illuminated the vehicle. A truck. Aiden yanked the wheel to the right again and was rewarded with a clunk. "Shit," he murmured. The lights went away and, when he checked the rearview mirror, the truck disappeared around the corner.

Aiden's hands shook as he limped his car into the closest lot. He parked in the gravel and left the car to check the damage. He rounded the hood. The scent of burned rubber curled in his nose. He choked back a cough and examined the passenger side of his car. "Fucking hell." He squatted beside the front wheel. "I'm not even sure how to fix this." He touched the deflated tire and bent rim. Getting to the wedding was now going to be even harder. He stood and whipped his cell phone from his pocket. Who was he supposed to call? Most mechanics would be closed by now. He'd have to phone Whit. He groaned. Whit Sherman was a nice man and a decent enough friend, though not dating material. But he was also invited to the wedding, so if he hadn't left yet, maybe Aiden could beg a ride.

Aiden stood on the side of the road. He could've sworn he'd seen the advertisements for an auto mechanic near the hospital. He spotted the neon over the garage and hope blossomed in his chest. If he wasn't mistaken, the sign read OPEN. He retrieved the keys from the ignition and locked the vehicle, then sprinted down the road. "Just don't close before I get there." He pushed himself, pumping his legs and praying. "Please stay open."

Part of him wished he'd seen the license plate number or markings on the truck that had run him off the road. But what would he be able to do? Turn the guy in? How was he going to prove the incident other than his bent rim and blown tire?

Aiden bounded across the asphalt to the front of the garage. At the door, he stopped to catch his breath.

A man strode out of the first garage bay and wiped his hands on a soiled rag. "Can I help you?"

"Hi." Aiden stood upright and puffed. Shit, he was out of shape. "Do you have a tow truck?"

"We do. What happened? Usually people come here in a vehicle. You seem to be without one." The man smiled. The five o'clock shadow darkened his cheeks and his blue eyes sparkled. He'd combed his hair into a short mohawk and the inch-long spikes glimmered in the pink light of the neon sign.

Aiden read the man's name tag. *Matt.* Funny, the guy didn't strike him as a Matt. More like a Roscoe or a Boss. He smoothed his palms over his thighs. Blood rushed through his body and his nerve endings tingled. Each time he swept his gaze over Matt, his pulse reacted. Either he needed a date and sex, or he'd lost his mind from sleep deprivation. He straightened his shoulders. He wasn't there for a date. "I ran over the curb down the road. I ruined my tire and probably more."

"If you hit the curb on Walker Road, then you jacked up more than a tire. If the rim isn't a mess, I'd be shocked." Matt disappeared into the garage bay, then stepped back out again without the rag. He snorted. "Most rims are a mess and if you did one hell of a job on it…" He whistled, then grinned. "Nice."

Aiden swayed on his feet. Go figure, he'd found the one mechanic in town to make a lewd joke about rim jobs. "Can you fix it?"

"I'll get the truck. I doubt I'll be able to get to it today because I need to find the right rim to fit your car. That'll take me at least a couple of hours tomorrow to locate. The tire will be easy—unless you did more damage. I won't know that until I get a look at the car." Matt tugged a set of keys from his overalls. "Where did you leave it?"

"Where I collided with the curb." He pointed down the road. "You're sure it'll take that long?"

Matt narrowed his eyes. "Guessing from your outfit, you're late. For a date or your wedding?" He knocked on the frame of the garage bay. "Aaron? I'll be right back. I'm retrieving a job."

"What?" Another man strode into the middle of the door opening. "We're backed up, man."

"Enough. It's right down there," Matt said. "I'm taking the job, so it's not your headache."

"I'll pay extra to get it rushed," Aiden added. "I'd say I'm desperate, but you've probably guessed that."

The man Aiden guessed was Aaron rolled his eyes and ducked back into the garage.

"The truck is over here." Matt pointed to the massive vehicle. "You're the black car about a quarter of a mile away?"

"It's dark blue, but yes, the sports car." Aiden toyed with the hem of his suit coat. "It was a splurge. A hiring bonus I bought myself." *Shit.* He sounded like an ass. "I'll shut up."

"Right now, I just need the keys. I'm going to assume you've locked it." Matt held out his hand. A tattoo showed from beneath the cuff of his overalls. "Even if you didn't, I need the keys to unlock the steering column."

"Sure." He yanked the ring from his pocket. "Sorry."

"You're fine, but like I said, I can't get it fixed tonight. You might want to call someone to give you a ride. I'm out of loaners. Is it a wedding? Or a date?" Matt asked.

"What?" Aiden tripped in the gravel. He caught himself and appraised Matt's body again. He liked the way the overalls clung to Matt's muscular frame. Sweat glistened on the back of his neck. Aiden shivered. The vibrant blue of Matt's eyes and his facial hair appealed to him. He wasn't a fan of men with earrings, but the thick silver hoops worked for the mechanic. "I—it's not my wedding. I'm not getting married." He was babbling. *Fuck.*

"Oh, sorry." Matt opened the door of the tow truck and grinned. "I'll get your car. Feel free to wait in the lobby. We've got free Wi-Fi if you want. Aaron will set you up with the paperwork so we can expedite the process." He climbed into the truck and closed the door.

Aiden stood in the parking lot for another moment as Matt drove away. He should move. If he wanted to get to the reception on time, he needed to call Whit. His mind wandered. What would Matt look like without the overalls? Was he a T-shirt and jeans type or did he prefer cargo shorts and polo shirts? *How about naked?* Aiden shivered again. Yeah, he wanted to see Matt in the buff. *Like that's gonna happen.*

He shook his head and crunched across the gravel to the building. Once in the lobby, he tugged his phone from his breast pocket. The wedding should've started by now. Instead of calling, he texted Whit.

Need your help. Car trouble. Can you pick me up after the wedding?

He sighed. Fuck. He'd made a mess of the night and it was only eight o'clock.

"Here. Fill this out." Aaron offered over a clipboard. "Nothing exciting. I'll be out helping Matt."

"Sure. Thanks." He scrawled the information onto the form, then put the clipboard onto the counter. His phone buzzed in his hand. Not a text, but a call from Whit. He groaned, then answered. "Why aren't you in the church?"

"I ducked out," Whit grumbled. "You're late. Where are you?"

"I had car trouble. Didn't you look at the text?" He massaged his forehead. "It's a long story."

"Seriously? You? Nothing is ever easy with you."

"It's not by design." He had to think fast. "If you're not in the church, then the ceremony is running late? Or is it over?"

"Farin's a little behind. Do you need me to get you?" Whit asked. "I'm available."

He swallowed past the groan rising in his throat. "Are you able?"

"Wait. You're asking me to come and get you? Uh…yeah. I'll be there in five minutes. Where are you?"

"Um…" He turned the stack of magnets around on the counter. He'd never read the name on the garage when he'd passed it over the last two years. He'd seen the sign, but hadn't retained the information. "The Alpha Auto Shop." *Alpha? Is Matt the so-called alpha? Is he gay too?* Aiden could only wish.

"The one on Walker Road? Okay, I'll be there. Just… don't touch anything."

"Why?" Aiden asked. *What's wrong with the garage?*

"It's dirty," Whit said. "Grease, dirt, grime. You don't know what you'll pick up there."

"I don't know. It's pretty clean." Compared to the hospital, yes, the lobby wasn't sterile, but it could've been worse.

"Right. It's a repair shop. Those places are always filthy. Just hold on and I'll be there." Without another word, Whit hung up.

Aiden groaned again. He'd done that too much in the last half an hour. If he'd had his way, he would've called anyone but Whit. Walking would've been preferable. Whit tended to get the wrong idea about his level of interest. Aiden wasn't in the market to date, didn't want a quickie fuck in the hallway or a suck-off in the bathroom—and not from Whitman Sherman.

When Aiden looked up from his phone, Matt pulled into the lot with his car attached to the back of the truck. He drove through to the gated area to the left of the building and disappeared. Aiden crept over to the window and watched Aaron and Matt unload the car.

He wasn't sure of the conversation between the two men, but from Aaron's body language—shaking his head and frowning—he guessed Aaron wasn't thrilled. Matt didn't say anything, or if he did, Aiden didn't notice his lips moving. His expression stayed still. Aaron waved his arms, then stormed back to the building.

Aiden forced his attention from Matt and the truck in favor of staring out of the window at the few cars on Walker Road. He hated weddings and relationships too. Men expected too much from him. They wanted things like for him to change his hours at the hospital to suit those relationships. *Not possible.* He didn't set his schedule. Dating another doctor made no sense. He knew the other ER doctors too well and considered them his brothers, and he spent almost no time outside the emergency room. If he hooked up with a doctor from another ward, they'd probably never see each other, either.

He bowed his head. The last guy he'd dated had admitted after four months that he'd only stuck with Aiden for that long to cash in on the doctor paycheck. He'd wanted a sugar daddy. Too bad Aiden wasn't bringing in huge bucks. The car—the damn thing—had been a splurge but a very second-hand item. The sports coupe looked good on the road and made a statement in the parking lot. But appearances meant nothing when the vehicle was attached to a tow truck.

Aiden rubbed his forehead and looked up when bright lights infiltrated the lobby. A sigh stuck in his throat. He'd know that expensive car anywhere—Whit. Instead of parking in the lot or the gravel, Whit stopped right beside the door and honked the horn.

Aiden bit back a growl. He left the lobby and opened the passenger door, but didn't get into the car. "Hello, fire violation? Move."

Whit shrugged as Aiden closed the door. Whit zipped forward into the closest parking spot. His brakes screeched.

Aaron hustled to the doorway and stopped beside Aiden.

"Sorry," Aiden muttered. He couldn't meet Aaron's gaze. "He's a little pushy."

"I'd say entitled." Aaron sighed. "Whatever. About your car. Matt'll hunt down the part and we'll see. If I know him, he'll call around until the junk yards close or his contacts stop answering the phone. He's relentless like that. Anyway, it should take about twenty-four hours to get the car back to being drivable. No guarantees."

"Thanks. I appreciate his relentlessness and your honesty. Have a good night." He went out to the lot and found Matt beside the tow truck. "Hi," he said. "Thank you." Aiden offered his hand to Matt. When they shook hands, Aiden's tingled. His breath caught in his throat and power surged within him. He'd never felt quite like this before. His thoughts muddled and he forgot what he'd come out to talk to Matt about. "Uh...I filled out the paperwork Aaron gave me. Call me when the car is done." He'd never heard himself sound so mechanical. *Yuck.*

"Will do." Matt smiled. "I'll see what I can do to get it back to you faster. I know what it's like to not have a car."

"No worries, but thank you." He lingered beside the truck longer than he should, but he couldn't make himself leave the spot. Something between him and

Matt had started. Was he falling in lust with the mechanic? Or was his radar locating interested guys broken?

Matt leaned against the door of the truck but didn't say anything.

Shit. He'd been standing there for too long. Aiden nodded once. "I should be going." He'd said the words more for himself than anything. "Thanks."

"Aiden," Whit snapped. "Let's go. We're late and Farin will kill us."

"Right." He smiled but wished Whit had kept his mouth shut. He wanted to keep talking to Matt — or at least sharing the moment with him. Aiden forced himself across the lot to Whit's car and climbed into the passenger seat. He waved at Matt. Fate was a fickle bitch, but if this was the start of something, then he didn't mind.

"Why did you wave? He's the help." Whit sped out of the lot, spewing gravel from the back of his sports car. "You pay them, respect them, but don't get cushy."

"He's nice."

"For a mechanic." Whit's voice dripped with disdain. "Seriously. You can and will do better."

"Stop." He massaged his temples. Listening to Whit caused a dull ache behind his eyes. "I don't want to hear it."

"Are you okay? Is your head hurting? From the crash?" Whit zipped down the road past the hospital and blew through a yellow light. "I'll just take you home. If you've got a concussion, then you need supervision."

"I don't have a concussion. Christ, I'm getting sick of you. I appreciate that you came all the way out here to get me, but you're acting like an ass. He's a nice guy and while he's a mechanic, he's got feelings too." The throbbing increased. He closed his eyes. "How about we be quiet and maybe it'll go away." *Fat chance, but worth a shot.*

"You know…I'm tired of this." Whit smacked his hand on the steering wheel. "You wanted me to rescue you. I did. I've seen the way you eyeball me. Don't try to deny it."

"I've never looked at you that way." He didn't open his eyes. Since when had he been appraising Whit as date potential?

"I've noticed. I also told you we'd end up at the wedding together. Maybe I come on too strong, but that sizzle between us is real. You should really listen to me more." Whit brought the car to a stop. "We're here. The wedding should be over by now. It wasn't supposed to be a long ceremony."

Aiden opened his eyes. He'd rather have aspirin and time to crash in his armchair, but he had to see his friends. He'd power through the headache for them. Soft white lights twinkled in the trees and jazz music played. White flowers had been strung on and from poles surrounding the guests. Aiden left the car but paused before he entered the party. His breath lodged in his throat again. This was what he'd asked for. Not to marry Farin or Steve, but the desire. The passion the two men had and the opportunity to share it with their friends. He wanted someone to join him on life's journey. Whit eased up beside him and grasped Aiden's hand, but he swatted his friend away. He had to get himself together.

"People aren't looking," Whit growled. "You can touch me."

"I need some air." Aiden strode away from Whit. He didn't care where he went as long as it was far from his colleague. He spotted Farin and Steve under a floral arch. No one seemed to be bothering them. *Great.* He'd speak to them quickly, then find a ride home. He rounded the gathering of tables and guests. Farin spotted him first.

"You're here. I thought you'd skipped out on us." Farin grasped Aiden's hand. "You really need to be less important at the hospital."

"I had car trouble." He hugged Farin, then Steve. "Congratulations. I can't think of two better people to be married."

Steve winked. "Thank you." He rolled his eyes. "I need to take care of something. Looks like my great-aunt found the wine. Excuse me. Thanks for coming, Aiden. Hopefully we can talk later." He darted away, leaving Aiden alone with Farin.

"I'm glad you made it and I'm sorry to hear about the car." Farin dipped his head. "Saw you arrived with Whit. You're playing with fire."

"Don't remind me." He turned his back on the party. "It wasn't my best idea."

"He's not your type," Farin said.

"Not at all." He wasn't about to argue. He and Whit would never work as a couple.

"Um...then why? Because he had a car? Come on. You could've taken a taxi." Farin leveled his gaze at Aiden. "Or are you having a lapse in judgment?"

"I just needed a ride and wasn't doing so hot under pressure."

Farin said nothing, but frowned.

"I wrecked my car on the way." He held up both hands. "My fault. I swerved to miss a truck that had gone left of center. The truck came right at me and I jumped the curb to not collide with it. That huge-ass curb by the hospital is dangerous. Anyway, I bent the rim and ruined the tire."

"Where'd you take it, Doc?" Farin asked. "Tell me you stayed away from Coby's. That bastard overcharges for everything."

"No. I know it wasn't there." He hooked his fingers in his pants pockets. "Alpha Auto Shop...that's the name. A guy named Matt is working on it. Seemed like a nice guy."

"Matt Phillips?"

"Maybe? I didn't ask for his last name."

"You just handed over the keys to someone you don't know?" Farin shook his head. "I'm kidding. How else will he fix your car? Doc, we really need to talk about getting you out of the hospital more and into the fresh air."

"Yes, we do, and yes, I did. But he was working at the shop and I think he owns it." Although now he was having second thoughts about his decision. "Was that a bad thing? Taking it there? I didn't have a whole lot of choice."

"Not at all." Farin rocked on his heels. "Matt is a good man. He looks like he'd kill someone — people see his tats and piercings and I've heard plenty of people claim he looks rough, but he's nice. He'll work hard for you."

"Good." If Farin liked Matt, then that was a plus.

"His turnaround time is awesome," Farin said. "Once he's on a case — or a car, whatever — he doesn't rest until it's fixed."

"That's good to hear. I can't handle Whit for much longer. He drives me crazy and he'll want to be my personal taxi." He sneaked a glance over his shoulder. Whit stood with a couple of muscle-bound men and two women at one of the round tables. At least he'd found someone to talk to instead of dogging Aiden all night.

"I can see why." Farin scrubbed his hand across his mouth. "He's hitting on the busboy."

Embarrassment washed over him. He should've gone with a taxi. *Fuck.* "Oh well, he's given me a reason to escape. My townhome isn't far away. I'll just walk home."

"The hell you will." Farin snapped his fingers. A waiter strode up to him. Farin nodded once. "Let Gareth know he's got a fare."

Without a word, the server disappeared.

"The taxis are still running this late? I guess they would still be running until midnight or two." Aiden watched people on the dance-floor area. "Or were you planning ahead?"

"Steve and I met this fellow, Gareth. He's nice and offered to ferry people who've had too much to drink. He's got a '57 Chevy with a red-and-yellow checkerboard design on it. He feels important and no one is driving home blitzed." Farin shrugged. "I hoped maybe he'd meet someone. He's sweet and cute, but shy."

"You're not trying to pair me up, are you?" He wasn't into shy men. He needed someone who could hold their own.

"Nah. You're not his type. He likes guys who are shorter than he is and he's only five-eight. Come on. He's parked out front." Farin waved. "I hate seeing you miserable."

"What's that supposed to mean?" Aiden asked. "I'm not that awful."

"No, but you're here with the wrong guy. Someone will let Whit know—if he doesn't run off with the busboy first."

"Thanks." He followed Farin to the driveway and the yellow Chevy. "Farin?"

"That's me." Farin faced him. "You don't want to go back and chase Whit, do you?"

"No." He shook his head. Not a chance. But he had a question. "How…how'd you know Steve was the one? That he was interested and it could work?"

Farin paused. "Wow. You know how to knock a man down." He folded his arms. "Well…at first, I didn't. He was so young. Still is, but I didn't think it'd work. We were so different too. But we started talking and those differences weren't so big after all. It's hard to explain. We just clicked. I swim more because of him and he's more open about his love of comic books."

"So it could be out of the blue?" He doubted that would happen. Life liked to throw him curveballs rather than make anything easy.

"Sure." Farin knocked on the window of the taxi. "Heya, Gareth. Would you take my friend Aiden home?"

"Sure," Gareth said.

Farin opened the back door. "I'll see you in a week. We're heading off to Fire Island for five days of just us. I love Genie, but I can't wait."

"Sounds fun." Aiden sighed. He hated to go home so early, but he couldn't be there any longer. "Well, congrats. I'm ecstatic for you."

"Thanks. Have a good night. I know we will." Farin wriggled his eyebrows.

"I'm sure." Aiden bit back a snort.

"You're jealous as hell. You should be." Farin clapped him on the shoulder. "Doc, it'll happen. I know. Cedarwood is for gay lovers. Trust me."

"Okay." He ducked into the car and settled on the seat. He wasn't sure what to think about Farin's comment. *Cedarwood is for gay lovers. What does that mean?*

"Where are we going, Doc?" Gareth smiled via his reflection in the rearview mirror.

"It's Aiden," Aiden said. "But you can call me Doc, I don't mind, and you can take me to Honeysuckle Avenue. I'm in the Briarwood Estates."

"You've got it."

Aiden rode in the back seat in silence. He'd missed the wedding and ducked out of the reception. Hopefully, the night had been magical. He rested his head on the back of the seat and closed his eyes. Was he wrong to want what Farin and Steve had? Maybe. But he did. Jealousy and longing filtered into his brain. His dates never turned out right. The guy was either too greedy or needy. They were jealous of his job or wanted an open relationship. They didn't give a shit about his desires or needs. He craved a companion. Someone he could share a great love with, but was that man out there? He wasn't sure. Mr. Wonderful had to exist. Had to.

Chapter Two

Matt worked through the night to locate the rim for Aiden's car. He slept for a few hours, then ventured back to the shop. Although he needed the rest, he couldn't shut his brain down. Every time he closed his eyes, he thought about Aiden. *Holy hell.* How had he been so lucky to run into a man like Aiden? Most of his clients didn't walk into the shop in suits. The way Aiden's suit clung to his frame and the cut of his hair... He wasn't like the other men Matt had been attracted to. He tended to gravitate to gruff guys — ones covered in ink and metal. Aiden didn't strike him as a tattoo kind of person.

He finished up the paperwork on Aiden's car, then headed into the garage bay. "How are you coming on the tire?"

"I'm almost done." Aaron grinned. "This is record time for us. If the good doc isn't happy, I'll karate chop him. I hate working on Sundays."

"Nah. He'll be happy." Matt twiddled with the cell phone. "I'm not wild about Sunday work, either, but it's when a lot of others have the time to bring their cars in. Speaking of cars, we've got a job. Do you want to retrieve it or should I?"

"Sure. I'm tired of looking at the undercarriage of this car." Aaron wiped his hands. "I'll need your help to get this belt on later."

"Deal." He returned to the office and took care of the tow call. He jotted down the information. Running the tow truck didn't bother him, but he'd prefer to see Aiden. If he didn't hang out at the garage, he risked missing him.

"Shit." Aaron strode into the office. "I need you to get the car. I just got the fuel line taken apart and I don't want to stop while I'm ahead."

"I thought you didn't want to look at the underside of the car?"

"I lied." Aaron shrugged. "No, I'm finally in a groove. Sorry."

"It's fine." He grabbed his coat and the truck keys, then made his way across the lot to the massive vehicle. *Well, shit.* He headed out on the call. The coupe was waiting in a ditch on the state route north of town. After an hour of wrangling with the vehicle and arguing with the owner, he pulled back into the lot at the garage.

"What do you have?" Aaron met him in the empty bay. "Crashed?"

"Broken fuel line." He unchained the car. "It'll be a pain to fix, but it's not impossible."

"Nice. I'm done with the Toyota and Mrs. Hayes is coming by in an hour to pick up her car." Aaron rested his hands on his hips. "Speaking of picking up… Your doctor was here. About an hour ago. He paid and left. I got his number, if that helps."

"It's on the invoice," Matt snapped. He shouldn't be mad at Aaron. His coworker had done his job. It wasn't his fault that Aiden had stopped by before Matt returned.

"Still. You could call him." Aaron waved the phone at Matt. "You should."

"No." He squared his shoulders. This wasn't how relationships—even ones that hadn't started yet—worked. For all he knew, Aiden wasn't gay or even looking for a date.

"Why?"

"I'm not...dating anyone." *There.* He'd said it. He barely knew Aiden. Christ, Aiden was his client.

"Why? You've got to move forward," Aaron said.

"You know why I..." He almost said *won't,* but the truth was he couldn't.

"Because of Ted?" Aaron asked. "Be serious. One asshole shouldn't ruin everything."

"Well, he did," Matt snapped. He'd never get over the feeling of hurt and embarrassment when Ted had walked away.

"No. This isn't all on him. Yeah, he acted like a dick. He was a total...mismatch for you. I mean, Jesus. I had no idea he'd screw you over and around like he did. But forget him. I saw how you looked at the doctor. I also noticed how you reacted to me when I said you'd missed him. I can see it in your eyes. You like him. That's freaking awesome and there's no crime in trying again."

"No." He hadn't wanted Aaron to see any of that.

"Asshole." Aaron tossed a towel at Matt.

"Dick."

28

"Fine, but I told the doctor that you'd call him." Aaron rushed out of the office and laughed along the way.

Fuck. "Did you?" He'd thought the tension between him and Aaron was done after they'd called each other names. *No luck.* "What did you do?"

"I didn't do anything." Aaron ducked behind the vehicle lift. "He's not expecting you to call, but I was right. You like him."

Well, yeah. He did like Aiden, but a doctor wasn't going to hook up with him. They were too different. He had ink, piercings and seemed to have grease under his nails at all times. The doctor was clean, pressed and put together. They'd never work and that was his luck. He'd never realized he liked polished men, and the guys he'd dated hadn't been as into him as he was into them.

Matt sank onto the stool behind the counter. He needed to make calls and should hire a receptionist. Unfortunately, his bare-bones budget didn't allow for extra workers.

* * * *

Eight hours later, Matt returned to the counter. He checked the spreadsheet on his archaic desktop computer. He and Aaron had completed work on four cars, which were now with their respective owners. Two new vehicles had come in and five were scheduled for simple repairs tomorrow. *Not bad.* If he and Aaron worked hard, they'd hit his goal for the month.

He saved the spreadsheet, then switched programs. Paperwork was his least favorite part of the job, but someone had to do it. He filed the completed invoices, then paid bills. When he tore the check from the pad, he sliced the side of his index finger. "Fuck," he murmured. Just what the tool company wanted to see—him bleeding for his work. *Jesus.* He sealed the envelope and moved on to the parts needed for the next day. He'd have to pull some from the stockroom and compile a list of what should be ordered. His pen ran out of ink partway through the task and he groaned. Maybe he should invest a few dollars in a tablet. The electronic device would probably make inventory easier.

Matt jotted down the rest of the parts and retrieved them from the stockroom before he returned to the office. His back ached. He stretched and sat behind the rusty metal desk. He was almost done. *Thank God.* He hated being at the shop past ten at night. Aaron had mentioned getting a dog so he wouldn't be by himself. That was probably a good idea, but he never seemed to have the time to head down to the shelter.

Lights flashed and illuminated the office portion of the building. He glanced up from the stack of papers. *Who needs service at this hour?* He abandoned his post at his desk and eased up behind the counter in the lobby. Had he arranged for someone to drop off a vehicle tonight? He couldn't remember. Not that someone leaving the keys in the box and the car outside was against type. He preferred to have the car or truck there so he could get started first thing in the morning. But he didn't remember anyone being on the schedule to drop off a car.

Oh, well. The sign on the door read CLOSED, so the owner of the headlights would have to deal. He tucked his keys into his pocket and swiped his finger across the screen of his phone. No calls and no scheduled drop-offs. *Good.*

The lights didn't extinguish, but a shadow darkened the door. When Matt looked up, a figure knocked on the glass.

"We're closed," Matt said. "Sorry. Come back in the morning."

The man—cloaked in a black jacket and with a ball cap covering his eyes—knocked on the window again.

A shiver ran the length of Matt's spine. Few things scared him, but when the feeling hit, he didn't argue. Besides, if he didn't recognize the person at the door, then he doubted he'd set up an appointment for the vehicle.

Matt left the counter and strode up to the door but didn't open it. "Do you have an appointment?"

The guy shook his head and pointed to the handle, but didn't speak.

"Do you have an emergency?" Matt asked. He still wasn't opening the door.

The man didn't move.

"I'm sorry. We're closed." Anger crept into his brain, despite the uneasiness. He wanted to go home, and the sooner the guy left, the sooner he could too. Matt checked the security system. He hadn't splurged on much, but the digital security system had been a must and had saved his ass more than once.

The man knocked again, not leaving Matt alone.

Matt's blood chilled. The shadowy object wasn't the guy's hand. It was a gun. *Where in the hell did that come from?* Matt kept his expression as steely as possible and stepped behind the counter. He'd installed a silent alarm for this sort of situation and thanked God Aaron hadn't talked him out of it. He'd hoped he'd never have to use it. Too late now. He pressed the button.

When Matt met the man's gaze, something boomed. The shriek of glass shattering echoed in the lobby and shards landed on the carpet. Matt collapsed behind the counter and his shoulder ached. *What the hell?*

"You made this harder than it had to be." The guy stood over Matt and aimed the gun at him. "You're supposed to hand over the money."

Matt's heart hammered. He'd never expected this — to die at the shop with no one around but the man who'd taken his life. Another shot rang out and Matt cracked his skull on the floor. Pain exploded in his brain and he closed his eyes. He should fight back but didn't have the strength to do so. His limbs weren't cooperating. The ringing in his ears damn near deafened him. A bone-deep ache seeped through him and his hearing muffled. He couldn't breathe.

Shit. He was dying. He had to be. For what? Money and parts. If the fucker would've asked and explained, he would've given him whatever he needed. Matt fought to open his eyes, but failed. He couldn't fight back and succumbed to the darkness. He needed to sleep. Yes, a nap would be good. He just hoped the slumber wasn't going to last forever.

* * * *

"Matt? Mr. Phillips?"

Matt struggled to open his eyes. He didn't recognize the voice and wanted to argue. Mr. Phillips was his father. He blinked and groaned. The bright light hurt and the stinky smell of antiseptic curled around in his nose. Did heaven smell like cleaner? *Nah, that's not possible.* But he swore he detected the stench of sanitizer in the air. He couldn't be at the shop. He and Aaron used an orange soap to clean off the grease.

He gritted his teeth. His head ached and his tongue felt fifteen sizes too big, as well as dry. He managed to open his eyes, but didn't recognize his stark white surroundings. Where was he?

"Hi." A figure blocked the light over Matt.

He knew this voice. *Aiden?* Was the doctor in heaven with him? He blinked again and focused on Aiden. Instead of the navy suit, sickly green scrubs covered Aiden's body. The awful color seemed to swallow him up. A bandana with a cartoon cat covered his hair, but his eyes shimmered. He must not have shaved recently. A dusting of five o'clock shadow covered his cheeks.

"It's good to see you awake." Aiden touched Matt's forehead. "How do you feel?"

"Like I've been punched in the head, shoulder and gut." Matt groaned. "What happened?"

"I was going to ask you that." Aiden stood beside Matt's bed. "You came in last night with a gunshot wound to your shoulder and the side of your head was grazed. Do you remember any of the last twenty-four hours?"

He winced. He pieced through what Aiden had said. "Wait, I was shot?" *Like a bullet through my body and could've died shot?*

Aiden nodded. "The wound on your scalp is superficial, meaning it grazed your head. The one on your shoulder was a through and through. I closed the wound and bandaged you up."

"I see." Matt massaged his forehead. The IV tugged on his skin and against the pole. "What's this for?"

"You've been assaulted. You're bruised on more than half of your torso." Aiden rearranged the tubing on the pole, giving Matt more slack. "I haven't seen so much black and blue in a long time."

He had to think. *Beaten? Shot?* "Oh shit." He remembered bits and pieces of the night before.

"What?" Aiden's eyebrows rose. "I'm here."

"The shop was robbed. A guy—wore a black jacket and ball cap—he came into the shop. He knocked on the window and I ignored him at first. When I refused to let him in, he shot. I hit the deck and the silent alarm. I remember him standing over me and aiming the gun. After the second shot, I blacked out." *God. What did the guy take? Were there cars stolen? Just money?* He needed an update. "My shop."

Aiden rested his hand on top of Matt's. "It's fine. Your coworker came in to be with you. The only reason he left was to get some coffee. He'll be right back."

"Oh." He understood Aaron having to take a moment, but he wanted his lone employee there now. Not that he didn't like Aiden sticking around. He appreciated Aiden's kind tone and apparent worry over him.

"He'll be back. Promise." Aiden smiled. "I'm glad you're okay."

He took comfort in Aiden's comment, but he wished he were anywhere else with him. The spark felt real. He glanced down at his hand. The IV hadn't gone anywhere. "Can we get rid of this thing? It's in the way."

"The IV?" Aiden asked. "In the case we had to do surgery on your shoulder, I wanted to be prepared, so no. I wasn't sure how long you'd be out and you needed fluids."

"Take it out." He wanted to go home. Yes, he'd just been shot, but he couldn't shake his desire to get the hell out of the hospital and heal in familiar surroundings. *Thank you, Doc, for helping me, but I'm done.* He struggled to sit up and yanked on the tubing. "Now."

"Not yet." Aiden moved the IV pole, giving Matt more room to maneuver. "I can't, even if I wanted to. I'm not the doctor on call any longer." He dragged the thin blanket over Matt's torso. "By the way, we had to remove your piercings in case you went into cardiac arrest. The nurse put them in a baggie for you. I'm sorry."

"You're a doctor," Matt snapped. "You have the training to take this out." Fury welled within him. Removed his piercings? *Shit.* He'd have a bitch of a time getting the damn things back in. He stared at the ceiling. Impatience wasn't a good color on him. He controlled things, didn't give them up to others. *Fuck.* He faced Aiden. "Please?"

"My friend Dr. Ramos is in charge. He'll check you over and discharge you—if you're ready." Aiden folded his arms. The sleeves of the scrubs tightened against his biceps and chest. "You're not ready to go. You just woke up and need another round of tests. Hold tight, let Ramos give you an exam and, while you're at it, wait for your partner to return. It won't kill you."

Men in ugly green scrubs weren't a usual turn-on for Matt, but Aiden managed to work the look with finesse. Matt groaned. He didn't belong at the hospital and Aaron wasn't his partner. "I'm not with Aaron."

"I meant business partner." The tips of Aiden's ears burned and the rosy glow spread down his cheeks to his throat. "Never mind."

"I'm sorry." Matt settled against the bedding. He wasn't going to get his way at the moment and might as well stop fighting. Besides, he wanted the pleasantness back with Aiden. "Aaron just wants to get paid. I can count on him to keep the shop running and to put a transmission back together without fail — but us being a couple wouldn't work." He'd pushed himself too much and a groan erupted in his throat.

"What?" Aiden perched on the side of the bed and placed his hand on Matt's shin. "I can answer any questions — except if you can go home."

He hated that the doctor was right. Leaving wasn't happening soon. "Well..." He should keep his mouth shut, but why bother? He'd never been shy about going for what he wanted any other time. "Would you stick around? If you're not busy. I like the company."

"Then it's a good thing I'm not busy." Aiden left the bed and dragged a chair close. "When I got off work, I came up here to check on you. I won't lie. You had me worried."

He felt a little better and also wanted some conversation that didn't revolve around him being hurt. "You said you'd answer questions, right?"

"Fire away." Aiden rested his elbows on his knees and met Matt's gaze.

"Why'd you assume I'm gay?" He'd lost his sense of suave. *Fuck.* He'd blame the incident at the shop. *Sure.* He'd lost his ability to be cool when he'd had his guts kicked in.

"Oh, well...that would be your business partner... er...Mr. Berger's fault. He came in right after the ambulance and filled us in on what had happened. He kept using the word partner, so I just assumed. My mistake." Aiden's blush deepened.

"It's okay. Aaron would like to be more, but it won't happen, and yes, I'm gay." He wasn't sure why he'd disclosed all of that information, but didn't regret doing so.

"I understand." Aiden grinned. "The flag at your shop clued me in too. I guessed you were either an LGBTQ-friendly establishment or proud of your sexuality. I liked your attitude and work ethic. The next time I need something fixed on my car—and trust me, it'll be sooner rather than later—I'm coming to you." He patted Matt's shin. "It's hard to find people who take pride in their work and it's good when it happens."

Matt fumbled for a moment. Pride in his work and coming to him. *Damn.* He wasn't one to give in to flattery, but he wanted to hear Aiden say more nice things. He could listen to Aiden all day. He cleared his throat to buy himself time to compose his thoughts. "Thanks. After this, I'll need the business. We're bare bones and even though I've got insurance, the bills will be a hardship." He hadn't wanted to admit that.

"I understand. Like I said, you've got a customer in me. I'll need new brakes soon and I haven't the slightest idea how to change my oil." Aiden shrugged. "I can heal the human body, but I don't know how to switch the dirty oil out in favor of clean. Sad, isn't it?"

"Nah. It's all about strengths. Mine have to do with motors and gaskets. Yours are hearts and kidneys." The spark he'd felt wasn't part of his imagination. "Have you talked to Aaron about the shop?" He needed to keep Aiden talking.

"I did. He mentioned the broken windows being boarded up by his brother this morning. He said two cars were stolen from the lot, but that seemed to be it." Aiden grasped Matt's fingers. "At least it was just two cars and glass."

He ran through his mental inventory from the lot. He couldn't be sure, but he'd bet the stolen vehicles were the Cadillacs. *Fucking balls.* "Shit was stolen. What if the customers don't trust me after this?"

"I think they will. You don't know what might happen. Look at the Gay Alliance. They took some serious negativity from the newly renamed Coalition for a Clean Cedarwood and proved being a melting pot is the best way to go. Talk to Colin Baker. I'm sure he can help. He's great at organizing." Aiden squeezed Matt's fingers. "Especially after this. People love to pitch in after an unfortunate event. I'm happy to bring my car to you. No worries."

"How are you so positive?" Matt asked. "Didn't you just come off a shift? You have to be tired. My brain isn't even processing positivity right now."

"Good company helps to buoy the spirits." Aiden chuckled. "The large coffee an hour ago might have something to do with it too." He nodded once. "I'm sorry we removed your piercings, but it's better to have them out than to be electrocuted." He paused. "I noticed your ink too."

"Kind of hard to miss it." He rubbed his arm. "Each used to have a meaning, but not after a while. I got off on the pain and went overboard. I'd get them as a coping mechanism." He pressed his lips together. Once again, he'd disclosed so much. But Aiden made talking easy.

"Huh. I'm not big into needles."

Matt stared at Aiden. "What? You're a doctor. You work with them. How can you not like needles?"

"Using them isn't the same as having one inserted into your skin." Aiden shivered and let go of Matt. "I'm a horrible patient. Not only do I self-diagnose, but I tend to tell the doctors what to do. Yeah, don't give me an injection or tell me what's wrong with me."

Matt laughed, despite the ache in his head. He liked Aiden's attitude and how the conversation flowed between them. For the first time in a long while, Matt wasn't touchy about his body art and wanted to discuss it. "I'll assume, then, you don't have any ink. Is it against the hospital regulations or just not your thing?"

"We can have tattoos, but it's preferred for them to be where they can't be seen. I don't see the difference. If you're doing your job, it shouldn't matter what color your hair is or what you've got inked onto your body." Aiden shrugged and yawned. "But even if I wasn't squicked out by needles, I'm not sure what I'd get. I thought about it once, but I couldn't decide, so I never got beyond the idea stage."

"Makes sense." The tiredness filtered into his brain again. He still wanted to go home, but he wasn't so apprehensive about being at the hospital. He also didn't want Aaron to come back. "So...do you have someone special at home?" *Please let him be gay and single.*

"No." Aiden shook his head. "I'm very unattached. I'm never home and if I'm not here, I'm probably dead asleep at my townhouse from being here for too long. I wish I had time for a cat. I've always wanted one, but I don't think it'd be fair to the kitty to be left alone so much. Still, I'd like the company."

"I'd like to get a dog. Probably will once I'm healed." Matt shifted his hips. He couldn't roll onto his side. *Damn.* "Is there anyone in particular you're looking for? Blond? Brunet? Male?"

"My ex-boyfriend would say I've got a type. He'd also say I'm an ass for staying at the hospital so often."

He's gay. Thank you, God. Hell yes. Matt tried to sound nonchalant to hide his joy. "His loss."

"I agree." Aiden nodded and clasped his hands together. "Which tattoo was your first?"

He hadn't discussed his tats in forever. Matt shifted and bit back a moan. Fucking balls, his shoulder hurt. "The stars on my lower back. I wanted something to make me look tough but settled for the stars." Memories of that night at the tattoo parlor rushed into his brain. He'd been so young and wet behind the ears.

"Settled?" Aiden's eyes widened and he smiled. "Didn't you have enough money for what you really wanted?"

"No. I was on the fence—a dagger between my shoulder blades or the stars." He chuckled. Back then, the needles had hurt like a bitch, but he'd refused to show his discomfort. "The dagger would've made me look like a badass, but I had plans for the future too. Being a badass wouldn't last forever, but aiming for the stars would. I'm not ashamed of my choice. I ended up getting the dagger too, but down my arm instead." He hadn't realized how corny he sounded until now, but oh well. "I wanted to play football professionally and was pretty good until I blew out my knees during my senior year. Since I couldn't follow that dream, I aimed for another set of stars and vowed I'd open my own auto repair shop. So…yeah…" He refused to talk about his father and his past beyond what was easy to say.

"I see."

"Well, if you did my exam, then you probably did see them." He laughed. The joviality between him and Aiden pleased him. "They're my way of dealing. When I wasn't working on cars and serving as an apprentice so I could open my own shop, I got more ink."

"To dull the pain?" Aiden asked. "That's what you said."

"You listened. Nice." Men who not only heard what he'd said but understood and offered an ear were one of his weaknesses. "I feed my need for pain." He didn't want to explain that he needed the pain to feel normal and to level him. If he had enough money to put more art onto his skin, he could subject himself to the mild torture and not deal with the shit in his life.

"I don't understand, but I kind of do." Aiden met his gaze and held it a little longer than he should've, but Matt didn't mind.

Getting close to Aiden, although scary, worked for Matt. He wanted to know everything about the doctor. But first, he wanted to change the subject. "So. Your car is still good, right?"

"It's fine." Aiden laughed. "You did a great job. I said I'll bring it back for the next issue. You do change oil and rotate tires, right? Maybe put on new windshield wipers?"

"We do." He relaxed. "Whatever you want." He caught himself. *Talk about a loaded statement.* He almost wished Aiden would reply with something like, *'I'd like you.'* But that would be too much to ask. "So. You're not involved?" *Fuck.* He'd asked that already and gotten an answer. *Damn nerves anyway.* "I mean…shit."

Aiden's eyes widened again and he laughed a little louder. "Like I said, I'm very single. Are you...looking to mingle?"

He had an opening. Matt stared at Aiden. "It's not against the rules to date a patient, right?" He craved a chance with the doctor. "I wouldn't be your patient any longer once I'm discharged."

"I don't think many doctors and patients are hooking up and I'm guessing there's a rule about not dating current patients, but I don't see why we couldn't once you're not in my care." Aiden leaned forward in his seat. Fire lit in his eyes. "Do you want to go out socially with me? I have a horrible track record with dates. If you're just trying to get business for your shop or you want money from me, just be honest."

"You think I'd do that?" Matt blurted. "That's low."

"I think I've found too many frogs and I've had to be careful." Aiden half shrugged.

He melted a little more for Aiden. "If you're interested in being seen with a tatted-up mechanic, then yeah, I'd like to go out with you. I don't want your money or the status of being with a doctor. I've got my own cash and status never meant much to me anyway."

Aiden didn't speak right away, but he grasped Matt's fingers. "You've got a deal. Rest up and we'll plan a night out when you're healed up."

Matt wanted to lean forward and kiss Aiden, but he noticed footsteps in the hallway. When he glanced over at the doorway, a man in a lab coat strode into the room.

"Aiden," the doctor said, "I thought you went home."

"You know me. I can't seem to leave this place." Aiden stood. "Del, this is Matt. I'm sure you read that on his chart. Matt, this is Del...er...Dr. Ramos. I'm going to step out so you can do the exam."

"Thanks." Dr. Ramos stood beside the bed and waited for Aiden to exit before he started the examination. He checked the bandages on Matt's shoulder and the bruises on his face. "You've been through a lot. Do you remember what happened?"

"I do." Matt recounted the story again. Little details, like the color of his attacker's hat and the scent of his cologne, came back to Matt. Once he finished, he wanted a nap—but in his bed. "I'd like to go home."

"Of course. Sleeping at the hospital isn't the easiest." Dr. Ramos tapped something on his tablet. "First, do you have a ride home? Aiden, maybe? I didn't realize he was dating, but he likes to keep to himself."

"We'll make plans when he comes back." Or he'd ask Aaron if Aiden said no. He paused. *Good Lord.* He'd started thinking ahead with Aiden and didn't blink when the doctor mentioned dating him. Sure, he wanted to hook up and it seemed like they'd made progress, but things were so unstable and new.

"Okay." Aaron bounded into the room. "Do you know they don't have soda or tea that's not diet down there?" He stopped short. "Whoa. Sorry."

"I'll send the nurse down with your paperwork," Dr. Ramos said. He smiled but didn't appear pleased. "It was nice to meet you, and I wish you the best." He left without another word.

"Wow." Aaron sank onto the chair Aiden had abandoned. "You got an old doctor. Too bad you didn't get that hottie one who wrecked his car."

"We can't win them all." Matt settled on his back. "What did you mean about the diet...what?"

"Oh, the drinks in the cafeteria. There isn't a regular soda or tea to be found and don't ask for sweet tea. They don't have that, either." Aaron laced his fingers together on his belly. "Want me to take you home? I heard him say you were going to be discharged soon."

"If you can. I don't want to leave the shop unattended for too long." Every day he remained closed, he lost money and would have to deal with irate customers wanting their vehicles like he'd promised.

"It's fine. The windows are boarded up and the security footage went to the police. I made sure there's a new memory card and everything was uploaded to your computer at home." Aaron toyed with the tubing on the IV. "I'll get you home and settled. Then I'm at your service until you're better."

"Aaron, you don't have to." *Shit.* This wasn't supposed to happen. "I just need a ride home." Not a servant. He'd be great on his own, and if he wasn't, then he'd see if Aiden might drop by.

"You can't lift anything and you're down an arm. You've got a sling." Aaron rolled his eyes. "You'll be crap at the shop. We might as well just stay closed for now."

"Yeah, but I've got shit to do. Customers want their cars and we've got bills to pay. I can't afford to be closed for God knows how long," Matt protested. If he knew anything, he knew exactly how close to the edge he was and when he needed to bring more cash flow in.

"Then what do you want me to do?" Aaron snapped. "Run the whole thing myself?"

"No. I want you to work on the cars and I'll do what I can manage while keeping the lights on." Ordering parts, payroll and invoices couldn't be that hard with one arm, right? "Give me two days to sort things out and we'll be rolling again."

"Then I'll take you home. I've got lots of room and I'm all on the first floor." Aaron stood. "It'll be great."

Christ. "I want to go to my house. I'm not putting you out." And he'd deck Aaron if he didn't stop pushing.

"No, you'll stay with me." Aaron grinned. "You've got to have supervision and this is my chance. I'm taking it."

"Whoa, Aaron. I want to go home. My home. Don't make this harder or weirder than it has to be." He managed to sit up. "Please?"

"You need care."

"Not at your house. I'm going to be fine at my own." And he wasn't interested in giving Aaron a chance to be with him. They were friends and coworkers, not each other's love interest.

"Asshat," Aaron snapped. "I'll bring the truck around. But think about my offer. I'm willing to stay. Just say the word." He clunked out of the room, grumbling the entire way.

Well, shit. Matt settled against the pillow again. Everything was fucked up. He had no idea who'd shot him and he guessed the cops would want to take his statement sometime that day. He was interested in Aiden, not Aaron, and doubted he had a chance with the doctor beyond one date. *Damn it.* He needed help too. He hated being dependent on anyone. He groaned. His body ached. He hoped things would work out. No question. He had little choice. He needed to ride this storm out in order to see the rainbow on the other side.

Chapter Three

Aiden watched Aaron leave Matt's room and a pang of jealousy hit him. He'd just gotten to know Matt and the connection was real. Was Matt the kind of guy who made everyone feel invited? Was he the type to click easily? Aiden scrubbed the back of his hand across his mouth. Man, he was overthinking things. The situation with Matt was new and fragile. *Suck it up and stop expecting something so fast.* But could he listen to his own advice? He ducked into Matt's room and hoped for the best.

"Hi." Matt sat on the edge of the bed. He'd managed to put his jeans on and wrangled a button-down shirt over his shoulders. "I really don't like this thing." He waved his arm in the sling. "Motherfucker, that hurts."

"Which is why you're not supposed to." Aiden helped him finish putting the shirt on. "Don't do that again without help."

"Then be my help." He wriggled his eyebrows. "I don't want to be snarled up in this sling. I like to move."

"You'll be able to move before you know it. It gets easier." He stood beside the bed and folded his arms. He sounded like a damn greeting card. "You're waiting on the paperwork?"

"Yeah. I'm glad to get rid of the IV. I hate that stuff. You said saline, but it could've had something else mixed in." Matt shook his head. "When you know addicts, you vow not to be like them. I don't mind a beer every so often, but never pharmaceuticals. If I can't have control, I'm not doing it."

"Makes sense, I suppose, but it wasn't mixed with anything. You like pain but on your terms." Aiden notched his chin in the air. "Have you ever considered getting implants? The discs or whatever? They give me the heebie-jeebies just thinking about them."

"Wow. No." Matt struggled to his feet, wobbled, then sat back down. "I like the art and the pain, but I'm not into dermal anything. I'm also not used to being upright. Wow." He leveled his gaze at Aiden. "I can't stay here. I need to get out."

Aiden recognized the pleading in Matt's voice and couldn't argue. He believed the best healing took place when the patient was the most comfortable—and usually at home. "The attendant will be here in a few with a wheelchair." He paused. "It shouldn't be much longer."

"Are you leaving?" Matt asked.

"Yeah, soon. I'm late for a nap." He didn't move. He had to deal with his twinge of jealousy concerning Aaron. "I saw your business partner came back. He'll take you home, right?"

"Yeah." Matt toyed with the edge of the sling. "Would…would you be interested in stopping by my place? Say it's to check on me or because we're friends and we want to talk. I don't care. Just come by."

"Aaron isn't staying with you?" He'd hate to impose.

"He'd love to be, but I told him no." Matt tipped his head. "What do you think?"

"I think you're supposed to have someone staying with you for the first twenty-four hours in case you have complications. You should have Aaron sleep over for a precaution." He hated arguing and encouraging Matt to be with Aaron.

"Then you come over. We'll talk more and you can watch me all you want. I'd planned on asking you to take me home so we could get to know each other better." Matt reached for Aiden. "It's forward and pushy, but it feels right to ask you."

"But what about Aaron?" He heard the clicking of the wheelchair on the tile floor. "Your ride is here."

The volunteer, a high school girl, pushed the chair into the room and smiled. She hesitated and flexed her fingers on the handles. "I'm here to spring you." Her grin faltered. "Got your stuff?"

Aiden helped Matt into the wheelchair. Once he was satisfied Matt had settled, he scooped up the labeled bag and placed it on Matt's lap.

"Can I have one more second?" Matt asked. "Just a second. Then I won't complain or give you hell. Promise."

She toyed with the cuff of her shirt. "Uh..." She switched her gaze between Matt and Aiden. "Sure. I'll be right out here." She left the room, plunging Matt and Aiden into silence.

Matt turned his attention back to Aiden. "Well?"

"Well what?" Aiden asked. Matt's question stunned him.

"I was trying to have a moment with you. I'm at 327 Oakdale. You can't miss the house. I'm the only one with a wrought-iron fence." Matt folded his hands on the bag. "I don't expect you to come over tonight — you're dead on your feet. But maybe tomorrow?"

Aiden had been up and down Oakdale a hundred times and didn't remember seeing a house with a fence.

"Please?" Matt grasped Aiden's fingers. "It's just a check-up. If we talk more and you hate me, then that's it. No strings. If things do work out, then good. I'd like to spend more time with you."

He couldn't say no. Besides, he was a sucker for blue eyes and facial hair on handsome men. "I'll do it — but after I catch a nap. If I'm too tired, I'm a pissy mess."

Matt sat back in the chair and nodded. "I don't know how doctors run for so long with so little sleep. I'd be dead by now if I were you."

"Adrenaline gets us through a lot, but there are plenty of days when I would rather be sleeping. If you're ready, let's go." Aiden didn't give Matt the chance to argue. He grabbed the handles of the wheelchair and steered Matt into the hallway. "He's all yours."

The girl took control of the chair and blushed. "Thanks," she whispered.

"Bye," Aiden called.

"Bye." Matt waved with his good arm. He didn't look back.

"Sending another patient home after the super care of Dr. Connor?"

Aiden tensed, then whipped around. "Colin, hey." He hadn't heard his friend in the hall. He prided himself on listening. "How are you? How's Gage? The group?" *Shit.* He needed to stop talking.

"Matt Phillips." Colin gripped Aiden's shoulder. "He's an interesting choice. Were you going for the most opposite award?"

So much for small talk about anything but Matt... "No." He hadn't thought about Matt as being his opposite, but now that Colin mentioned it....yeah, he and Matt didn't have that many similarities.

"Good. You're more alike than you realize," Colin said. "To answer your questions, Gage is great. He made the honor roll for the first grading period. The group is fine and you should know...you were just there. As for Jordan, even though you didn't ask, he's fine too. We missed you at the reception. Thank goodness Whit filled us in." He rolled his eyes. "But back to why I hunted you down... Del said I'd find you here."

"Did he?" He'd never get that nap. "What'd you need?"

"First, don't hang out with Whit. If I have to deal with him again, I might string him up. He never stops talking and boasting." Colin held up both hands. "Second, I'm supposed to tell you to go home." He steered Aiden toward the elevator and pressed the button to call the car. "Del's worried you're overworking yourself. He thought I'd be able to convince you to leave. You've put in your time and deserve a break."

"You're both right, but don't tell me I'm not that important to the hospital that I can't leave. I know. I can. I stopped to see Matt and stayed longer than I'd planned." He stepped into the car with Colin. "But why didn't Del tell me this himself? He's got higher seniority and knows damn well I'll listen to him." He hated feeling so irritated. Colin hadn't done anything wrong and neither had Del.

"He could've, but like I said, he thought I'd be more convincing. Plus, I needed to see you, so I offered to help him out and relay the message." Colin shrugged. "It wasn't that big of a deal."

"Oh." Now he felt sheepish. "Sorry. What did you need?"

"We're having a party at the house. The support group, past and present members, as well as special guests are invited. Mostly, I'm trying to get rid of the tons of extra food left over from the wedding reception. I'm up to my eyeballs in cold cuts."

He couldn't help but laugh. "I'm sorry. When is it? If it's tonight, I'm booked."

"You've got a date? Does Matt know?" Colin asked.

The bell dinged and the elevator opened. Aiden stepped out first, then tugged Colin over to the curving set of steps. "I'm sleeping with my blanket and pillow." *Yeah, not a hot date.*

"Sounds reasonable." Colin winked.

"Del is right. I've tried to do too much and it's kicking my ass." He scratched the back of his neck. "I can't seem to get out of here most days. Today has been a long one, for sure."

"Well, the party is Wednesday at six. Bring your appetite, your willingness to answer questions...and Matt." Colin stuffed his hands into his pockets. "We've got a new member, Ian, and his son has lots of questions. I guess Ian's partner left him last year and they've both had a hard time adjusting. Payton would probably like to know he's not alone."

"How old is he? I'd think Gage would've made friends with him."

"He's sixteen, and while Gage has tried, Payton's quieter. It just doesn't work." Colin shrugged. "I bet Ian would like to have someone to talk to, too. He's going back to school, working at the library full-time and trying to raise a teen. He's about as crazy busy as you are."

"Sounds like." Confusion filled his brain. Was Colin trying to set him up with Ian or convince him to stick with Matt? He and Matt had only had a few conversations, but there was a spark between them. Aiden sighed. He could be reading too much into the chat. "I'm not dating Matt. It's talking." Not fucking, although he'd like to after Matt healed. "Besides, I'm not sure he can make it. He'll probably be working. Matt said something about trying to get the shop open again after the shooting."

"So soon? He was shot. Shouldn't he be resting? They haven't caught the shooter." Colin's eyes widened. "Jordan isn't supposed to talk about it, but I can tell. He's tense and he can't talk on the phone in anything but a shout."

"I'm sorry." He tried not to laugh, but he could just see Officer Jordan Hargrove practically yelling into the receiver. "As for Matt, he's like you — he owns his own business. If he's closed, he's not making the money needed to stay open."

"True enough." Colin rocked on his heels and nodded. "If he can't make it, I'll have you take him a plate. You're not getting off easy."

"If I'm off, then I'll be there." Aiden twisted his watch around his wrist. "I'm not that great of a speaker, but I'm willing to help."

"We appreciate it." Colin walked with Aiden out to the parking lot. "I'll see you Wednesday. Be there." He waved, then climbed behind the wheel of his car.

Aiden watched as Colin drove away. He shook his head and navigated through the lot to his own car. Late-day sun glittered on the hood. He trailed his fingers over the fender. Del and Colin were right. The hospital would survive if he wasn't there. Still, he loved his job and helping people. His drive kept him working long after his shift ended. He opened the car door and plopped behind the wheel. His phone buzzed in his pocket. Annoyance crept into his brain. He didn't want to listen to the voice mail. Truth be told, he didn't want to do much of anything. Instead of grumbling, he tugged the phone from his pants and checked the screen.

"Restricted number," he murmured. "Wonderful." He tapped the icons to bring up the voice mail, then switched to the speaker setting.

"Hey, Aiden. It's Lucky. I haven't talked to you in forever and I missed you. Are you working?" Lucky chuckled. "You're always working and I'm babbling. Well, hon, call me back. You've got my digits now. I'm waiting…and horny."

Aiden bit back a gag and deleted the message. He wasn't calling his ex-boyfriend back—the number had come up restricted. Lucky hadn't been much of a charm but more like a curse. The only time he wanted Aiden's attention was when he needed something…like all the time. Lucky craved cash, privilege and to be taken care of without giving much back in return. Aiden hadn't been able to give Lucky what he wanted from the relationship. He hadn't been rolling in money or the time to spend with his boyfriend, so Lucky had left. Unfortunately, he also came back every so often and, although Lucky wasn't a catch, Aiden struggled with letting go.

Aiden drove home and, along the way, considered his options. Lucky was bad for him. Horrible. He used people and didn't care who he hurt. The sex had been decent. But would Matt be any better? Aiden kept thinking about the tattoos and piercings on Matt's body — his appearance could be a turn-off for some, but the modifications intrigued Aiden more than anything. Despite the fascination, he barely knew Matt. The pain thing, the quick connection and Matt's eagerness to spend time together bothered Aiden a little. When he moved too fast, he tended to get burned. But he and Matt hadn't fucked. They hadn't gone on a date or even kissed. What if they didn't connect outside the hospital situation? They'd get into the real world and his tendency to find flaws in everyone would pull him and Matt apart. Everyone had flaws and they always showed them at the worst time.

He pulled into the garage and parked the car. He needed to stop analyzing the situation with Matt and Lucky. Christ, he could barely keep his eyes open.

Aiden trudged into his townhome and stripped along the way to the master bathroom. He switched on the shower and stood nude in the room as the steam built. His brain ached and wouldn't shut off. He thought about what Farin had said. *'Cedarwood is for gay lovers.'* He'd met Lucky in Cedarwood and that relationship hadn't worked out all three times they'd tried. Lucky's neediness had been too much for him to handle. He eased into the stall and rested his head on the tiles. Water slid down his face. The spray stung and relaxed him, but the tiredness in his bones threatened to overwhelm him. He should hurry through the shower so he could crash. Instead, he scrubbed himself and took his time to wash away the stress from the hospital. He slid his hand over his dick and stroked. Most of the time he preferred solitude, but right now he wished he had someone to join him.

When he closed his eyes, he pictured Lucky with him in the shower. Being with Lucky hadn't been awful. They'd fucked often and Lucky hadn't minded switching roles. He opened his eyes. The only good part of his time with his ex had been in the sack. Why did he want the arguments, the pouting and the hassle back into his life? *I don't.*

His erection wilted. *Well, shit.* Aiden ducked under the water again to rinse the soap down the drain. Instead of thinking about Lucky or even Matt, he finished the shower. He'd never get any rest if he were still upright.

Aiden turned off the water, toweled himself and wandered into his bedroom. He collapsed on the bed and buried his face in the pillow. The scent of his fabric softener comforted him. Having a soft, safe place to land was better than a gigantic paycheck. He dragged the blanket over his body and sighed as he succumbed to sleep.

* * * *

Aiden jerked awake and sat up. He scrubbed both hands over his face, then glanced over at the clock. Four in the morning. *Shit.* He needed more rest. He flopped backward onto the bed and yawned. His dick formed a tent in the sheets. *Great.* He had a boner from the dream. The vision in his brain wasn't going to fuck him…but the moment he'd shared with Matt had felt real.

Sleep sounded like a good idea, but when he closed his eyes, he couldn't nod off. *Damn it.* Aiden slapped the bed for his phone. Maybe if he engaged his brain, he'd be able to go back to sleep? *Who am I kidding?* He knew the science behind blue screens and their effect on the brain. He'd make the situation worse. Still, he left the warmth of his bed and retrieved his phone. He checked the icons. Two missed calls—one from Colin and another from a number he didn't recognize — no voice mails, fifteen emails — all things he could deal with later. Plus notifications from his various social media sites. He swiped the reminders away. He wasn't in the mood to be social.

Aiden abandoned his phone on the nightstand and crawled back into bed. He stared at the ceiling. He'd counted the swirls in the ceiling paint the hundred or so times he'd been desperate for sleep but couldn't settle down enough. According to the clock on his phone, he'd nabbed seven hours of sleep. Too bad he needed more to refresh. Christ, his muscles ached and if the hospital called him in now, he'd probably lose his shit and his job, he'd been wound so tight.

He shoved the sheets out of the way and slid his hands over his dick. He closed his eyes, allowed his subconscious to take over and imagined Matt there. He might as well embrace the fantasy.

* * * *

"Stroke yourself." Matt grinned and stretched out beside Aiden. The sheet covered Matt from the waist down. The barbells in his nipples glinted and the tattoos on his chest flexed as he propped himself up on his hand.

Aiden rested on his back and planted his feet. He wrapped his fingers around his cock and stroked. He grunted and a shiver slid down his spine. His thoughts blurred as he increased his speed. His nerve endings sizzled and fever racked his body. He gasped. "Oh fuck," he murmured.

"That's right. Faster. Get dirty. Come. You want to, and I want to see it." Matt splayed his hand on Aiden's belly. "Come for me."

Shit. He'd never last. Not now. He gritted his teeth and palmed his balls with his free hand. His belly tightened. "Matt." He arched his back and his stroking turned frantic. "Matt," he said, drawing the man's name out.

Matt rolled onto his back and tweaked his nipples. "Yeah. That's so hot. Makes me want to climb on for a ride." He slid his palms over his abs but didn't move the sheet out of the way. "I want you to come apart."

"Uh-huh." He focused on Matt. He caressed his cock with one hand and massaged his balls with the other. A groan ripped from his lips.

"I want you to play doctor with me," Matt said. "I've been bad and need the doctor to take care of me. Check my vitals, give me mouth-to-mouth and cool my fever."

"Oh fucking fuck." Aiden opened his eyes and stopped stroking. *Cool his fever?* Even in his fantasy, he couldn't turn off his job. He closed his eyes again and resumed fucking his hand. Sweat prickled on his skin and the tingles flooded his veins once more. His movements turned frantic. He slid his hand up to his chest and pinched his nipple hard. He grunted. *No holding back now.*

"Fuck yeah. Come for me," Matt said. "Do it."

* * * *

Aiden didn't need any more encouragement. He grunted again and the orgasm overtook him. Cum splattered all over his hand and streaked across his belly. A laugh bubbled in his throat. He settled in the sheets. Having Matt there would've been better. Still, he'd always said he'd rather come alone than not come at all.

God, he sounded so lame. Still, he laughed. He needed to get out more.

Aiden snagged a shirt from the floor and dried the cooling cum from his body. He tossed the article of clothing out of the way. Leaving a mess wasn't his style, but he wanted sleep. He'd put things back in order once he woke up.

The post-orgasm slumber hit Aiden hard. He dragged the blankets over his body and nuzzled the pillow. If he wasn't careful, he'd sleep his life away — at least the life he had while he wasn't at the hospital. If he couldn't be with someone, then he'd be happy on his own.

Aiden woke four hours later, refreshed and happy. Orgasms tended to help his mood. He'd prefer a good climax to nothing at all. At least he couldn't let himself down if he was the one stroking his dick.

Once he'd gathered his bearings, he showered. Not just a rinse-off, but even shaved, too. The water stung his face and the scent of his soap kicked his senses into working order. He dressed in a T-shirt and sleep pants then, phone in hand, headed into the kitchen.

When he grabbed the box of cereal from the cupboard, he laughed. Lucky would've made fun of him for his penchant for having cereal in the morning instead of just coffee like other adults, as Lucky put it. Kids ate cereal. Adults had regular breakfast. He amused his coworkers at the hospital with his habit and, last Christmas, the nursing staff had bombarded him with mini boxes of cereal as snacks. He'd loved not having to buy cereal for the next six months.

He flipped the switch on his coffee maker and, while the java brewed, dumped milk into his bowl of corn flakes. His phone flashed.

Aiden eased onto one of the stools and swiped his finger across the screen. He ate and checked the icons again. He'd missed another phone call. At least it wasn't from the hospital. He played the voice mail and continued to eat.

"Hi. It's Matt. I wasn't going to bother you, but I had your number. It was on the invoice. I promise I'm not stalking you." He paused. "I'm not... Shit. I'm still figuring the whole dating thing out. Damn it. If you're not too wigged out by me being forward, call me back. My number is 555-8026." He paused again. "Oh shit. You're probably wondering if I'm okay. I'm fine. I don't need a doctor visit, but I'd like one so we can talk again. Fucking hell. I'm not good with this kind of phone call. I'll stop talking now. Bye."

Aiden laughed and wiped his mouth. He'd made Matt uneasy? Wouldn't Matt be happy to know the feeling was mutual. He'd assumed Matt was more composed. The new info pleased him. He didn't want to be the only one struggling. He twiddled with the phone and dialed Matt's number. Eating while talking on the phone wasn't his idea of polite, but he wanted to finish the cereal before it turned soggy. He switched to the speaker setting while the call rang. After six rings, he reached for the phone to disconnect. *Matt must be busy.* He'd try later.

On the seventh ring, Matt answered. "Are you still there?" he puffed.

Aiden swallowed his cereal and laughed again. "I called you. Yeah, I'm still here. I got your message. I was crashed out for—I'm not sure how long, but my phone says it's Tuesday. How are you feeling? What's your level of pain?"

"You can't shut off being a doc, can you?" Matt chuckled. "I can't not diagnose what's wrong with an engine, so I get it."

"Yeah, I'm not good when I'm not at work." He gripped his spoon. Jesus, he sounded so smooth.

"To answer your questions, I'm feeling good. Sleeping helped. My body needed time to recharge. My level of pain is low. I've had tattoos that hurt more than this. Sure, my shoulder aches and my bruises look gnarly, but I'm still here."

Aiden abandoned his cereal bowl, left his stool, poured himself a cup of the coffee then leaned against the counter. "Good. I'm glad. Don't strain yourself. Trust me, if you try to do too much…you'll do more damage."

"Yes, Doc." Matt laughed. "I've got my tablet and went to the shop this morning. Aaron and I are working well together considering." He paused. "Doc?"

Aiden hated the nickname most of the time, but coming from Matt, he didn't mind. "Yeah?"

"When do you go back on duty?"

"Tomorrow morning. I'm on a twelve-hour shift. Six to six at night." Just saying his schedule tired him out. And he was supposed to be at Colin's dinner after work. He groaned.

"I don't know what's making you grumpy, but I'd love to go for a walk. Would you like to go with me?"

"Yeah, I would." He wanted a date—it would be the easiest way to find out if things between them would fall apart before it got going too fast.

"Because you want to keep an eye on me?" Matt asked.

Smart man, but not the exact reason. "I'd be lying if I said no. I mean, yes, I do, but I'd like to spend time with you." He finished his coffee. "Give me fifteen minutes. I'll be there."

"I'm at the shop. Make it half an hour."

He stopped short. "I wasn't kidding about taking time off."

"All I did was sit at the desk and counter. I did a lot of the paperwork and made phone calls. No lifting or straining," Matt said. "Trust me. I'm pissing off Aaron as we speak. He says I'm too needy but not in the right way. I just want to keep my business running."

"Men." Aiden chuckled to mask his true emotions. He shouldn't be annoyed, but he kept getting the feeling Aaron was more of a pain than he was worth. "I'll probably annoy you too." He placed the bowl and his mug in the sink, then snatched the phone from the counter and switched back to the regular setting. "I can't turn off who I am." He headed upstairs and kept the phone tucked between his ear and his shoulder. Being a doctor tended to be the flaw everyone else found in him because he spent so many long hours at the hospital.

"That's expected. You're not pissy because I don't want to date you. You're doing your job. I'd be angry if you didn't check on me. You're the one I want worrying about me."

Aiden shrugged out of his T-shirt but paused. "Wait...what?" He had to be hearing things. Matt wanted him around? He'd said as much before, but until now, Aiden had dismissed it.

"I don't want to be with Aaron. He's cranky and I can't handle working with the man I'm sleeping with. It doesn't work. Is he a whiz with a crankshaft? Yes. I trust him with any car repair, but not a relationship. As for you...I'd like to date you." Matt chuckled again. "Just meet me at my house. I'll be home by then."

"How? You're not supposed to be driving." Even if he hadn't taken any more of the pain meds, he probably still had some in his system. Driving—even with one arm—wouldn't be a good idea.

"Aaron's taking me home. He says I'm useless here. Plus, I've got a meeting with the police."

"Oh." He shrugged into a new T-shirt and switched his sleep pants for boxer briefs and a worn pair of jeans.

"Yeah, Jordan Hargrove's coming over. Him and someone else. I can't remember."

"Cool. I like Jordan." He unballed his socks. "Give me fifteen to twenty and I'll be there."

"I'll see you." Matt hung up, leaving Aiden in silence.

Aiden waited until the phone went dark before he sat on the edge of the bed. A date. A walk. Matt liked him—at least enough to give him a try. He should have his head examined. As fast as the twosome was going, he didn't want it to stop. After the disasters of his past, he'd sworn he wasn't going to try again. The fumbling and quickness of Matt made him remember the fun of dating. Maybe Matt felt beholden or an attachment because Aiden was his doctor. He didn't want to think about that right now. He'd rather focus on the good feelings and keep them going. He needed companionship and wanted it with Matt—at least for now.

Half an hour later, Aiden drove down Oakdale Avenue past the split-level houses that lined the street. He'd gone down this road a few times to reach the freeway, but he'd rarely noticed the homes. Each of them had seemed to look the same. Maybe he hadn't been looking close enough. Now he had to pay attention if he wanted to find Matt's house. He hadn't seen any fences other than wooden ones.

He kept driving until he came to the curve at the city-limits sign. Where was Matt's home? He noticed the grove of trees on the left side of the road and how the pavement changed from perfect and well-kept to crumbling on the edges. The scene reminded him of Cedarwood – for all the worries of the city council, the town looked great, but if one peeled back the layers, they'd see just how much work Cedarwood had to go. The Gay Alliance had done wonders and reduced the violence and protestations against the LGBTQ community, but there was more work to do.

Aiden slowed down a little and surveyed the landscape. A series of stone pillars caught his attention. *The fence.* He turned on his signal and veered left. Sure enough, there was the house. He'd seen the place a few times and wondered who lived there. The wrought iron and tall trees concealed the home from the street for the most part, but what he could see reminded him of a Gothic church, all tall windows, pointy eaves and dark colors. He pulled into the driveway and stopped in front of the imposing gate. *Good Lord, does a vampire live here? Someone looking for locations to shoot a horror movie would have a field day with this place.*

He hadn't expected Matt to live at this particular house. His nervousness overwhelmed him. Was he supposed to ring the bell? Was there a bell? An intercom? Aiden opened his car door and considered his options. He'd have to look for button or something.

"Hi." Matt stood on the other side of the fence. "I told you it was a crazy fence."

"You weren't kidding. It's original." He stood beside his car. "This place reminds me of a vampire house."

Matt laughed. "Next time I'll have the gate open. I thought you weren't going to show. I usually leave it closed so I can keep out the nosy people who think it's a horror house or whatever. Give me a minute and you can pull up to the garage." He disappeared behind the fence and the gate swung open.

Aiden climbed back behind the wheel and drove forward to the garage. He parked, then left the vehicle.

"I can see why people would think this is a scary house. It's spooky." Aiden folded his arms. "I got stuck in traffic. The soccer games just got out and everyone seemed to be leaving the fields at the same time."

"I forgot about that." Matt grinned. "My house does have the spook feel, but it's not that bad. Come along and I'll show you around."

"Done." Aiden stood beside Matt. "I've got to ask — do you have vampires or something? Tell me you do the place up right at Halloween."

Matt closed the gate. "I do. I love to dress up like a vampire and scare the hell out of the trick-or-treaters. Whoever makes it to the main gate gets a full-sized candy bar. Not too many make it, though." He nodded to the house. "I get the strobe lights going, fake spiderwebs everywhere and lots of dark netting. The ambience is fantastic."

"So you're the spooky-vampire type, or do you sparkle? You don't strike me as a romantic vampire." He walked along the property with Matt, but instead of looking at the scenery, he only saw Matt, the way his shirt clung to his muscular frame and how his jeans stretched across his ass. Even the sling made him handsome. He knew how to work his look.

"I have to be scary. That's the only kind there is. Don't tell me you prefer the sparkly ones." Matt snorted. "Those are awful."

"No, I'm not big on being scared, but vampires should be dangerous — not cutesy." He loved watching the old black-and-white movies featuring the original monsters and the vampires ranked at the top.

"Good." Matt's eyes flashed. "I can't be with someone who won't dress up with me and be scary."

"Right." He wasn't sure what to say. First, who'd said he'd dress up? And second, where did Matt get the idea they were going to last beyond Halloween? Good God, the man was pushy and more than a little forward. "Do you ever sparkle?" He chided himself for the silly question, but he didn't do well under pressure.

"I do when I'm at the clubs, but I haven't gone in ages. I like the music and the dancing, but the expectation to hook up drives me nuts." Matt stayed in step with Aiden. "Do you club?"

"Not since college and that was only a handful of times. I'm usually at the hospital taking care of the club goers who had too much fun. The music and dancing are great, but when you see the aftereffects of that good time and all the bad that can happen, it makes one think twice. Well, it did for me."

"Makes sense." Matt moved a tree branch out of the way and half the leaves tumbled off. "Did you put yourself through college?"

"And med school." Aiden breathed a sigh of relief. This he could talk about. "My folks didn't care if I was gay, purple, bi or anything. As long as I was happy and true to myself, they were happy. What they couldn't afford was college. Dad was a lawyer and did the best he could to keep the bills paid. Once my mother left, that was that. She never looked back. He met Keye and we all moved forward. I kept my grades up and went for every scholarship I could find. I'm up to my eyeballs in debt from my student loan, but between grants, scholarships and those loans as well as working in college, I managed. I can't complain. I'm doing what I love and I'm happy."

"Sounds like. I don't regret what I've done either. It's made me who I am." Matt stopped at the porch. "I just realized we got back to the house. We've done a lap around the property and I bet you've seen nothing. Sorry."

"It's all good. I got caught up and haven't asked how you are." If Matt wanted to talk, he'd open up in his time—not Aiden's.

"Such a bad doctor." Matt chuckled. He strode onto the porch. "I'm feeling good. I'm not pushing, but I'm not taking the pain meds, either. I don't see the need. Yes, things hurt, but it's not unbearable. Besides, taking those drugs makes me nauseated."

Aiden stared at him. Matt had been shot and beaten up. He should be on some sort of pain management— not nothing at all. "Do you need something else? I'm sure we can find something that won't make you sick."

Matt shook his head. "Nah. I'd rather not take something and risk side effects…you know?" He went quiet and bowed his head.

Aiden wanted to press but didn't. He had the feeling there was more to the story, but he wouldn't push— emotionally or physically. "Looks like we've had that walk."

"We did." Matt gripped the door handle. "Why don't you come in?"

"Sure." He followed Matt into the house and, as he stepped over the threshold, a strange feeling came over him, as though he was on the cusp of something big. He and Matt had fallen into conversation so easily and acted like old friends, even though they'd just met. He liked it. What bothered him was Matt's tendency to talk in terms of relationships and the future, like they were already together. They weren't. Not really. Things could be great for now, but the fall would come. He'd find something messed up with Matt or Matt would see something in him…and they'd split.

What annoyed Aiden more was the confusion. Part of him wanted to put distance between him and Matt. He didn't need the distraction or to get his heart broken—and that would happen. It always did. The rest of him wanted to give Matt a try. The odd pairing worked for him and he liked how Matt made him feel giddy and excited.

What should he do? Hold back or go for something possibly very special? He wasn't sure, but he didn't have much time to think. When Matt met his gaze, another piece of Aiden's resistance melted. Try as he might to fight his attraction, he was already hooked on Matt Phillips. He just had to hope the fall wouldn't be a true disaster.

Chapter Four

Matt breathed a sigh of relief. Aiden had come over and the conversation wasn't contrived. It flowed well. Beyond that, Aiden turned him on. He'd always been a sucker for the clean-cut types and Aiden fit the bill. He liked Aiden's slender but muscular runner's body, his piercing blue eyes and the way he carried himself with confidence. A shiver ran the length of Matt's spine. He'd been looking for someone like Aiden — smart, sophisticated and with his head on straight — for ages. He just hadn't expected that person to be a sharp dressed doctor type.

"Can I get you something to drink?" He ushered Aiden into the living room. "Sit. Make yourself at home."

"Thanks." Aiden stood in the middle of the nearly empty room. "I take it you don't spend much time in this room?" He gestured to the lone chair. "Did you forget, or wasn't furniture for this space important?"

Matt stood rooted to the spot. *Well, fuck.* He'd been so wrapped up in his thoughts and desires and hadn't realized he'd set Aiden up in the emptiest room in the house. "Join me in the kitchen. I promise there's more than one place to sit." Maybe he could salvage the moment in there.

Aiden followed him into the kitchen. "Hey. Stools." He winked. "It took me forever to buy the furniture for my townhome. I had milk crates holding up my coffee table for the longest time. My friend Melissa used to give me heck because I wasn't interested in decorating."

"Melissa?" He didn't want to show his hand or his jealousy. He pulled two glasses from the cupboard. "A friend?" God, he sounded like an ass.

"We were close in college." Aiden shrugged and plopped onto one of the stools. "She got married and her husband hated me."

"Jealous?" Not that he wasn't feeling a little of the green-eyed monster making its appearance. He was. He filled one glass and offered it to Aiden. "I've had my share of dealing with jealousy from the partners of my friends. It's not fun."

Aiden nodded. "He thought Melissa loved me more than him. Not the case. I was never a threat. We'd go out and I'd stick up for her, but I never put the moves on her, either. She knew she'd be safe and there was a better chance we'd both go for the same guy than anything. But Declan didn't care. She loved him and when he voiced his opinion, she listened. Once they were married, she went along with his line of reasoning—probably because it was easier than going against him."

"Was he dangerous?"

"No. Just set in his ways."

Matt rounded the counter and sat beside Aiden. He couldn't remember the last time he'd invited someone over. "Well, that sucks. You should be able to rely on your friends. Not that I can talk. Aaron is reliable in the shop, but he's getting weird on the relationship front." The more he thought about Aaron, the more he wanted to put distance between them.

"She'd been pulling away for a while before they got married. She told me that it didn't bother her that we weren't going to get together, but I knew otherwise. She got me drunk exactly once and tried to kiss me. I didn't give her what she wanted. No boner, no kissing back, just me lying there. When I sobered up, I apologized and tried to explain. She said she understood, but she didn't." Aiden toyed with the condensation on his glass.

"You shouldn't have to apologize. If you're not into someone, then you're not." He believed what he'd said, although he wanted Aiden to fall for him. He nodded. He'd known a few misguided souls too. Trying to let them down easily rarely worked. He sipped his water. His shoulder ached, but he refused to take the pain meds. Addiction ran deep in his family and within him. He'd rather not tease the beast. Christ, he was messed up. He wanted a man who might not want him back, had given said man advice and a shoulder to cry on, so to speak, and had more demons than most people should. He groaned. No wonder he couldn't keep a boyfriend.

"You've overdone it." Aiden abandoned his glass. "Let me look. Have you taken acetaminophen at least? Something for the pain I can see you're in?"

Not yet, but Matt would get one of the low-dose pills. "I'm fine. I'm just..." *Worn-out but not ready to accept defeat.*

Aiden checked the dressing and his brow crinkled. He met Matt's gaze. "You did too much." He sighed. "But your wound looks good. No extra bleeding and it's starting to heal."

"Good." He drank more water to hide his wince. "I'm not ready to quit, though."

"You should rest. Lie down a while." Aiden patted Matt's thigh. "It'll be worth it."

Matt set the glass on the counter. "Come with me. I'll do what you say, but I want you with me." Correction—he needed Aiden with him. The attraction wasn't just physical. He craved Aiden's attention and wanted to know they could give a relationship a try.

"Matt... We're going too fast. You need to get better, not think about sex or me." Aiden withdrew his hand. "I gave you the wrong impression. I'm sorry."

Matt swiveled on his stool and stilled Aiden with his free hand. "You're not telling me something. One minute, you're here and it seems like this is something that could happen. Now you're saying I'm going too fast. I never said we'd fuck. I believe I wanted you to lie down with me. Two of us, on the bed and talking. I like spending time with you, and if I have a problem, you're right there. I don't care if you're a doctor or a janitor. I like you."

Aiden pinched the bridge of his nose. "You're a distraction. You're dangerous."

His fury picked up. He hadn't realized he'd been irritated until now. "Because I have tattoos?" he snapped.

"No."

Matt tried to keep himself in check, but his frustration got the better of him. "Isn't that how it works? The truth comes out. You just wanted a tough guy for now."

"I didn't say that." Aiden recoiled from him.

"I'm too dangerous for you. That's what you said. I'm a nice guy with ink on my body and piercings in my skin. I've got issues, but I'm not awful." Holy shit, he had to stop while he was ahead. He'd already gone too far.

Aiden left his stool. "Okay. You're tired. You're hurting." He nodded but didn't look at Matt. "You're not thinking clearly and could use a rest. I'm going to head out. Get some sleep, take the stress off your shoulder and call me later." He still didn't meet Matt's gaze as he left the kitchen.

Damn it. Matt left his seat and hurried after Aiden. "I'm sorry."

"It's fine." Aiden's smile was tight and the lines around his eyes deepened. "Get better. I'll check on you in a few days."

"Wait." He touched Aiden's arm. When Aiden faced him, he gave into his urge to kiss Aiden. He mashed his mouth down on Aiden's. Instead of pulling away, like he thought Aiden might, Aiden kissed him back. He didn't touch Matt, but he wasn't fighting him.

Matt moaned, but not because of the pain. He wanted more from Aiden. Maybe he was moving too fast. He didn't care. He wanted to be with Aiden.

Aiden broke the connection first. A blush streaked across his cheeks and his eyes widened. "I should go." He nodded again and didn't look back. Within moments, he stood beside his car. The poor doctor seemed confused.

Matt sagged against the main pillar of the porch and groaned. He should check on Aiden and follow him to be sure the doctor got home okay. But he couldn't drive. Beyond that, he'd pushed too hard and hoped for too much in a short period. He'd thought he knew how Aiden felt and what he was doing. He'd believed he'd found something special. He still did. Aiden was unique. He was smart, funny and had a good head on his shoulders. Then there was his look—the man was gorgeous…and cautious. Matt didn't fault him for his restraint. He rather liked how Aiden didn't rush as much as he did. He just wished he knew how to get his attitude in check and for Aiden to trust him. *Well, shit.*

Aiden had said he'd check on him in a few days. *Not good enough.* He'd give the doctor time to simmer, but every cell in his body screamed for him to chase. He sighed. If Aiden wanted to lead the way, then Matt would follow.

* * * *

Twenty-four hours later, Matt didn't feel any different about Aiden. He still wanted Doc Cedarwood. Although he'd thought about his plans all night, he wasn't sure how to convince Aiden they should take a chance.

He'd cleaned up the house as much as he could and even shopped online for furniture. The prices bothered him and he hadn't purchased anything, but he'd looked. Once Jordan stopped by and he'd given his statement…yet again, he decided to follow Aiden's directions and got that rest.

Now, he sat up on his bed and twiddled with his phone. If he remembered right, Aiden had said he had a twelve-hour shift today. He wondered what Aiden had for plans after. Probably sleep. As he swiped between the screens, a call came through. He recognized the number and a lump formed in the pit of his stomach. *Not Aiden.* He connected the call and hit the speaker setting. "Hey, Colt. What's up?" He'd known Colt for ages. They'd tried to join the Cedarwood Chamber of Commerce at the same time and had run into the same barriers. He liked the café owner. "How's business?"

"Good. Since the Coalition decided to leave me alone, it's bounced back. But I called about you," Colt said. "How are you? My God, man. You've been robbed and shot. That's got to suck."

"I'm okay." *What a noncommittal answer.* He might not have been trying to be a shit, but he sure sounded like one.

"I'm glad to hear that. I've worried about you." Colt paused. "No temptation?"

Matt pressed his lips together to keep from answering right away. He should've seen this question coming, but he hadn't figured Colt would call him on the carpet for his past indiscretions. Colt had seen him through the bad times. He'd been a friend when Matt pushed everyone else away. He should've known Colt would check up on him.

"Well?" Colt asked.

"No. I've removed it." He'd tossed the pain pills he'd been given at the hospital into the toilet and ripped up the prescription for more. The only thing that might screw up his chances was Aiden, but Aiden had left before any irreversible damage.

"Have you? I've heard you hooked up with Dr. Connor. Don't you think that's inviting trouble?" Colt asked.

Matt nodded. He'd known this line of questions and warning was coming. "He's a good man," Matt snapped. "Smart, handsome, funny… I like being with him."

"Right. His proximity to pharmaceuticals isn't a draw?"

"Colton." *Fuck.* Aiden's ability to feed his habit hadn't occurred to him. He shook his head. He wasn't about to put Aiden in that position. Getting clean had nearly killed him and he refused to go back. Maybe Aiden was a temptation, but he didn't see him that way.

"Do you think he'll still want to be with you when he finds out you're a former addict?" Colt asked.

"Are you trying to convince me to leave him alone? Because it sure sounds that way." He gritted his teeth. *Fucking hell.* He wasn't going to use Aiden. The attraction was real. "I told him about the pain thing. He understood." But worry crept into his thoughts. He doubted Aiden would agree to many dates if he found out the full truth about Matt.

"So you told him half of your story." Colt sighed. "You agreed to full disclosure. You said the next time you got involved with someone, you'd be honest. Don't let me down."

"I'm not. I'll tell him." He paused. "I'm just… We're not together. Hooking up involved him coming to the house to check on me. I told him I refused to take the meds. I'm not going down that rabbit hole again. I can't. My life is good—well, mostly."

"Okay." Colt groaned. "I don't trust you. I can't, but I also can't keep you from living your life. I've got my eye on you, though."

"Understood and appreciated." He wasn't going to argue with Colt. He had a point. Matt had screwed up before and Colt had talked him down. Now that he had his life sort of in control, Colt had the right to be worried. Before, Matt would've taken the rejection from Aiden — even as small as it was — and ruined his life.

"Look, the other reason I called was because Ashley insists Colin and Jordan want you at the party tonight," Colt said. "It's a celebration of single parents, the kids and Cedarwood. It's also a reason to get rid of the extra food from the wedding. I guess there was tons left over."

"When and where?" Like he'd give up the chance to get out with his friends?

"Oh, and Aiden should be there."

"Okay." He needed to contain his enthusiasm and not blow his chance. Even though he could be on the cusp of letting Colt down, he refused to give in. He'd beaten his addiction to painkillers and his overwhelming need to tattoo himself in order to feel level. He'd found other ways to deal with his problems. He wasn't about to screw up the opportunity this time. If he had to grovel to get Aiden to let him try again, he would.

"Are you coming? It's tonight at six at the community center."

"I'll be there." Matt nodded. "Count me in."

"Fine. See you at six." Colt clicked off the line, leaving Matt in silence.

Last night, he'd thought his chance with Aiden had thinned to almost impossible. Call him overly dramatic, but he hated going for the long shot. The party was another way to show Aiden he wasn't a cranky guy prone to losing his temper. He could do this.

Matt left the bed and debated his next move. He'd forgotten the doctor's rules on showering. *Shit.* He'd have to do a glorified sponge bath.

What the hell should he wear for a community dinner? Something sexy enough to grab Aiden's attention but not so showy that he appeared to be trying too hard. He opted for a button-down black shirt and jeans. He'd wear his cowboy boots since they were easier to put on.

Matt hurried through the bath and dressed. Driving was out of the question, but he could take a taxi. Not only would he get there, but maybe he'd score a ride home from Aiden.

Half an hour later, he stepped out of the car and stood in front of the community center. He paid the driver, then headed in. His hands shook and he hesitated in the foyer. The last thing he needed was for Aiden to turn him down. He'd screwed up by losing his cool Aiden.

"Hey." Aiden strode into the foyer. "Hi, Matt." He smiled. "I didn't know you'd be here."

"Is that a good thing or bad?" Matt asked. "I'm glad to see you. I'm sorry things started out rocky."

"It's good. I've been thinking about you since yesterday. I'm sorry I walked out." Aiden tucked his keys into the pocket of his scrubs. "I'm not good with relationships. Most of the guys I've dated have only wanted me because they wanted to be with a doctor. I'm not rich and I work ridiculous hours. If you're willing to be with someone who won't have tons of time for you because of my work, then maybe we can give this a shot."

Matt's eyes widened, but he didn't pull away. "I'd like that. I'm usually at work more than I'm at home, so this might work." He offered his hand. "Would you like to head into the party with me? It doesn't have to be our debut or anything. Just two friends who showed up at the same time."

"And we can figure out the dating thing later? Like after the party?"

"Yes." Matt squeezed Aiden's fingers. "One question. Were you just freaked out about a possible date, or did you think I'd try something when I mentioned resting with me? I wasn't thinking sex. I meant conversation with the pressure taken off my shoulder."

Aiden smiled. "I should've understood. I'm used to guys who go from friends to sex at warp speed. I like the slower tempo."

"Good." He kept hold of Aiden's hand and strolled through the foyer. The pressure subsided. Now he could relax and enjoy himself and his time with Aiden. "But that doesn't mean I don't want to sleep with you. I'd love it."

"I would too." Aiden blushed again and the tips of his ears reddened.

Thank you, God. Matt's heart swelled and the pain in his shoulder decreased. Life wasn't perfect, but it was good. Hell, it was better than that. He'd been given a second chance.

"So you know, I'm the child of gay parents. That's why they invited me. I work with the other kids of gay parents and help them understand they aren't different because they have two dads or two moms." Aiden opened the door for Matt. "Colin keeps me around because I help."

"I'm not the child of gay parents, but I'd like to be a parent one day. Does that help?" Matt asked. He'd thought long and hard about what he wanted out of his future. The chance to help a child on their path and to be the father he'd wished for... Yeah, those were on the list.

"You're swaying me." Aiden remained beside him as they ventured into the main room.

Matt knew many of the people there. He'd worked on the cars of quite a few of the guys or had come across them at the gym. For once, he didn't feel so out of place. Aiden strolled up to a pair of men sitting together.

"How are you?" Aiden offered his hand. "Still good after that bout of pneumonia?"

Matt smiled from behind Aiden. He sort of recognized the men. Part of him wanted Aiden to introduce him, but the rest of him wanted to simply exist. They were just there together. They weren't a couple or anything yet.

"Hey, Matt? This is Daren and his partner, Stone. Guys, this is my friend, Matt. He's a mechanic." Aiden placed his hand on the small of Matt's back. "He's also my knight in shining armor. He fixed my car when I ran over a curb and messed up the front end."

"Hi," Matt said. "It's a pleasure to meet you." *Never let it be said I don't have manners.* The longer he stared at Stone, he finally remembered where he'd seen him. Stone ran the printing company in town. He'd only talked to Stone twice, but the handsome bald man was hard to forget. Unfortunately, that was what Matt had done. He also didn't know the pair well enough to engage in deep conversation.

Aiden spoke to Stone and Daren for what seemed like forever, not that Matt minded. He observed the people in the room. Plenty of children of all ages were there. Some of the men sat together in pairs, others in fours and fives. He marveled at the sight. The community — not just gay or straight or whatever — had come together.

Although he filled a plate and sat beside Aiden, he didn't feel very close to him. Aiden always had someone to talk to or someone coming up to chat. Matt could've been angry, but why? Aiden was a doctor. He'd probably seen plenty of these people at one time or another at the hospital. He finished his dinner and sat back in his chair.

"Hi." Jordan eased onto the seat on Matt's left. "How are you feeling?"

"Not much change since yesterday." He managed to laugh. "Looks like there's not much food left. That's good, right?"

"It is." Jordan nodded. "We won't have much to take home." He scooted closer to Matt and lowered his voice. "I wanted to talk with you about the robbery. We've narrowed down a few suspects and will need you to come in to see if you can possibly identify the alleged robber."

"I can." He'd do whatever he needed to in order to get the whole thing sorted out. "Say the word and I'm there."

"Good. The security footage from your shop has been valuable." Jordan folded the edge of the paper placemat. "More businesses should have surveillance like that installed."

"It wasn't cheap, but if it's helping, then that's what matters." He flexed his right hand. "I'm ready to get the hell out of this sling."

"I know nothing about that. When I got shot five years ago, I broke my arm too and was a mess. They had me in the most irritating shoulder-slash-arm cast." Jordan rolled his eyes. "Well, I'm glad you made it. Glad you got something to eat. Feel free to come to the support group. We say we're for single gay parents, but we'll take anyone as long as you're willing to share your story."

"Thanks." He wasn't sure what story, but oh well.

"I need to chase down Gage. He's a good kid, but I saw him tailing Genie. He's one gigantic ball of hormones. He's not old enough to have hit puberty and shouldn't be so girl-happy, but he is." Jordan shook his head. "I forgot how much fun it is to be a teenager — almost — or raising one." He stood. "I'll talk to you tomorrow."

Matt scrubbed the back of his hand across his mouth. Having kids had crossed his mind plenty of times, but the idea of them becoming teens hadn't occurred to him. Of course, they'd be teenagers eventually. Everyone had to grow up sometime. But would he be a good parent for a teen?

"You're deep in thought." Aiden waved his hand in front of Matt's face. "Are you tired? You look beat."

"I'm getting there." He forced a smile. "Going home would be good. Think you could give me a ride?" He'd been too forward. *Oh well.*

"I can, but I can't stay long." Aiden left his chair and stretched. "I've got another six a.m. shift. Once I get back to my townhome, I'll probably collapse on the couch."

"Makes sense." He stood and the bones in his back cracked together. He hoped no one heard the horrible sound.

"Let me bring the car around out front and we'll go." Aiden winked, then strolled away.

Matt sighed. He could watch Aiden's ass all day and night. The man worked his scrubs like a champ.

Colt stepped between Matt and the door. Matt bit back a groan. He should've guessed Colt would make an appearance. *Fuck.*

"I have something for you." Colt tugged an object from his pocket. "I haven't trusted you the way I should. You've been clean for more than four years. It's high time I give you a break." He opened his hand. A silver coin shimmered in his palm. "I'm not done busting your balls. Once an addict, the desire never totally goes away. This is to remind you that I'm watching, but from a distance. Aiden's a good man and he deserves the best. I don't know him all that well, but I'm protective of you. I don't want to see you blow this chance. You could be good for each other. Don't let your anger, your former vices or anything else screw this up."

He stared at Colt. Sometimes he hated the man and other times he wanted to be Colt. Right now, his respect for Colt grew. He couldn't promise he'd be perfect, but he'd try. "I fell off the path a couple of times, but I have no plans to do it again. Aiden's safe in my hands."

"That's all I can expect." Colt shook hands with Matt. "Have they made any headway with the shooting?"

"Jordan said the surveillance tape was promising, but I don't know anything else." He blew out a long breath. "I should see if Aiden's out front."

"By all means." Colt nodded once. "You've got the coin. It's my year one sobriety coin. I don't just pass those out to anyone. If you'd show up to the meetings, you'd have one of your own."

The gravity of what Colt had done washed over Matt. He should feel pressured, but he didn't. He felt honored. "Yes, sir." He held his head high and left Colt in the main room. By the time he stepped outside, Aiden was waiting in the fifteen-minute spot in front of the building.

"I thought you'd never come out." Aiden opened the door for Matt. "I can't talk though. Every time I turned back to you, someone else wanted me."

"You're popular." He settled on the seat. "It happens. How many of those guys have you seen at the hospital? If it's not there, then you've talked to them for the group, right?"

"You're not jealous?" Aiden pulled away from the curb. "My last boyfriend hated when I talked to anyone who wasn't him."

"Really?" Matt stretched his fingers out on his thigh. He wanted to reach for Aiden but held back. He had to be honest. "I won't lie. When we first walked in, I was a little jealous. Everyone knew you. But the longer I sat with you, the more I didn't care. You're supposed to be a people person. If you weren't, it wouldn't work." He frowned. Somewhere in what he'd said, he made sense. "I'm not insulted or jealous. I liked watching you schmooze."

"I like that." Aiden grinned. "I'm sorry we didn't get the chance to talk more."

"There will be time." If he'd figured anything out, it was not to push but to let fate take its course. "We can plan a proper date."

"We can…just not this weekend. It's my weekend on." Aiden pulled onto Matt's street. "If you can wait a few days, then it's on."

"I'm trying to heal. I can certainly wait a little while. I'd like to see you and would love to spend time together, but I'm always game for texts and phone calls." He waited until Aiden got to the end of the driveway. "Stop here. I didn't remember to bring the fob to open the main gate. Next time, I'll remember." He sounded awkward. *Damn it.*

"Works for me," Aiden said. "One question."

"Anything." Well, most anything. Right then he wasn't sure he wanted to answer, but he'd do it.

"When you asked me to lie with you, you really meant for conversation, didn't you?"

"I did." He nodded. "I knew I was losing steam, but I didn't want the connection to fizzle." He didn't want the fun times to disappear.

"If I hadn't been so cautious, then I would've stayed." He brushed the back of his fingers against Matt's cheek. "Would you mind if I kissed you?"

"Nope." He leaned across the console and feathered his lips over Aiden's. He might have decided on slowing down, but not at that moment. Right then he needed Aiden. The taste of the doctor, lemony from the water and the chicken as well as the tartness of the Caesar salad. He liked the way Aiden's lips fluttered on his. He moaned into Aiden's mouth, pushing the connection deeper. His thoughts muddled and the ache in his body dissipated. If this was what he needed for his drug of choice—Aiden—then he was all for them being together.

Aiden broke away first and puffed. "Wow."

"Yeah."

"If I had known it would be like that, I would've kissed you the night we met at the shop."

Matt grasped Aiden's fingers. "Just wait until I'm back to eighty percent. It'll be even better."

Aiden shook his head and laughed. "I'll do that. Hell, it might take me that long to get back to you. I work crazy hours, but yeah, a few texts and calls would be good."

"I changed my mind. Would you help me into the house? Just hold the gate and the door for me. I promise I won't try to proposition you." Matt twisted the handle on the car door.

"Whatever you want." Aiden hurried out of the car and rounded the hood. He offered his hand. "Come with me. We'll get you inside."

Matt allowed Aiden to usher him through the main gate, then up onto the porch. He unlocked the front door, then turned to Aiden. "I had a good time. I needed the lesson in humility and patience. Here's to another date when we're both ready."

"I don't know what to say, but absolutely." Aiden kissed him, this time leading the way. He didn't linger the way Matt had wanted, but Matt wasn't going to argue. He'd been given a taste of Aiden and was now addicted. He needed more. If he bided his time, he had a gut feeling he'd get what he'd always wanted and more.

Matt braced his good shoulder on the door and watched Aiden stroll down the steps. "Good night, Doc Cedarwood."

Aiden paused. He tipped his head and chuckled. "That's a new one. Doc Cedarwood? I'm not sure I'm helping everyone or befitting of that name, but…okay. Good night, Matt. I'll come up with a catchy nickname for you later." He waved, then closed the gate behind him and opened the door to his car.

Matt waited until Aiden had zipped away from the house before he closed himself into his home. He couldn't be sure when he'd see Aiden again, but he held on to the hope that they'd get together sooner rather than later.

Chapter Five

Aiden stretched and cracked his neck. In the last two weeks, he'd called and texted Matt almost every day. Despite his best efforts to get together with Matt, his schedule and Matt's didn't gel. If he wasn't at the hospital, Matt was at the shop. He should've been annoyed but wasn't. Things weren't working out—for now.

"What are you doing?" Madison asked. The nurse stood beside Aiden. "Your patients have been transitioned to the next shift and you're allowed to go home."

"I know." He completed the rest of his paperwork and groaned. "I know I'm done for now, but sometimes I wonder why I go home. As soon as the requisite time between shifts is up, I'm called right back."

"You're not invincible." She patted his shoulder. "I get it. We need more staff."

"We do."

"You've got one of the best sets of bedside manners I've ever seen and everyone needs your brand of kindness. That said, right now we don't, and you need to go home to get some rest." She nudged him away from the computer. "I hear you've got a boyfriend."

"What?" He stared at her. Going to the dinner with Matt had been rather bold. But he'd kept the texts and phone calls private. "We went out once to a public event. It wasn't that big." He'd minimized whatever was going on with Matt. Not good. "But yeah, I guess we're seeing each other."

Madison snorted. "How nice." She didn't look at him and typed away on the computer. The longer she remained quiet, the more his heart sank.

That was one of the reasons he shied away from relationships. He always screwed up.

"Aiden?" She turned to him. "Do you like Matt?"

He didn't think. Instead, he just answered. "Yes."

"Do you want anyone else?"

"Why? Are you offering?" He wasn't attracted to her, but Madison had a tendency to beat around the bush.

"No." She frowned. "Yes, you're cute and most of the nursing staff wants to play with your thermometer, but I'll pass. What I meant was, you're not being casual with him, right?"

"I'm not sure." He sat on the closest stool. "I'll level with you. The whole thing with Matt has been interesting. It's not usual. We met because I had an accident and needed the car fixed. He did and I kind of blew him off because I haven't had a whole lot of time for anyone and I have issues with relationships. When we got together for a chat…he moved too fast. I felt like I knew him, but I wasn't sure if I wanted to take that leap. I freaked out and ran."

She narrowed her eyes, then sighed. "Aiden, hon, you can't let the problems with Lucky or whatever issues you've got cooked up in your head taint what you're doing now. Matt moved everything so fast, yes. He might be eager, but that doesn't mean he doesn't respect you. I'm sure he does."

Or he just wants a quick fuck before he walks away from me. "What do you think I should do?"

"Give him a shot." She smiled, then flipped her blonde ponytail over her shoulder. "If you date a few times and it falls apart, you're not out anything but some time. If you fit together and it's good, then...even better."

He raked his fingers through his hair, then sagged on his stool. "Okay. I'd already sort of planned to give it a shot. You just made me feel better about my decision."

"Then go and find your studly mechanic and let him play with your...thermometer." She laughed and nudged him. "Go."

"Deal." He left his seat and patted her arm before leaving the nurses' station. Aiden made his way through the bowels of the hospital to the locker room. Madison's encouragement had helped but wasn't the last push. He'd struggled with his feelings since the first night. Matt made him happy and gave him reasons to enjoy his time away from the hospital, instead of looking forward to going back. His heart ached after he got off the phone with Matt. *Why aren't I giving Matt more of a shot?*

Aiden changed his clothes and considered what to do. He should leave the hospital and go to the shop. If Matt wasn't there, then he should be at home. Part of him wanted to call the visit a check-up and claim he was there to make sure Matt wasn't going without the sling all the time. The rest of him knew better. The longer he'd been away from Matt, the more he'd grown attached to him. He hated himself for how he felt — when things finally blew sky high, he'd be even angrier for trying again.

Aiden tossed his dirty scrubs into the hamper and grabbed his bag. He headed out of the locker room and ducked through the back entrance. His back ached, his muscles hurt and he wanted quiet. He snorted. Matt kept telling him he thrived in the public eye. Madison said he had a great bedside manner. Even Aiden, the man who seemed to live at the hospital, wanted to be alone — unless Matt was involved.

He trudged across the lot to his car. Once he got closer to his vehicle, Aiden noticed a figure next to his front fender. The light shone down on the man and his hat obscured Aiden's view of his face.

"What's going on?" Aiden asked. "Who are you?" He strode up to the car. Within seconds, he recognized the man — Matt. His heart leapt, and the tiredness melted away. The spring returned to his step. He hurried to Matt. "Matt?"

"Yeah." Matt adjusted his fedora. He wasn't wearing his sling. The shirt and jeans clung to his body like a second skin. He offered up a bouquet of flowers. "I heard you had a rough day." He offered up the daisies. "For you. I wasn't sure what you'd like, so I got these."

"Wow. I love them. Thank you." He couldn't remember the last time he'd been given flowers. "What are you doing here?" He wanted to appear excited but sounded silly. The giddiness within him had gotten the better of him. Matt made him happy. He lurched forward and kissed him hard on the lips. Electricity zapped in his veins. The kiss lasted longer than it probably should've, but he loved being this close to Matt.

Matt rested his forehead on Aiden's and wound his arms around him. He caressed Aiden's lower back. "Are you happy to see me?"

He nodded. "Yeah, and that's not a gun in my pants." He breathed in the scent of Matt—clean but with a little musk. Once the intoxication of being together with Matt dissipated a bit, Aiden met his gaze. "What about your arm? You're straining yourself." *Fuck it.* For now, he'd keep his worries in check. They weren't gone, just in check.

"I'm fine. I've been taking it easy. I read everything the doctor sent home and I've been following your directions. I know my limits and have been staying within them." Matt slid his palms into Aiden's back pockets.

Aiden's ass tingled and his cock throbbed. He bit back a groan.

"I feel the same way. The phone calls are good, but I wanted to catch you in person." Matt paused. "Plus, I heard it's been a rough week."

"You could say that." *Rough... Try awful.* He'd helped the patients from three car accidents, a man with a wooden handle stuck in his ass, another who'd voluntarily swallowed five dollars in quarters, and a football player who'd passed out on the field. The poor kid had died on his way to the emergency room. Aiden hated when bad things happened to kids and hated to spend his week this way. When he'd gone home after each shift, he'd called Matt, then collapsed.

"Then let me cheer you up," Matt said. "I want to."

"Already done." He'd have one hell of a time getting out of his own head later, but for now he'd be all right. "You being here has done wonders for me." *Until you leave and I'm fucked.*

"I mean, yeah, being together, but not only here." Matt squeezed Aiden's ass. "Come home with me."

"Unless you drove, I'll have to take you home." He laughed. He should be irritated with Matt's lack of wheels, but he wasn't. Matt shouldn't be driving anyway. He preferred to help his friend out.

"Sorry. I had to be at the shop. I hired a kid from the vocational school to help Aaron out, at least until I'm back up to working order. According to Aaron, I'm now the office bitch." Matt shrugged. "When we closed, I walked over."

"I'm glad you were willing to get help — I'm betting the kid is too — and that you're here." He needed the break. "Hop in." Aiden looked forward to time alone with Matt. "I'm ready to get out of here."

"When I saw you leave the hospital, I called Colucci's. Our order should be ready about the time we get to the house." Matt settled on the passenger seat and rested his hand on Aiden's thigh. "I know it was pushy, but I wanted to make the night special."

Aiden sat beside him and sighed. "What's on the menu?" He stuffed the key into the ignition. "How'd you know what I'd like?"

"Besides me?"

"Nice." He pulled out of the lot and onto the street. Aiden drove down the road past the dangerous curb and away from the hospital.

"Spaghetti. That's what I ordered. I wasn't home and couldn't cook something myself. Next time I owe you a home-cooked meal." Matt squeezed Aiden's thigh. "Promise."

"I love it, but you don't have to." Aiden sped across town to Matt's house. "No, I appreciate it. Most of the time I eat those boxed dinners. Not the best or the most flavorful, but they're healthy-ish."

"Ish doesn't sound tasty. Sounds awful and like it doesn't make anything better. So you're healthy... If you're not happy, then who cares?" Matt caressed Aiden's leg.

"When you're stressed and don't have much time, you'll eat cardboard." Aiden cringed. Most of the stuff he made himself for lunches and dinners wasn't all that exciting.

"How do you deal with the stress at work? The kid is doing a great job, but Aaron's driving me crazy. I'm open to suggestions to de-stress."

Aiden turned onto Matt's street. "In your case, you should lay off the strenuous stuff until you're healed. No marathons, racquetball tournaments or wrestling matches."

"Well, shit. I'll have to reschedule my whole weekend." Matt laughed and palmed Aiden's leg, higher up on his thigh.

Aiden hadn't expected that answer from Matt. They'd been so serious before. He gave in to the full-blown belly laugh. He hadn't been so happy in forever — not like this.

Matt sobered. "But seriously. How do you do it? You've got to be stressed. It's life as a doctor, I assume. How do you keep level? A secret addiction? Yoga? Anything? I'm trying to balance out my life — between the crap at the shop with Aaron, my shoulder and whatever this is happening between us...I'm overwhelmed."

Aiden didn't understand how Matt made the connections, but sometimes things he thought would make sense didn't. "Unless you count my need to run down on the track in the therapy wing. Three miles every day I'm on at the hospital. Pushing myself in the ER, at the track or wherever frees my head. I know that doesn't make a whole lot of sense, but that's me. Plus, I have a minor obsession with jazz music from the 1930s."

"Interesting." Matt laughed. He pressed a button on his keys, opening the gate. "I'm not familiar with that genre of music."

"You should check it out." He pulled into Matt's driveway. "You can see a lot of what's going on now in those songs." A car parked behind his. Aiden pointed to the rearview mirror. "Is that the food?" He noticed a lit-up sign on the vehicle. "I think it is."

"Looks like." Matt left the car and stood behind Aiden's. After a few moments, Matt strode up to Aiden's door with a bag.

Aiden sighed and watched the other car leave. He didn't care where he was. He'd keep an eye out. He wasn't big on trust, even if he was in the town of Cedarwood. Matt being shot had scared the shit out of him.

Matt leaned on Aiden's door. "Take these and pull forward to the garage." He stuffed the bag through the window then strolled away from Aiden.

"Will do." He continued up the drive to the garage and parked. He left the vehicle and picked up the bag.

"Thanks." Matt rested his hand on the small of Aiden's back. "Do you need help?"

"I should be asking you that. I'm fine." He locked the car, then followed Matt into the house. "You've strained yourself."

"Nah." Matt tossed his keys on the bar. "Make yourself at home." He kicked out of his boots. "I got some new furniture so the house isn't quite so…empty."

"You didn't have to." Aiden placed the bag on the counter. "Unless you were planning on doing it to begin with."

"A couch and television aren't that much." Matt winked. "Sit at the bar with me and we'll watch something on that new TV. Want some water?"

"Please? And yes, I'd like that." Aiden had washed his hands before leaving the hospital, but extra washing was part of his nature. He pumped plenty of soap onto his hands and kept them under the faucet until the hot water scalded away the germs. If nothing else, he was cautious. He unboxed the food and arranged it for two settings. He pulled out the stools and waited for Matt. "This is a gothic house. A bar, while nice, doesn't seem to fit," Aiden blurted. He should've kept his thoughts to himself.

"I agree. The previous owner did that. The house was part of her family for over a hundred years and by the time it came down to Jasmine, she didn't know what to do with it. She tried renovating, but the costs were larger than she thought because she wanted modern everything. I'm switching it back a little at a time. I like the bar, but it's not historical and it's falling apart." Matt arranged his napkin on his lap. "It'll take time and money I don't have, but I'll do it."

"I'm sure you will." He toyed with his fork. "Thanks for dinner. This looks fantastic." He wasn't sure what else to say. The conversation wasn't going the way he'd planned. Embarrassment washed over him. When they'd talked before, everything had flowed. Now? He wanted to impress Matt and be cool. Instead, he sounded like a fool, blurting things out.

"Bet it tastes good too." Matt twirled spaghetti onto his fork, then stopped and stared at Aiden. "You're tense again. Are you okay?"

"I'm fine." He picked at the slice of garlic bread. "Matt...what are we doing here?" He needed to know what was happening, to see how everything fit together and where the variables were so he could prepare himself.

"Eating, I believe." Matt turned in his seat. "Talk to me."

"Your arm. You've got to be straining yourself. You should have that sling on." God, he couldn't turn his inner doctor off. "I'm sorry."

"No, you're being a good doc. According to my physical therapist, I need to sleep in the sling, but he's been weaning me off it for the last week. If I rely on it too much, I'll do more damage." Matt held up his fork. "It's very sexy how you worry about me."

"Yeah." He fumbled. *Shit.* "Matt..." *Oh, fuck.* Where were the flaws? Where were the warning signs to turn around and get the hell out of there?

"What's going on between us is two guys having dinner. We'll kiss some more—if I get my way—and touch. I want to be with you. Are we going too fast? Depends on who you ask. I think we're fine. This is the speed it's supposed to be," Matt said. He polished off the bite of spaghetti. "Is that what you want?"

"I do." His hands shook. "Matt."

"Finish your dinner. I'm dying to use that couch." Matt returned to his dinner.

Aiden ate in silence. He could get used to this closeness. He finished his spaghetti. Being with Matt and acting domestic soothed him.

"Happy?" Matt closed the foam box. "I'm not only happy, but I am full. This is the most I've had to eat in days."

"It's the tastiest thing." When Matt tugged him from the stool, Aiden didn't fight him. He made sure to move on his own free will and not strain Matt's shoulder.

"I'm not going to break." Matt snorted. "Check out the new stuff." He grasped Aiden's hand and led him into the living room. "It's amazing the things you can find online."

"I've got friends at the hospital who swear by Internet shopping." Aiden settled beside Matt on the couch. The cushions gave way, pushing him closer to Matt. "It's comfortable."

"Sure is." Matt grinned. "I like it."

Aiden bumped into Matt's shoulder. "Sorry. I should've moved onto the other side." He should've been thinking about Matt and not savoring the squishiness of the sofa.

"I'm a little tender, but I'll live."

Aiden jumped up from his seat. He wasn't using his head. *Good God.*

Matt snatched his hand, tugging him back to the couch. "I never said to go." He eased Aiden onto his lap until Aiden straddled his thighs. "Better."

The bulge in Aiden's jeans rubbed against the one in Matt's pants. The delicious friction sent heat straight to Aiden's core. His nerve endings sizzled. He and Matt should be going slower than this, but he couldn't stop now that they'd started.

"Don't you want to kiss me?" Matt asked.

"I do." He leaned forward and used the back of the couch for leverage. He feathered his mouth over Matt's. The sizzles increased. He wanted Matt to feel the same passion flowing through his veins. He broke away but didn't go far and stared into Matt's eyes. The man personified sin and his cologne kicked up Aiden's need even more. His thoughts muddled. He liked kissing Matt, and pushed deeper. Matt nipped his bottom lip and, when he opened his mouth, Aiden sucked on Matt's tongue. He'd never tasted anything so divine as Matt.

Matt groaned and grabbed Aiden's ass.

Holy shit. He loved when his lover took control. He tilted his head to feast more on Matt's mouth. The scruff on Matt's cheeks abraded his face and he loved every moment. Their teeth clashed and they bumped noses twice, but Aiden didn't mind. He ground his hips, needing to be closer to Matt.

Another groan ripped from Matt's lips. He broke the connection. "What can I not do?"

"Huh?" He needed to think clearly and his brain wasn't cooperating. "What?" He fumbled for another moment. *Not do? Oh! With his shoulder...* "Don't overexert yourself."

"How?" He palmed Aiden's chest. His eyes widened and a wicked grin spread across his face. He whipped Aiden's shirt up over his head. "Can I fuck?"

"I wouldn't suggest swinging from the ceiling fan." His nipples hardened in the chilly air. He wanted to be naked...now.

"Good thing I don't have a ceiling fan." Matt cupped Aiden's cheek and brushed his thumb across Aiden's bottom lip. "I want to be inside you."

He nodded. "I want you there." Aiden paused. "Are you clean?" He hated to screw up the moment, but he had to know.

"Uh-huh. You?" Matt's eyebrows rose.

"Yes." He got himself tested religiously. Even when he wasn't sleeping with anyone, he went through the tests.

"Then what are we waiting for?"

Aiden scrambled off Matt's lap. He had no idea where the bedroom was and didn't want to barge up to the second floor uninvited.

Matt snagged Aiden in an embrace. He kissed Aiden. Raw desire filled Aiden's body. He loved a man who pushed him and made him think. One who cared about more than just himself. Being with Matt energized and overwhelmed him. But not having had sex in a while made him wary. What were Matt's expectations? Would he be good enough? Why in the hell had he eaten an extra donut at breakfast? He wouldn't be able to hide his lack of exercise over the last two days.

Matt rubbed his nose along Aiden's belly. He didn't kiss — more like he seemed to use Aiden's body to mark himself. "What are you worrying about?"

"How can you tell?" *I'm not telegraphing that much... am I?*

"You stopped kissing me and your forehead is all wrinkled. There's a faraway look in your eyes. Oh, and you lost your boner." Matt slid his hand over the front of Aiden's jeans. "I'll get it back."

"I bet you will." He had no doubts at all. Aiden didn't struggle as Matt popped open the front of his jeans.

Matt chuckled and resumed kissing Aiden's torso, but instead of the frantic movements like before, he took more of a leisurely pace. He dragged his tongue along Aiden's ribs, then swirled around Aiden's navel. Was Matt learning him?

Aiden slid his fingers into Matt's spiky hair. Despite the gel, the man had soft tresses. Aiden whimpered. He couldn't remember the last time he'd been given so much attention by his beau. Usually he was the bottom and wasn't invited to move beyond that role.

Matt opened Aiden's pants and shoved the denim down his hips. "You've been holding out on me." He moved Aiden's boxer briefs away from his cock. "I'm in love."

A shiver streaked down Aiden's spine. *In love.* Guys weren't in love with him. They fell for his status, not the man.

Matt rubbed his face over Aiden's cock and slid his right hand along Aiden's belly to his chest. He tweaked Aiden's nipple.

The pain morphed into pleasure in an instant. Aiden rocked on his heels. His throat ran dry and he wanted to get closer to Matt. Not just a physical connection but a mental one too. He wanted to know what Matt was thinking. How he felt. Was he confused and excited too?

"My, my, my. You're beautiful." Matt left a bite on Aiden's love handle.

Aiden nearly choked. "Liar." He couldn't handle the compliment. He wasn't anything special. Hell, he had chub where he shouldn't, and other flaws.

"Would I lie about this?" Matt held Aiden's cock in his hand. "You're beautiful inside and out. You might not see it, but I do. And this?" He pressed his thumb against the blunt head of Aiden's dick. "Smells good, looks delicious and I bet you taste fantastic."

He should argue. Should explain why Matt was wrong, but he couldn't. "I'm all yours," he blurted. He wanted to belong to Matt and to believe that them being together was a matter of fate. He didn't want anyone else. "Yes, all yours."

"Good." Matt encircled Aiden's dick with his fingers and stroked him. He flicked his tongue across the knobby head. Damn, his man did taste good.

Aiden shivered. "Shit. Sorry." He fumbled with his hands. "I…"

"You're fine." He winked. "It didn't hurt."

"Are you sure?"

"Uh-huh."

Aiden rested his palms on Matt's shoulders. "You know how to bring me to my knees."

It was good to know Aiden was just as off-kilter as him. He plunged his mouth down on Aiden's cock and bobbed his head. He tasted Aiden all over and groaned. *So yummy.*

Something within Matt changed. Being with Aiden was more than a simple blowjob or a quickie. It wasn't even just a date. He deeply cared about Aiden. Love wasn't there—well, not yet. He liked to move fast, but this was too quick for the emotion to be love. Still, this was something more. He hadn't expected to fall for Aiden—not like this. Sure, his feelings had developed at warp speed, but that was Matt. He made decisions within seconds and stuck to his guns. No looking back, just dealing with the choices he'd made.

He continued to bob his head and curled his tongue around Aiden's shaft. Sucking cock was one of his favorite activities and Aiden was like candy. He buried his nose in Aiden's pubic hair. The man smelled good and he loved the way Aiden's fingernails scraped his shoulders.

Aiden groaned again and moved his hips. Matt might have been in control, but Aiden knew when to push. He eased his dick in and out of Matt's mouth.

A thought occurred to Matt. *Why Aiden?* Why was the somewhat mousy, not-at-all-his-type guy getting to him? *Loneliness? The need for a new fix?* He wasn't sure. They'd connected on a deeper level. Aiden hadn't been afraid to come to his home and hadn't blinked when he'd showed his tattoos.

Aiden shivered and rammed his cock into Matt's mouth. His grasp tightened on Matt's shoulders. "Fuck." He curled forward. "Matt."

He swallowed Aiden to the hilt and hummed. When Aiden gasped, he placed his left hand on Aiden's hip and the other on his chest. He pinched Aiden's nipple.

"Matt." Aiden's knees buckled and he tipped onto Matt, putting pressure on him. "I'm right fucking there." He tensed and whimpered. His breathing turned ragged.

Matt rubbed Aiden's hip. He wasn't sure how to tell Aiden it was okay to come, but he hoped the soothing gesture did the trick.

"Fuck," Aiden said and drew the word out. Aiden let go of Matt's shoulders and yanked his cock from Matt's mouth. Cum splashed onto Matt's shirt and chin.

Aiden closed his eyes and wobbled. "Damn."

"That's one way to put it." Matt bit back a chuckle. He wasn't a fan of being jizzed on, but Aiden doing it didn't seem to bother him. He used his shirt tail to clean off his chin.

Aiden opened his eyes and his lips parted. "Oh, shit. I'm sorry." He tripped on his pants and stumbled onto the couch. "Damn."

"What are you sorry for? Coming?" Matt unbuttoned his shirt. "Don't be."

"I came on you." He kicked out of his pants and wadded-up boxer briefs. He scooped his shirt up from the floor and wiped Matt clean. "I wasn't thinking."

"You were coming." He laughed and stilled Aiden's hands. "It's okay. Better than okay. It was beautiful."

Aiden blushed from his hairline to his chest. He leaned forward and rested his elbows on his knees. "Matt."

"Babe—and yes, I'm calling you that—never be ashamed to come." He caressed Aiden's back. "I don't know what happened that you're embarrassed, but don't be."

Aiden opened and closed his mouth, but no sound came out. He stared at Matt, then placed his head on Matt's lap.

Matt petted Aiden's hair. He loved sharing little moments like this—the bonding after intimacy and knowing he'd affected Aiden down to his core. Now if he could only get Aiden to open up a little ... "Hey, Doc?"

"That's me," Aiden murmured.

"Are you falling asleep?" He knew better but had to ask.

Aiden laughed. "No, but you overwhelmed me."

"Oh. Good." He paused. "Would it be bad to mention I've got a raging boner and I want to fuck you?"

"Nope."

"Good, 'cause I'm loaded and ready to blow."

"You already blew." Aiden sat up and faced Matt. "Take me to your room. I'm dying to be fucked."

Things had definitely changed between them. He'd done more than fall for Aiden. The connection was stronger than he'd imagined. "That's my kind of guy."

"Me?" Aiden's eyes flashed.

No turning back. He'd gone head over heels. Matt dragged a deep breath into his lungs and let it out slowly. He needed to tell Aiden everything, but not yet. Right now he wanted to indulge in the man he could see himself loving forever. "Yeah, you."

Chapter Six

Aiden abandoned his clothes downstairs and followed Matt up to the second floor. He marveled at the architectural nuances of Matt's home. He couldn't understand why anyone would want to get rid of the curved doorways or the wide molding around the doors. Even the maroon of the hallway seemed perfect for the house.

"Here she is—my bedroom." Matt stopped at the second door on the left. He nudged Aiden into the space first, then stood behind him and wrapped his arms around Aiden.

He gazed around the room and sighed. "You have rounded walls," Aiden blurted. The curves fascinated him. "Sorry. I've never seen that except for in magazines."

"I know. Those were selling points." Matt scratched Aiden's belly. "Those and the rounded windows."

He hadn't noticed those. Still, the uniqueness of the room wasn't lost on him. "Beautiful."

"That's my line." Matt kissed the side of his neck. "What's beautiful is having a naked man in my room. You're so comfortable. I love it. Like you've always been here."

He realized what Matt had said and winced. "Yeah...fully naked and you're clothed." *Damn.* He wanted to run back downstairs and retrieve his pants. Better yet, he wanted to get out before he lost his heart to Matt.

"Then I'll join you." Matt let go of him and held his head high. He slid the buttons free from the holes in his shirt until it hung open. He shrugged out of the garment. Being half-nude meant all his tattoos were on display.

Aiden sank onto the bed and stared at Matt. He'd seen the ink before but hadn't really appreciated it back at the hospital. The calligraphic letters across Matt's chest glistened in the light. *Phillips.* Stars decorated the ends of Matt's last name and another pair were on his lower back. A detailed set of skulls covered his shoulders. The word *triumph* stretched down the inside of his left arm and *desire* had been written on the right one. "I never noticed the spiderwebs design between the other tattoos."

"Oh. Those are filler." Matt held up his left arm and turned his wrist over. "I've got an engine block here and pistons on either side."

"Because of the shop?" *Of course they'd be for the shop. Duh.*

"Exactly. The words are what are important and they're motivation. The webs were something light to fill in the gaps. Speaking of gaps..." He nodded to the bed. "I want you on your hands and knees. I want to see your ass. I bet it's even better without clothes."

"You didn't look already?" Aiden did as told and crawled onto the bed. He glanced over his shoulder. "What do you think?"

"I think you've held out on me." Matt palmed Aiden's butt. "You've got enough to grab and hold on to during sex."

"You can't bottom yet." Aiden squeezed his eyes shut. *Christ.* He needed to get out of doctor mode.

"Not yet, but I will be ready soon."

Aiden shivered at the sound of Matt's belt buckle popping. He opened his eyes and rested on his hip. He needed to see what was going on and experience Matt in the raw.

"Just a second. We need rubbers and lube." Matt strolled over to the nightstand and rummaged through the nightstand for the needed items.

Aiden snuggled in the blankets. He kind of liked not being in charge. He spent so much time telling others what to do and dealing with overwhelming stress at the hospital. Having someone else take command was nice. He appreciated being able to decompress and not having to think. Matt would take care of him.

* * * *

Matt stretched out on his back. His shoulder ached, and it was only a matter of time before Aiden chewed him out for overexerting himself. Aiden draped his arm across Matt's belly, but he didn't seem relaxed. He balled his hand.

"Going home with someone is out of your comfort zone, isn't it?" Matt asked. He tucked his uninjured arm under his head. "Am I good enough?" He hated asking the question, but with the way Aiden tensed, he wasn't sure what to think. Was he only okay until they fucked, or was there something else on Aiden's mind?

Aiden tipped his head and met Matt's gaze. "What do you mean? I wouldn't be here if you weren't good enough."

"Are you sure? You're this close to jumping and running." Matt stared at the darker blue flecks in Aiden's eyes. "Hon, be honest with me."

Aiden stilled. "I owe you an explanation."

Ah. Here it comes. Matt bit back his frustration. If Aiden said 'this was fun, but I gotta run,' he'd scream.

"Slow." Aiden flattened his palm over Matt's heart. "It's about my past."

Even better. He wasn't ready to share his issues and hoped Aiden didn't expect him to reciprocate. "Okay," he managed.

"I grew up in the gay community for the most part. To me, it was the community. I never saw people based on their race or orientation. We're all people. When I was a kid, my dad was married to my mother. That's how they had me." Aiden shook his head. "I mean, they weren't in love with each other. She wanted a baby, and he… I don't know what he wanted. I remember seeing him with his 'special friends'. Until I was twelve, I didn't see the same guy come to the house twice. Looking back, I understand they were his boyfriends or guy for the night. It bugged me. Not only was he stepping out on Mom, but he couldn't seem to stick with one guy. Anyway, when I hit thirteen, he came out, Mom left and never looked back, and I got to stay with my father the smoothie. For a year, he kept up the 'special friends' bit—probably because he didn't think I understood. I don't know. But when he met Keye, things changed. There weren't guys in and out of the house. I liked that he'd found someone, but all those men… The situation left a mark on me."

"One of them hit you?" Matt blurted. "No one has that right."

"No, they didn't." Aiden smiled. "What I mean is, I didn't want to be like my old man. I swore I wasn't going to be the guy who went through boyfriends like water. I don't like trying everything before I buy."

"You're smart." Matt rolled onto his side and twined his legs with Aiden's. "I'm sorry I jumped to conclusions. It just made me angry to think someone would hurt you. You're a sweet man and deserve the best." He wasn't sure he could be that best, but still.

"I learned too much about germs and communicable diseases through my studies. I'm not petrified of germs, but I'm not fond of them, either. It's easy to keep yourself clean at the hospital. There is sanitizer everywhere. But in life? You can't trust anyone. One of my hang-ups—which I seem to have forgotten with you—is to keep it in my pants because I don't know who has what or if I'll get it."

"No, I get it." He had the same feelings. Many of the guys he'd dated hadn't been forthcoming and had ended up pissed when they didn't fuck at the end of the night.

"But to answer your question in my odd, roundabout way, I don't date much because I don't have a whole lot of faith in humankind. I don't like putting myself out there unless I can control the situation. I'd rather be alone than hurt." Aiden shrugged. "Still think I'm so great and wonderful?"

"Your last boyfriend said you were missing a few marbles, didn't he?" Matt trailed the back of his fingers down Aiden's chest. "And you're worried I'll be the same way?"

"With you, I'm normal." Aiden groaned and closed his eyes. "I don't have to impress you or prove I'm anything but me. Weird, nerdy, complicated, afraid of more than I should be…but you seem to get me."

Aiden seemed to understand him in return. "I agree." He kissed the tip of Aiden's nose. "You make me feel like myself again." He'd have to tell Aiden about his past sometime, but not now. Things were going too well. He refused to screw it up, even though he had the notion a clusterfuck was on the way.

"You don't mind if I sleep over, do you?" Aiden opened his eyes. "I'm beat. You wore me out."

"Doc Cedarwood, I'd be angry if you didn't." Matt chuckled.

"Good. I'll check your shoulder in the morning. It'll probably be sore." Aiden kissed Matt. "You should take something, though. It'll help."

"You're big on the meds. I'm okay. If I'm not, I'll tell you and let you do whatever you think is best. Promise." Matt knew damn well he'd be hurting by the time he woke up. His shoulder already ached. But he wasn't about to take drugs to dull the pain. Aiden was worth any hassle.

"Okay." Aiden turned over and pressed his ass into Matt's hips. Within seconds, his breathing evened out and he was snoring softly.

Matt snuggled against Aiden's backside and held him. Sleep filtered into his brain, but he couldn't shut down enough. He'd never experienced anyone like Aiden. So smart and funny, but uptight and on the verge of losing his cool when he wasn't at the hospital—at least as much as Matt had seen. Aiden seemed to have so much love to give, but his fear kept him from opening himself up. Not that Matt could expect a whole lot in return. He hid his past and his troubles with addiction because he was worried about what Aiden might say. He didn't want to lose Aiden when the doctor learned the truth. He noticed the coin on the nightstand. Colin, Jordan and his friend at the newspaper, Remy, seemed to be cheering for him. Colt seemed to be doing the opposite. Matt pinched the bridge of his nose. He wanted to be good for Aiden. The sex was hot and he loved the way Aiden looked in and out of clothes. Aiden felt perfect in his arms. He wanted to protect Aiden and cherish him.

If Matt kept the pills out of his life and ignored the urge to drink, he'd be fine. Aiden was his new vice. If he had to succumb, then Aiden would be a good addiction.

Chapter Seven

Matt snorted and rolled onto his side. He reached for Aiden. When he touched the sheets instead, he jolted awake. "What the hell?" He sat up and blinked until his vision cleared. Where was Aiden? He couldn't have bailed on him...right? Matt crinkled his nose. The scent of bacon hung in the air. *Bacon?*

Matt scrambled out of bed and put on a clean pair of boxers. If there was a robber in the house, the fool wouldn't be cooking. He rushed down the stairs and bolted into the kitchen.

Aiden stood at the stove with his back to Matt. He'd donned a T-shirt and his jeans. The scent of the bacon as well as toast and eggs wafted around Matt. His stomach growled. He couldn't remember the last time a guy had made food for him.

"What's this?" Matt crossed the room. "Are you cooking for me?" Excitement and gratitude filled him. Aiden certainly made the house feel more like a home.

"Of course." Aiden glanced over his shoulder. "I like to be in the kitchen, but eating alone tends to take the fun out of getting creative. I hope you like the works. Eggs with peppers, onions and cheese, bacon and toast. There's even oranges."

"Where'd you get it?" He eased up behind Aiden and embraced him. Matt rested his chin on Aiden's shoulder. "I don't have any of these things in the house." He hadn't before now.

"I ordered it." Aiden tipped his head enough to kiss Matt on the cheek. "My friend, Lennon, runs the Sunset Foods grocery store and owed me a favor. I stitched up his thumb after he sliced it with a box cutter. Anyway, I called him, placed an order and forked over a little more for quick delivery. Voilà. We have breakfast and lunch. I hope I'm allowed to stick around to have lunch with you, but it's there. You could get sick of me by ten."

"I doubt I will." He dragged his nose along the side of Aiden's neck. "I love it."

"Good. How's the shoulder?" Aiden moved the peppers and onions around in the pan. "Feeling good or stiff?"

"I'm stiff, but not in the shoulder region." He ground his semi-hard dick into the seam of Aiden's ass. "The wound is fine and I'm a little sore, but nothing I can't handle. I'm not used to sharing my bed. I wouldn't trade last night for anything, so don't think that's the case."

"I can go." Aiden dumped the chopped veggies into the pan of whisked eggs. "I know when I'm not wanted." He laughed. "But I'm not going until after I eat."

"You're not leaving in the middle of all this fun." He swatted Aiden's butt hard. "Now that I've got you, I'm not ready to let go."

"I suspected as much."

"I'd ask if you need help, but it looks like you've got it all under control." Matt let go of Aiden and rounded the island to sit on one of the stools.

"It's all part of my evil plan." Aiden wriggled his rump. "If I look good, then you'll keep me around. Scoot a plate over here. This is done."

Matt pushed one of the dinner plates across the counter. "Oh, I plan on keeping you around."

"Perfect." Aiden scraped the eggs and veggies out of the pan, then parceled out the bacon. "Hope you like it."

"I'm sure I will." Matt munched on the bacon. The taste overwhelmed him and the bacon melted in his mouth. "Damn." He bit back a groan. He'd planned on asking more questions, not having a virtual orgasm over the food. "So, just because you work a lot, that's why you can't keep a date? Because you're careful about who you sleep with? You should be snapped up by now and married. You're a catch." He had the motto that if he found the guy he wanted, he'd push himself hard to make things work. Love meant sticking it out through the good and bad times. His ex-boyfriend Theo didn't believe that. If Matt wasn't strung out or drunk, then Theo wasn't happy. Matt doubted Aiden would be like Theo, but still. He had to be his own version of cautious.

"I might be a catch to you, but Lucky, my ex, didn't think so." Aiden broke a new set of eggs into the pan. "He thought I was made of money. I'm a doctor, so I should be rich and keeping him in the best lifestyle. He forgot I'm in debt up to my eyeballs and I'm a simple guy. I work in Cedarwood, Ohio. This isn't New York or Chicago. I'm happy and not rolling in the dough.

Lucky never believed that. We split because he needed more money than I'd ever make. Then, because he was such a sweet fellow, he kept coming back into my life. If I started to get close to someone, he appeared and worked his Lucky magic. Bell said no before we even kissed. Drake was a dead end. I heard he took up with Lucky for a while. I don't know. I guess I gave up and stopped looking for Mr. Right."

"Until you ruined your car and needed a rim job." Matt winked when Aiden glanced back at him. "Hey, I'm happy to oblige anytime." He'd kiss Aiden's lips, chest, ass, dick…whatever.

"Likewise." Aiden switched off the burners and plated his food. He settled beside Matt. "Enjoy."

"Already done." Matt devoured the rest of his breakfast, then leaned back on his stool. Aiden's decision to surprise him had hit the mark. He liked being with Aiden and acting like an old couple, despite the relationship being so new. The silence between them didn't bother him. He didn't feel compelled to keep talking.

Aiden sopped up the remainder of his eggs with his toast. "Well?"

"You're hired as my personal physician and chef." Matt pushed the plate away. "I'm stuffed and I'll have to put in double time at the gym once I'm cleared to work out again. Think you'd ever want to run with me?"

"I would."

Matt sighed and rubbed his belly. "Now for a shower and a second round of sex. Are you in?"

"Uh…yeah." Aiden grasped Matt's fingers. "I'm not sure I want this to end."

"Doesn't have to." As far as he was concerned, Aiden could move right in.

A ringing sound echoed in the house. Matt tipped his head. He didn't recognize the tone. "Is that yours or mine?" Matt asked.

"No clue." Aiden gathered the plates and placed them in the sink, then wiped his hands. "I'll check my phone." He disappeared upstairs, then returned with the phone in his hand. "Guess it was me, but the number isn't one I know. They can leave a voice mail."

Matt flattened his hands on the bar. "It's not the hospital with an urgent request for you to come in?"

"Can't be. I have the numbers programmed into my phone. Besides, they know I can't come in today or tomorrow. I might be salary, but I've worked too many hours in a row. These are my mandatory days off." Aiden sat on the edge of the stool and twiddled with the phone. "They did leave a voice mail. Let me check it."

"By all means." Matt rested his arm across the back of Aiden's seat.

Aiden held the phone to his ear. He narrowed his eyes, then frowned. The color in his face drained away and his lips parted. He collapsed back in his seat. "Fuck."

"What?" Matt focused on Aiden. "Doc? What happened?"

Aiden shook his head. "My dad…" He held up both hands and gasped for air.

Matt rubbed Aiden's back. Whenever Aiden wanted to talk, he'd listen.

"Uh…it sounds like my father had a stroke." Aiden scratched his forehead but didn't look at Matt. "The person who called is his new partner, Ross." His voice dropped an octave. "Two nights ago, Dad and Ross were at the condo, and Dad said his arm was numb. He exhibited all the signs of a stroke. Ross called nine-one-one, and Dad was rushed to the ER in Springdale, where I grew up. According to Ross, the medical staff in Springdale has him under observation because his oxygen levels were too low. He's stable, but they aren't sure how much damage was done." Tears slipped down Aiden's cheeks. "Fuck."

"Doc." Matt gathered Aiden into his embrace. "We'll get cleaned up and go to him. I'm going with you so you have some support."

"The thing is, Ross said in the message that this was one hell of a way to introduce us. It's not funny. Why would he say something like that?" Aiden's chin quivered.

Matt wanted to kiss away the pain and frustration, but he wasn't sure how. "Maybe Ross isn't good under pressure and he knew his joke was shit, but he tried anyway? If he's worried, then he's probably not going to say the right things."

Aiden wiped his face with the back of his hand and squirmed in Matt's arms. He pulled away and paced the length of the kitchen. "Matt, the man had my father rushed to the ER two days ago. No one said anything until today. What if he'd died? Would Ross have kept it to himself?" His voice cracked. "Who does that?"

"Probably a guy who'd been told by the doctors that his partner was in trouble but going to make it. I'd bet he waited until your dad was stable so you wouldn't worry." Not the best decision, but Matt hadn't made it. If he were in Ross' position, he would've called right away.

"That's no excuse," Aiden snapped. He paused. "I'm sorry. This isn't your problem, and I'm dragging you into my family drama." He wiped his face again. "Fuck. I'm crying too. Jesus. I'm a mess."

"You're human." He left his stool and tucked Aiden to his chest again. "No one is excusing what Ross did. I can't say what I might have done in his place. But your father is stable."

"I lost one dad. I can't afford to lose another," Aiden whispered.

"I can't guarantee you won't, but I will be right here with you. Come on. We'll get cleaned up and drive to Springdale. I'm sure he'd like that, and it'll set your mind at ease to know exactly what's going on." Matt steered Aiden to the steps.

"You've got to get to the shop." Aiden bucked against him halfway up the staircase. "You need to be at your business."

"That's what I have Aaron and Deighan for." He'd probably have hell to pay from Aaron, but fuck him. Aiden needed him right now.

Matt steered Aiden upstairs and started the water in the shower. "I'll join you in a moment." He held up his phone. "Once I call Aaron, I'm yours."

"What if…" Aiden scrubbed his hands over his face. "I'm scared. I know he's stable, but what if he doesn't make it?"

"Slow down." He left the phone on the counter and grasped Aiden by the shoulders. "You said so yourself—he's stable. He's at the hospital, and the doctors know what they're doing. Trust them the way you want people to trust you. I'll—we'll get you to the hospital as soon as we're cleaned up. If we drove straight there right now, we'd only buy a few minutes.

You might as well be clean and have some time to gather your thoughts before you go."

The worry in Aiden's eyes didn't dissipate. His shoulders sagged, but he allowed Matt to undress him. "Matt. I'm not used to being scared. I'm the one taking care of people. Not the other way around."

"Trust me. Once we're there, I'm handing control over to you. We do what you want for as long as you want. Until then and because you don't want to show up smelling like sex, get a shower so we can go. Besides, I've got one of the most interesting showers." He helped Aiden over the side of the clawfoot tub. "Okay? I'm here for you." He yanked the curtain around the tub, then grabbed his phone. Through the translucency of the curtain, he saw Aiden dunk his head under the spray. The poor man seemed as forlorn as he probably felt.

Matt's heart ached for him. Aiden needed him or someone to help him get through this situation. First, Matt had to get his life in order. He dialed Aaron.

"Hey," Aaron said. "Comin' in?"

"Do you need me?" He kept his attention on Aiden. "Or are you good?"

"I always need you, but Deighan and I have things under control. Are you hurting? Did something get pulled, or did you overdo it?" Aaron asked.

"I need to take Aiden to the hospital down in Springdale." He rested his free hand on his hip. He hadn't worn his sling in a while, and his shoulder let him know that wasn't smart, but he couldn't wear the damn thing all the time. He had to get used to being without it for longer periods of time.

"What the hell is in Springdale that's not in Cedarwood?" Aaron paused. "Jesus, you didn't?"

"Didn't what? Aaron, I don't have time for your bullshit." His frustration rose. Aaron wasn't always clear with his comments and right now was a bad time to be joking about anything.

"Just promise me you're not using again and you haven't dragged him into it. That's the only reason I can think of why you'd have to go to a hospital far away from here," Aaron snapped.

"Sometimes I really don't like you," Matt said. He stepped out of the bathroom but stood where he could see Aiden still. "I quit using years ago, okay? I'm not getting back into that. Trust me. Colt read me the riot act. Besides, I'm not interested in being that guy again. It sucked, and Aiden deserves better."

"Okay, then."

"I'm going with him because his father was rushed to the hospital in Springdale, where he lives with his partner. I guess Aiden's dad had a stroke, and Aiden wants to see him, but he doesn't want to go alone." He forked his fingers into his hair. He'd leveled with Aaron but didn't feel much better.

"I'm sorry to hear that," Aaron said. "You're going to take the whole day, then?"

"If you can hold down the fort for that long, then yes. He needs me."

"This is your business. You said you couldn't just leave it."

"I'm not just leaving it. I hired Deighan and I've got you, so in case this stuff happens, I know the shop is being managed. I'm not supposed to be lifting and driving, so I'm not much help beyond the books and answering the phone. Once this is handled, I'll be back...probably tonight because I wanted to check on some inventory. Before you know it, things will be back to normal." Matt leaned on the door frame to the bathroom. "Okay?"

"Yeah, whatever. You owe me." Aaron sighed. "I hope it's nothing too bad with Aiden's dad."

"Me too."

"Take care of Aiden. I don't like it, but I get it," Aaron said. "You're blunt with hints."

If the hint was the fact that they'd never hook up, then good for Aaron. If not, then nothing was resolved. "I'll check in with you tonight. Promise."

"Sure."

"Thank you, Aaron. You're saving my butt and you're the best friend I've ever had. That's huge. I do owe you," Matt said. "Big-time."

"Yeah. Hey, before you go and I forget. Jordan came by. He didn't get real specific, but he mentioned the surveillance footage was clear but the police department can't seem to find the guy. It's like he vanished," Aaron said. "They've got posters up and I saw a frame from the video on the news with an 'if you have any information' number listed too."

"Shit." He clunked his head on the doorframe. "Well, I'm sure they're doing their best to get it solved." *Fucking hell.* He'd hoped they would've made progress by now. *Over two weeks, and nothing? Come on.* They had to know something. The guy couldn't just disappear.

"Business is down too. Mrs. Handleman's Caddy was recovered and the Lexus was found, but both were stripped. Deig and I are doing our damndest to get them back to showroom quality, but Handleman swears the insurance shouldn't have to pay for our negligence. Thinks we should since it was your fault, according to her. Matty, we had the lot locked up.

Unless the shooter knew to grab the keys for that car, it shouldn't have been stolen. It's not our fault."

"I know. People think we're targets, I'm assuming too." A lump formed in the pit of his stomach. The initial downtick in business wasn't a blip but more like a downward turn. *Damn.*

"Some people just want you here so they know it's all good. Others won't come back until he's caught and others swear we did it for publicity."

"Right. Getting shot was a stunt." Matt groaned. "Shit."

"Just...come back. When you're here, it'll be better," Aaron said. "We'll run one of those big oil-and-brake-change promotions, and things will be okay."

"You're right. We'll talk about it tonight. I'll see you then."

"Thanks." Aaron clicked off the line.

Matt paused a moment. His head swam. He'd learned too much he wasn't sure how to deal with but had no choice. If his business was going to survive, he had to get the books into the black again. He tossed the phone onto the bed, then headed back into the bathroom. He tugged the curtain and drank in the sight of his lover nude.

Aiden stood in the middle of the tub, his hair wet and suds sliding down the middle of his chest. "You're right. This is the coolest shower ever. How did you not tell me you had a clawfoot tub?"

"It didn't exactly come up in conversation." He eased in behind Aiden. "But now you know. I love the tub. It's huge and holds two people."

"I thought you said the woman remodeled the house." Aiden leaned back in Matt's arms. "I would assume this would be the first to go."

"That's the beauty of my house—well, one of them. She ran out of cash before she got up here, so it stayed as-is. As for the bathroom being attached to the master bedroom, that was in the original plan of the house." He added soap to the washcloth and cleaned Aiden's belly. "The man who built the house had four daughters and a lot of money. He wanted the girls to have two bathrooms to share and the master bedroom had another. It's all historically accurate if you're a millionaire and want things your way."

"Nice." Aiden rinsed, then faced Matt. "I'm done and going to get dressed. Was Aaron okay with being there alone?"

"He didn't like it, but he's got Deighan there." Matt hurried through washing himself off and shampooing his hair. He didn't like the way Aiden seemed so numb. If there was a way to fix things, he wanted to do it, but he wasn't sure how. He rinsed, then turned the water off and toweled himself. When he stepped into the bedroom, Aiden was wearing only a shirt and boxer briefs. He wrestled his way into his jeans. The tight denim accentuated his toned legs and butt, while making him appear about five years younger.

"Damn." Matt stared at Aiden. God, the man was so hot. He reminded Matt of a male model. Sure, he'd seen Aiden plenty of times in and out of clothes, but he still stole Matt's breath.

"We should go." Aiden wound his belt through his jeans, then secured the buckle. "We'll have missed rush-hour traffic."

Matt glanced down at his arms. For the first time in forever, he wasn't sure what to do about his ink. "Aiden?" He paused. "Do you…want me to cover my tats?"

"Why?" Aiden stepped up to him and flattened his palm on Matt's chest. "You're not ashamed of them and neither am I."

The gravity of the moment and what Aiden had said washed over him. *Not ashamed.* If he wasn't turned on by Aiden already, those words would've done the trick. He held the towel tight. "Are we a couple?" Probably a little quick to ask that, but oh well.

"You're asking me that now?"

"Sorry. I can deal with a timing belt and pistons, but my personal life... I'm horrible with timing there." He shrugged out of the towel and turned his back on Aiden while he dressed. He wasn't ready to see the disgust he swore would be in Aiden's eyes because he'd jumped the gun with his question.

Aiden didn't say anything as he went downstairs. Matt grabbed his keys, wallet, phone and the gate fob, then locked up and followed Aiden to the car.

"First, sorry about the awkward question. Like I said, I'm horrible with timing. Second, here's this. It's to open and close the gate without me having to punch in the code." He plunked the fob into Aiden's hand. "Now we can go."

Aiden unlocked the car but didn't move from his spot. "Matt. This is high tech."

"It was either that or waste the use of a perfectly good, perfectly scary gate." Matt rounded the hood and waited on the passenger side of the car. "Ready?"

"Yeah." Aiden pushed the button to open the gate, then slid into the driver's seat. He backed down the drive. "Why don't you close the gate, so I can make sure I don't pull out in front of anyone?"

Matt did as asked, then held on to the fob. He wished he hadn't opened his mouth. The subsequent apologies weren't helping.

Aiden drove through Cedarwood in silence. Once he reached the state route leading out of town, he finally spoke. "I think we are."

"Huh?" Matt didn't look up from his lap. "What are you talking about?"

"A couple? I think we are. Once you sleep with someone—not just fuck, but sleep with them—then that's kind of an official act. It is for me, anyway." Aiden gripped the steering wheel with one hand and reached for Matt with the other. "You stunned me, but I wasn't expecting you to be on my wavelength."

"I've been quick on pretty much everything. I assumed you'd know." He grasped Aiden's fingers. "But I'm glad." For the rest of the drive to Springdale, he and Aiden rode in silence. He hated that Aiden had to be behind the wheel. If he'd had another choice, he would've taken control. Aiden deserved to break down if he needed, not be strong right now.

Matt barely noticed the details of Springdale as Aiden sped through town. He kept his focus on Aiden. If his boyfriend showed any signs of needing a break, then he was determined to jump in. Once they reached the hospital, he allowed Aiden to take the lead.

Aiden stopped at the front desk. "Hi, Imogene. How are the kids?"

"Wonderful. It's great to see you again." She raced around the desk to hug him. "We haven't seen you in forever. Are you here for your dad? Didn't anyone call you?" She pursed her lips. "Someone should've called you before now."

"It's a mix-up, yeah, but we'll get it sorted out. Don't worry. Which room is he in?"

"Still, I'm ashamed and sorry we didn't get in touch with you. He's on the fourth floor, ICU. We've changed it a little. There's a waiting room up there, so your friend can stay there while you go in. We limit the guests to two at a time." Imogene grinned and laced her fingers together. "You should really come back to Springdale. We could use a few more great doctors like you."

"Maybe one of these days." Aiden waved, then took Matt's hand. "I'm sorry, Imogene. This is my boyfriend, Matt. Matt, this is my dear friend from high school."

"It's nice to meet you." Matt winked. "I'll try to remember to ask you later for juicy details about Aiden when he was a teenager."

She blushed. "He was a good man back then too."

"See you." Matt waved and followed Aiden to the elevators. He didn't say anything during the ride up to the intensive care unit. Aiden had better things to worry about besides him. When they reached the small waiting room, Matt stopped. "Want me to stay here?" he asked. "I don't mind."

"Would you?" Aiden bobbed his head. "I'm sorry. I just want to talk to Dad alone." He kissed Matt. "Thank you. You're one in a million."

"I'm just me, but I'll do anything you want me to." He waited until Aiden disappeared down the hall before he surveyed the layout of the waiting room. He'd expected a dark space with beat-up couches or worn-out chairs. Instead, he happened upon a bright, cheery room with two leather sofas and myriad black chairs. A large-screen television showed the local news, and a selection of magazines littered the coffee tables.

He chuckled. Springdale was considered a boring crossroads town by most of the people he knew, but if the hospital was any indication, the place was just as nice as Cedarwood — at least on the surface. He strode over to the window and stared out at the grassy space and pond. Ducks swam in the middle of the water and cattails surrounded one end. He almost wished he had a pond in his yard. But then he'd have to take care of it and landscaping wasn't his forte. He killed plastic plants.

A man stomped into the room. He growled as he made his way to the windows. "Son of a bitch thinks he can toss me out. Jesus. The little shit doesn't know I'm hurting too. He thinks he's the only one."

Matt turned away from the guy. He had enough to worry about and wasn't in the mood to listen to a tirade. Still, he couldn't totally ignore the man. The guy had to be over fifty but was fit and lean with silver hair. He appeared well-groomed. He could be a catch but was a little too old for Matt's tastes.

"Are you here waiting for someone?" the man asked. "My name's Ross." He offered his hand. "Sorry about my bitching. I'm stressed."

"Sounds like." Ross? *Isn't Aiden's dad's partner named Ross?* Matt returned to watching the ducks. He didn't want to know about Ross' problems.

"Who are you here to see?" Ross asked.

"My boyfriend's father." He smiled. Pride washed over him. Calling Aiden his boyfriend pleased him more than he'd realized.

"Oh? I'm sorry. My partner had a stroke." Ross stood next to Matt. "Scared the hell out of me when I found him. That kind of thing shouldn't happen to anyone."

"No, it shouldn't, and I'm sure it wasn't pleasant. I'd freak if the same thing happened to us." *Holy fuck.* Ross had to be Aiden's dad's partner. He was under stress, sure, but calling Aiden an asshole? *Come on.* Being a dick and calling Aiden names wasn't making the best impression, even if Ross didn't know the score.

"How long have you been together?"

Matt stuffed his hand into his pockets. He couldn't lie, but leaving a few details out wasn't awful. "It's new."

"I remember that. I've been with Len for a little over a year. We're in the comfortable old men stage." Ross chuckled. "I love him."

"Good to know." *Kind of.* He'd hope if they were together for a year that love would have already blossomed. If Ross treated Len the way he talked about Aiden, though, Matt might have to say something.

"Why are you out here? You should be in with your beau, or aren't you ready to meet the future father-in-law?" Ross laughed and rocked on the balls of his feet.

"Well, when the one you love has to deal with stress and asks for a moment to be alone with his parent, you let him. He needed time, and I will give him pretty much whatever he wants." Matt bit back the answer he wanted to give. *Drop dead. Stop giving my boyfriend shit. Shut up.* Not the best things to say and probably better to keep quiet. "We've got a great give-and-take. Besides, I wanted to make a good impression on the father-in-law, so to speak." Would he and Aiden get married? Too soon to say, but he could see it. The thought of having Aiden as his husband warmed him all over. He bit back a smile. Yeah, maybe it was jumping the gun, but sharing his life with Aiden looked awfully bright.

"Len's kid didn't make a good impression on me," Ross said, interrupting Matt's thoughts. "It's disgusting. He waited two days to show up, then pushed me out like I'm no one. The nerve of the ass."

He'd had enough. No one trashed Aiden — not like this — but he had to be tactful. "He's just as upset as you, I'd imagine. Len doesn't want you and the son fighting. Be compassionate." Because if he heard Ross say one more thing to insult Aiden, he'd blow a gasket. He knew Aiden hadn't waited and probably hadn't been rotten to Ross, either.

"I suppose you're right. I still think the kid is an ass. He's a spoiled brat, really." Ross snorted. "I've seen better-behaved children."

"Okay." Matt held up both hands. "I'm not sure who you're talking about, but I'm done listening. You're trashing someone you barely know and I don't want to be in the middle." He walked away, making a lap around the corridor before going to Len's room. Interrupting Aiden's time with his father wasn't right, but wasn't nearly as bad as allowing Ross to continue. Anything was better than being a witness to the character assassination of Aiden. He stood at the doorway to Len's room and paused for a moment. He couldn't tell what Aiden and Len were talking about. *Shit.*

"Hi." Matt waved. "Sorry for the interruption."

Aiden smiled and reached for Matt. "You're fine. I should've introduced you before now anyhow. Dad, this is my boyfriend, Matt. Matt, this is my father, Len."

Len offered his hand and a half-hearted smile. "Sorry we're meeting on these terms. Aiden's told me good things about you. He said you rescued him."

"Dad." Aiden blushed. "He towed my car."

"I did." Matt shook hands with Len. He couldn't remember the last time he'd met the parents of his boyfriend, let alone had a boyfriend, besides Theo, who cared to introduce him to the family. "It's a pleasure to meet you. Aiden told me nice things about you too. As for the rescue, I did tow his car, but I've got an automotive shop and he'd messed up the front end of his vehicle. It's good to see you're better. You freaked Aiden out."

"I'm right here," Aiden muttered.

"It was just a scare," Len said and seemed to ignore Aiden's discomfort. "The doctor called it a reminder that it's time to retire." He shrugged. "When Ross comes back, I'll introduce you." His eyes lit up. "You own your business? A chain shop, or is it something else?"

"Not a franchise. It's my own. Just me and two other employees." Matt widened his stance. He loved talking about his business. He'd also have to make things up to Aiden when they got back to Cedarwood—not that being alone together would be a hardship. "It's small, but we keep busy."

"Nice. We'll have to check out your rates. I can always use a good car man." Len beamed. "And you own it. Aiden, you've picked a good one."

Aiden's blush deepened. He sprang up from his seat when a man in scrubs entered. "A word, Dr. McLean?" He stepped into the hallway with the doctor, leaving Matt and Len alone.

Len nodded to the chair Aiden had just vacated. "Sit."

"Sure." He settled onto the hard plastic seat. His ass ached after just a few moments. *No wonder Aiden got up so fast.*

"How's Aiden doing?" Len asked.

"What do you mean?"

"Is he overworking himself? Do you get to see him enough?" The lines around Len's eyes deepened, and he frowned. "Is he good to you?"

"We've got a system that works for us. Yes, he probably spends too much time at the hospital, but I'm at the shop most hours of the day. When we're both off at night, we get together. We're not at the living-together stage or anything, but we're a twosome." He hadn't lied, but he wished he could've given Len a better answer.

"Keep an eye on him. He's a good man and a brilliant doctor, but he forgets to have a life." Len folded his arms. "My son had to endure a lot of crap. The divorce, me figuring out who I was, finding Keye, then us not having a ton of money. I know it wore him down. He thinks by working all the time, he won't realize he doesn't have a life. I don't want it to pass him by."

Matt couldn't agree more, but he had little to add. Good God, he spent more time than he should at the shop. Less now that he'd been hurt, but still.

"You're not his usual type." Len grinned. The sparkle returned to his gray eyes, and the silver scruff on his cheeks glistened. "I'm glad."

The tips of Matt's ears burned. He wasn't prone to embarrassment, but Len seemed to know what to say to disarm him. He could see a lot of Aiden in Len and knew Aiden would age just as beautifully. "We're a lot more alike than Aiden realizes, but I've gathered I'm not his norm." He rubbed his arms. "I'm just more colorful, but we both do our jobs with perfection. Anything less would mean he loses a patient and I screw up an engine. We're both dedicated and can't stand to get anything wrong."

"You're smart too," Len said.

Matt smiled. He wasn't sure what to say. If Len had seen his grades in school, he might have changed his tune. Book smarts weren't his forte. He shook his head. "By the way… Aiden came almost as soon as he could. I made him shower and breathe for a moment this morning, but right after Ross called, we were on the road."

"What?" Len tipped his head to the side. "That's what I assumed. Why do you mention it?"

"Nothing. Just…I didn't want you to think we'd blown you off." Matt shifted on his seat. *Well, shit.* Had Ross lied to Len too? Or had he saved the honor for Matt because he'd assumed Matt wouldn't care to check his story?

"I knew you hadn't." Len tensed, then fumbled. "Ross. Hi." He smiled, though tightly, as Ross strode across the room. "I didn't see you there. This is my son's partner, Matt."

"Pleasure," Matt said and offered his hand. He loved the way Ross' eyes widened. Had he realized he'd insulted Matt's boyfriend back in the waiting room?

Ross opened his mouth, then closed it without saying a word. He didn't shake hands with Matt, either.

Good. The asshat could be stunned and rendered silent. Maybe he'd learn not to blow off about Aiden to just anyone.

Aiden entered the room again and paused at the foot of Len's bed. "Ross."

Matt left the chair. "How about we run down to the cafeteria and get a couple of coffees so Ross and your father can be alone?" He grasped Aiden's hand. "Yes?"

"Sure." Aiden nodded. "We'll be back in a few."

"Take your time," Len said. "I'm not going anywhere."

Matt waited until he and Aiden were in the hallway and nearly to the elevator before he spoke. "Are you okay?"

"Me?" Aiden shrugged, then pressed the button for the elevator. "Yeah."

"Who else?" He stepped into the car with Aiden. "You're tense, and I know you're not happy."

"I'm better now that I've seen him." Aiden sagged against Matt as the doors closed.

Matt's heart swelled for Aiden. The longer he spent with him, the more he wanted to talk to Aiden and tell him all of his truths. But he needed the right time and now wasn't it.

"It wasn't a stroke. It was what's called a trans-ischemic attack, or a TIA. It's like a stroke, but basically the plaque in your carotid artery slows the blood flow to your brain. When they brought him in, his oxygen levels were lower than the doctors liked, so they've got him under additional observation. Springdale isn't the biggest town, but we do have a good hospital."

The doors opened into a larger room. The scent of baked chicken and coffee wafted through the air. Matt bit back a growl. He'd eaten breakfast, but damn, he was hungry again.

"The doctors handling Dad's care are great. I met Dr. McLean when I interviewed here after my residency in Westlake. I didn't get the job. Good because I did at Cedarwood and got to meet you, but bad because I wanted to be closer to Dad." Aiden massaged his temples. "I'm not totally okay with what's going on, but I feel better knowing McLean is on it."

"Good." Matt hustled Aiden through the line at the counter. "I'd like water and one of those brownies." His mouth watered. "Please?"

"Make it two." Aiden grasped Matt's hand. "Shit. I forgot my wallet."

"This was on me." He paid, then picked up the bottles of water. He didn't argue when Aiden carried the plates to a booth behind a potted palm. The privacy would be a good change of pace. Aiden sat opposite him and sagged forward.

"I'm glad you made me chill before we rushed down here, but I'm happier to be here." Aiden flattened his palms on the table. "God. You've got to think I'm such a drama whore. First the accident, now this."

"Um…I was shot and you saved my life. I think we're even." He unwrapped his brownie. "You needed to see your dad. I get it." Being around his own father wasn't an option, but he couldn't deny Aiden his wish.

"You've never said a word about your dad." Aiden twisted the cap on his bottle. "Is that okay to ask, or is it a sore subject?" He waved his hand. "Never mind. I'm being nosy, and it's none of my business."

"Nah." Aiden had to know sometime. Matt toyed with the edge of the brownie, then tugged off a piece. He nibbled on the dark-chocolate confection. *Damn, it's good.* He should've ordered milk to wash it down.

Aiden downed some of the water but said nothing. The awkwardness of the moment wasn't lost on Matt. But how in the hell was he going to handle the situation? He wanted honesty from Aiden but hadn't disclosed a lot of information. When he met Aiden's gaze, he knew. "You're my boyfriend, and we're together. Let me tell you about the bastard I called father."

Chapter Eight

Aiden reached for Matt's hand, then rubbed the back of his knuckles with the pad of his thumb. Matt had been a champ through Aiden's crisis. The least he could do was reciprocate. But he felt the tension from Matt and regretted his question. "I'm prying. I guess me having to deal with shit makes me stressed and nosy." That and he couldn't prevent himself from looking for the cracks and problems that could arise.

Matt's eyes flashed and a wolfish smile curled on his lips. "That's just a lack of sex." He held Aiden's fingers tighter. "Do you realize that's the first time outside of the bedroom that I've heard you swear?"

"Sorry. I try not to use foul language while I'm at the hospital. I'd rather not risk slipping in front of a patient and being rude."

"Good reason."

Aiden stared at Matt. Having such a good man in his life humbled him. Matt knew how to listen, to talk and just be with him. He couldn't say the same for his father and Ross. His head ached just thinking about his father's new partner. The man was crass, mean and not much fun to be around. But the fallout was always around the corner. Eventually something would happen. He had to stop looking for the imperfections, but damn it, he couldn't stop who he was.

"What?" Matt asked.

"I'm not happy about my father's situation or the deal with Ross, but I'm happy—if that makes sense." He wasn't sure anything he'd said computed.

"It does." Matt nodded. "The guy your father is seeing is an ass."

"You figured that out too? I knew from day one, but I kept my mouth shut. I'd only met him once and chalked it up to a bad day, but I guess my assumptions were spot-on." He sagged back in his seat, and the stress of the day weighed on him all over again. "My father claims Ross said the same about me. The words *ungrateful, spoiled jerk*, and *jackass* were mentioned too." He fought to keep his emotions in check. The man his father claimed to love seemed to hate him and enjoyed tearing him down. The throbbing behind his eyes increased. He didn't need Ross' kind of stress in his life, but he sure as hell couldn't take it out on Matt. *Damn it.* His father deserved a partner. If Ross was good to him, then fine. Aiden wouldn't argue.

"Ross said some choice things to me before he realized who I was." Matt finished off his brownie. "I didn't say anything I'd regret or that should get you into trouble with your father, but I straightened him out. I'm not listening to someone rip you apart the way he did."

"Thanks." Aiden picked at the label on his water bottle. Talking about his father and his feelings weren't his ideal, but with Matt, it was easier. "Dad and Keye were great together. Not just good, but great. They balanced each other out. Dad's serious and all about his legal practice. Give him a juicy case, and he's happy. Keye was a free spirit. He could get Dad to relax when nothing else would. They traveled together and it worked. If Keye bought him an ugly sweater, Dad wore it with pride. It's funny. They were fixtures at the pride parades in Cleveland. Once they were together, I decided I wanted a love like theirs. As for Ross, I'm not sure how I feel." That wasn't the truth. He didn't like Ross. Didn't like the way Ross seemed to know everything, the way he lied and the way his father seemed to go along with it. "I get a sketchy vibe from him."

"Because he's replaced Keye?" Matt stilled Aiden's hands. "Or something else?"

"It's the lying. According to Dad, Ross told my father I didn't want to be here. He's told him I demanded money and said I wouldn't talk to him unless I got my way. I call Dad every week." He still couldn't believe what Ross had told his father. "I've never felt so belittled in my life."

"None of that sounds like you — the brattiness, the demanding or the defeat." Matt held on to Aiden's hands. "You're ordered and dependable. I've never seen you outright... No, you're a little demanding, but you wanted your car fixed. It was expected. What Ross said was out of line."

He'd forgotten about the night he'd run over the curb. Yeah, he'd been an ass. If he'd been a jerk then, were there other instances he'd acted out and hadn't noticed? Maybe he'd been heartless all along and didn't know? There were the flaws — in him.

"Aiden?" Matt snapped his fingers in front of Aiden's face. "Hey. I see the wheels turning. I'm just giving you shit. Yeah, you wanted the car fixed, but you were a lot nicer about it than a lot of my customers. Don't sweat it."

Easy for him to say. Aiden scrubbed the back of his hand over his mouth. He'd over thought so much, but damn it. Ross had gotten into his head—maybe Ross didn't know that, but he'd messed with Aiden's concentration in a horrible way.

"I don't know the guy well, but he threw you under the bus to me. He had no idea you were connected to me, sure, but he still verbally abused you in front of a stranger. That showed his character, and it wasn't pretty. He seemed rotten and like he wants to bring everyone around him down." Matt curled his fingers under Aiden's chin. "I can spot these kind of people a mile away."

"Oh? How?" He tried to treat everyone the same and assumed Matt did too.

"My father. You asked about him earlier. I'll tell." Matt folded his hands on the table. "My old man was a lot like Ross. Remember how I said I'm a sucker for pain?"

"You said you needed it to be level." He held the bottle in both hands and leaned forward. Matt had his full attention.

"I do, but it's not like I want everyone to know." Matt kept his gaze on Aiden, but his voice cracked. "I can trace that need back to my father. See, he was the kind of guy who hated everyone who wasn't like him. He was angry, aggressive and straight."

"Nice." Not really, but he wasn't sure what else to say.

"Yeah, nice wasn't him. He settled everything with his fists and usually on me. Because of him, I played football even though I wasn't heart and soul invested in the game. I wrestled because he swore it would take the sissy out of me and I tried to be straight so he might love me again." Matt smiled, but the light didn't reach his eyes. He rubbed his forearm. "It sucked."

Aiden couldn't imagine being held back in so many ways and forced to do things he didn't believe in. He couldn't fathom anyone abusing their own child in such a manner, either. "Matt. Babe." He doubted Matt wanted sympathy, but any other words seemed irrelevant.

"I'm not a virgin. Not in the biblical sense. Dear old Dad made sure I had rubbers and a chick from the bar the night I turned eighteen. He told everyone that Nikki would make me into a man. I was of age, she was willing and we fucked in the back of her Saab. She thought I liked her. I went home and puked. I guess he told everyone about my new status and acted like what I'd done gave him greater standing in the community." Matt shook his head once, then closed his eyes for a moment. "She called me once, and I told her the truth. I like pole, not pussy. Nikki took it well, but Dad found out and beat the hell out of me."

"Matt." He thanked God he'd won the lottery with his fathers. They weren't a perfect example of how to be, but they were a damn sight better than Matt's father.

"I played football and wrestled through high school until I blew out my knees during my senior year." Matt collapsed his water bottle. "Sucked."

"I remember you said your father thought you playing ball was his ticket to fame and fortune. He didn't like what he perceived as your unwillingness to push yourself for his sake, did he?" Aiden asked.

"Bingo. Ross might not be physically abusive, but he's a bully. Like my father, he'll let you know he thinks you're beneath him."

"Did you ever talk to your dad?" Aiden tensed. He guessed the greeting-card moment hadn't happened between Matt and his old man.

"No."

"Too much damage?" He'd gotten too personal and nosy again. He really had to stop looking for the faults against him being with Matt, but still.

"He's dead. Can't exactly get a dead man to talk and I'm not sure I'd want to. Knowing him, he'd find a way to cut me down, and I don't have time for that. I've tried to focus on the present and future as well as healing." Matt forced a smile, though it was tight. "We didn't talk much when he was alive, but I'm glad he's at peace. I used to be angry I never lit into him, but now I'm relieved. He can't hurt me and he's gotten his."

His respect for Matt grew. "You're a strong man."

"Nah. I'm a survivor. Unfortunately, the way I dealt with my pain and frustration was through the body ink and piercings. They were something I could control. Once I had the needle in my skin, the pain made me feel something. The piercings were reminders I was still here. I thought I needed the pain to survive. I won't lie. I still get a fix from them and I doubt I'll stop." Matt shrugged. "I'd rather channel my energy that way than by doing other things."

"Where? You look good with what you have." Too much more would overdo it and Aiden preferred Matt with the edge. Any more art and he wouldn't be Matt.

"I don't want new ones. I let my tattoo artist touch up the color or fix the art that wasn't done right the first time." Matt straightened in his seat. "If you ever want to…you know…my friend Bix, er, Ben Armstrong, is great, and he's in Cedarwood."

"I'll pass for now." He'd met Bix once when he'd been on rotation to oversee the vaccinations at the health department. Bix had come in for a tetanus shot. He seemed like a nice guy—colorful but nice.

Matt rested his elbows on the table and folded his arms. "I don't talk about Dad. Aaron doesn't even know the whole story. He thinks my issues are because of Theo, my most recent ex-boyfriend. He's not, but I don't want to talk about him right now."

"You don't have to talk about him ever." Aiden finished his brownie, then his water. The gravity of the moment hadn't been lost on him. He cherished Matt and respected him more for how he'd pulled himself up. Maybe he wasn't someone else's ideal for sexiness. He fit the bill for Aiden. He made Aiden's motor run. Hell, Aiden wanted Matt to take him home right now for a few rounds of hot sex.

"Aiden?" Matt asked, drawing Aiden out of his thoughts.

"I think I'm in love," Aiden blurted. He didn't regret what he'd said. Hell, he felt free now that he'd admitted to his feelings. Maybe it was too early. Probably was, but he knew his heart.

"You're just tired. You'll say anything to get me into bed." Matt stood and offered his hand. "Come on. Let's see your dad."

"Sure." But he wasn't speaking out of weariness. Matt did something to him. Like finally understanding a test question from biology class or getting the man of his dreams to agree to a date... Something bizarre and not expected but totally right. He held tight to Matt's fingers as he and Matt went up to the fourth floor. He and Matt hadn't been together long, but they acted like an old couple. He'd thought love wasn't in the cards, but he'd fallen for Matt Phillips.

With Matt by his side, Aiden spent the next hour with his father. Ross, for reasons Aiden never quite got out of his dad, had vacated the room for a while. He didn't mind. He hadn't decided how he felt about his father's new beau.

Matt sat beside Aiden. With his father, they laughed, talked and simply existed. Aiden liked how his dad and Matt got along. *As if I need more reasons to like Matt!* He should be looking for reasons to split up so he could keep his heart under wraps. Aiden listened to Matt and Len discuss the finer points of car maintenance. He'd thought he'd never find a man who would respect him, want him for the man inside instead of the title and whom his father liked. He'd hit the jackpot with Matt.

Dr. McLean came back into the room and folded his arms. "It's like I've walked into a family reunion." He laughed, and the echoed around the space. "I'm glad. Len, you needed this. So...I'm going to keep you here for a few more days. I'd like to get your oxygen levels back up to where they should be. I'm not seeing any lasting damage from the TIA, but that doesn't mean something won't manifest." He turned his attention to Aiden. "You need to rest. Aiden, a word?"

Aiden followed the doctor into the hallway. "What's up? Did you see something that's bothering you?"

Dr. McLean bowed his head. "Yeah, you." He finally met Aiden's gaze. "I knew your father was gay. I've been treating him for the last four years and Ross for the last six months, but you? I had no idea."

"Is that a problem?" Aiden stared at him. He'd spoken with Isaac a few times since the interview and had thought they were friends at best. Talking about his sexuality had never seemed important. Besides, he had no idea Isaac might be interested.

"No. I just…" Isaac paused. "Your father will be fine. Ross seems adequate at taking care of him. He'll need to do a lot of resting."

"I agree, but I have the feeling that's not what you wanted to talk about." Aiden widened his stance. "I'll level with you. I'm gay. Have been all my life, but I didn't understand it until I was a teen. Mom was gone and Dad and Keye never told me I was anything but normal. I'm not a showy gay. I like men, yes, but I'm not at the clubs, wearing way too much eyeliner and cruising. I'm probably the most boring gay man you'll ever meet."

"But you're taken."

"No, I just dragged him along because he was the last man I slept with." Aiden frowned and the ache behind his eyes returned. "Yes, I'm taken."

"Thought so." Isaac stuffed his hands into the pockets of his lab coat. "When you interviewed, I was still so new here. I wasn't given the opportunity to put in my opinion on you or anything, but I would've loved to have had you here at Springdale. I think we'd have gotten along great and it might have been me with you in there."

"Isaac." *Where was he right after Lucky left the last time?* "Things happen in strange ways. It's not up to us to question why." He sounded like a bad hair-metal song.

"Guess not." Isaac dragged a long breath into his lungs and sighed. "Keep an eye on your father. He needs you."

Aiden stared at Isaac as he walked away. Guys weren't exactly crawling out of the woodwork to hook up with him, but he hadn't detected a vibe from Isaac. Not even now that Isaac had said something. He shrugged. Trying to figure men out, especially those he wasn't seeing, wasn't worth it. He headed back into the room and checked the time on his phone.

"Everything okay?" Len asked.

"It's fine. We should go, though." Aiden stretched, then put the phone back into his rear pocket. "I've got to work tomorrow night, and Matt has to take care of business at the shop. I'll call you in the morning to see how you're doing." He crossed the room to his father's bed and hugged him. "Get better."

"Had you worried, didn't I?" Len patted Aiden's cheek. "I expect to hear from you."

"You will," Aiden said. He might have forgotten any other time, but this was more important.

"It was a pleasure meeting you and getting to talk." Matt shook hands with Len. "But Aiden's right. I need to speak to my second-in-command and make sure he hasn't burned the building down. I hope to see you again soon. The holidays are coming in the next couple of months. It would be great to do something as a family." Matt rested his palm on the small of Aiden's back. "Ready?"

"Yeah." *Did Matt just mention the holidays?*

"I'll consider that an invitation, and I'm accepting." Len's eyes lit up. "I can't wait to tell Ross we've got plans for Thanksgiving, Christmas and New Year's. He'll be thrilled."

Aiden somehow doubted that.

"I heard my name." As if on cue, Ross appeared. "What's happening?"

"We're spending all the holidays with Aiden and Matt. It's all settled." Let sat up a little more. "Don't argue."

"I see." Ross brushed past Aiden, pushing into him enough to nudge him backward without making it appear forced.

"I'll call you later, Dad," Aiden said. "Ross, it's been nice getting to meet you." He'd lied. The only things he knew about Ross were those he didn't like, but if he made Len happy and wasn't an ass to him, then Aiden wouldn't argue.

"Bye, boys." Ross waved. He then turned his back on Aiden and Matt as if they weren't there.

"Okay," Aiden murmured. He left with Matt and didn't say anything until they were together in the elevator. "Was it just me, or was that super awkward?"

"Super awkward." Matt draped his arm around Aiden's shoulders. "Feel better?"

"I do. I'm not wild about Ross, but Dad sees something in him and doesn't seem to buy Ross' bull crap, so if it works for them...I won't argue. I'm sure my father wouldn't have picked you out for me, but since we make each other happy, he won't say anything, either." Aiden leaned into his boyfriend. He needed a nap.

"Why wouldn't he have picked me?" Matt asked. "I'm a pillar of society."

"You are, but he always pushed the clean-cut college boys on me. He and Keye used to say I needed a man who was laced tighter than me so I'd finally relax." He now understood the flaw in his father's choice, but when he'd been a college man himself, he'd wanted nothing more than a preppy guy to ask him out. Just like now, he looked for the flaws in everyone before even getting together to begin with.

"Got it. Next time wear long sleeves." Matt tensed. "Pretty boys aren't always nice. Just because a guy has tats doesn't mean he's horrible."

"I know." Lucky came to mind. For a while, he'd considered giving up medicine just to shut his ex-boyfriend up, even though Lucky had only wanted him for his money.

"I'm sorry for that. No one deserves a dick for a boyfriend or an asshole for a father." Matt strolled out of the elevator first, then stopped in the middle of the lobby. "Coming?"

Not yet, but I will be later. Aiden hurried up to Matt. "Maybe Ross is a great cock sucker. He's handsome — if you're into older men — and comes across charming, if you don't know him well."

"You're not into older men?" Matt kept in step with Aiden across the parking lot. "What if I'm older than you?"

"I'm thirty-five. I'll be thirty-six in June. You?" Aiden asked.

"I'm thirty-seven." Matt grinned. "That makes me older."

"Ah, but you don't have so many years on me that you could be my father." Aiden opened the door for Matt. "See?"

"True."

"I like my men refined, professional and handsome but closer to my age." He winked at Matt. "If he's got ink or a few piercings, then that's fine too." He still wasn't positive they could go the distance, but he wanted to put himself out there.

"Are you saying I'm your type?" Matt settled on the passenger seat.

"I am." He sat beside Matt and closed his door. He'd held on to his feelings for long enough and needed to get them out. "This might be way too fast, but I've fallen for you." *Until you fail me.*

"You have? Me?" Matt laughed. "It's not funny that you like me, but it's funny you mentioned the fast thing. You do remember I'm the one who practically pushed you into my bed like two weeks ago, right?"

"I remember." He sped out of the parking lot. "I had to do some thinking first."

"I'm still stunned." Matt grasped Aiden's hand. "But I like you too."

"The way you handled yourself after the shooting, the night we met, the way we fuck...how you acted around my dad...you're the one I want. I love being with you and I can't wait to get home so we can fuck."

"With care," Matt added.

"Of course." He sighed. "I'm the guy who thinks before he acts, but once I make the decision, I'm sure and I stick with it." Well, usually. He'd worried for three months before settling on a college and a med school, doubted himself for two weeks before he'd asked Lucky out and made himself sick debating his decision to accept the job in Cedarwood. Admitting his feelings to Matt had been the most impulsive thing he'd done in forever. But he'd been burned in the past. Relationships didn't always work. He knew that. He should've kept his mouth shut, but no. He'd keep his reservations in his mind for now.

"Aiden, you're... I'm honored." Matt kissed Aiden's knuckles, sending a shiver of excitement through Aiden's veins. "I'm a little choked up too."

"Why?" Was Matt having second thoughts? *Oh God. Please don't let him be questioning us getting together.* Part of him didn't want the rejection, but the rest of him expected it.

"You see so much more in me than I thought was possible. I'm the guy who uses ink and metal to hide behind. My tats are my shield. If you can't see the real me, you can't hurt me." Matt squeezed Aiden's fingers. "I don't like opening up, but you make me think it's not all that bad if I do."

Matt's words touched him. Aiden glanced over at Matt. "There's more to you than a tattoo."

"You make me want to be a great man—one who isn't afraid to be himself. I'm honored to be with you."

"Likewise," Aiden said. "You know, my father warmed up to you a lot more than I expected." He remembered the last time Len had accepted one of his boyfriends—back in college when he'd dated Greg. The relationship had lasted a whole two months, but Greg had proved he was a stand-up guy. Unfortunately, he'd also loved sex and had hated to be faithful. Between Greg and Lucky, Aiden had learned to keep his heart guarded.

"Really? I don't believe you. Len is a great guy."

"He hated Lucky. Abhorred Seth and told me if I stayed with Dillon, he'd cut me out of the will." When Len had lobbed the threats, Aiden had thought they were law. Looking back, he realized his father had just been trying to protect him—not very well, but he'd tried. Then again, Aiden's tastes hadn't been the best, and Len knew how to size people up after one meeting.

If Len liked Matt enough to encourage getting together for the holidays, then Matt must be all right.

"Maybe you just needed to bring me along," Matt said. "I'm a good-luck charm, Doc Cedarwood."

"You're the spark." Aiden grinned. Matt made him happy, relaxed him and he now looked forward to his time off.

"Now you're flattering me."

"I'm being honest." He couldn't wait to get home — his home or Matt's. They didn't have to fuck. He'd enjoy lying together naked, but he had the feeling that once the clothes came off, sex would follow.

"I like it." Matt scooted a little closer and palmed Aiden's thigh. Once they reached his house and Aiden pushed the button to open the gate, Matt sat up straighter and tugged his phone from his pocket. "I should call Aaron before it gets too late. Do you mind? Go in and make yourself comfy. Strip, bathe, find the lube… I don't care." He winked. "I'll be in once I'm done, then no interruptions."

"Sure." Aiden pulled through the gate and parked. He waited as Matt unlocked the door, then went inside while Matt wandered back to the driveway. Checking on Matt crossed his mind, but why? Matt was an adult and had a right to privacy. Besides, he didn't really want to know about the shop.

Aiden wandered through the kitchen to the front room. He'd forgotten the beauty of old homes like Matt's. *Is there a parlor?* The last Gothic-style house he'd seen — in a magazine — had a parlor and living-room area as well as a formal dining room and an enormous porch. He wandered around the house and realized just how much space Matt had as well as the scant amount of furniture. He noticed bits and pieces of what could be the original woodwork in the front room. The intricate carving seemed out of place against the bland white baseboard. He trailed his fingers over the wall in what he guessed to be the dining room. Spots in the middle of the wall seemed to sag. He'd seen that once in an old rental house. The woman must've painted over the wallpaper just like his former landlord insisted was important to freshen up the apartment.

Aiden stopped in the hallway. Of all the things he'd noticed — woodwork, wallpaper and the lack of furniture, save for the hulking television and lone sofa — there were a few things that stuck out because they weren't there. No photos on the wall. No artwork. Not even a mirror.

Who doesn't have some sort of decoration out?

Aiden's heart broke. Something felt off. The longer he wandered through the house, the more he wondered about Matt. Part of him wanted to help add more color to Matt's home. A few potted plants, some paintings or a poster or two, photographs and decent curtains. The rest of him swore he should take more of a hands-off approach. *Duh...flaws?* Where was his head? Besides, this was Matt's place, not his, and he had no claim to how it looked.

He headed back into the living room but paused in the archway to the kitchen. A collage of photos caught his attention. *How did I not see these before?* He touched the frame and studied the smiling faces. Some of the people were familiar — Colt Harrison from the diner, Ashley Willis and Farin Baker. Others were sort of familiar to him. One man in particular grabbed his focus.

Aiden's stomach clenched. The guy was certainly attractive. Black hair in a fashionable swoop over his forehead—almost like a fifties greaser—and his piercing blue eyes stopped Aiden in his tracks. The guy possessed the perfect amount of hair on his cheeks to be sexy and rugged without being overdone. Then there was the cleft in his chin. *Damn.* In one photo, he stood beside Matt and smiled. Then there was another where he was alone and smirking. When he smiled, he looked hot, but the smirk... Aiden didn't know him, but he kind of wanted to.

He noticed Matt and the black-haired man in one of the photos and in an embrace. Jealousy rose within him. Was this the kind of guy Matt normally dated? If there were photos of him still on the wall, was Matt maybe tempted to go back to him?

Aiden sagged onto the closest stool. He shouldn't be angry or jealous. Hell, Matt had had a life before him and would have one if they split up. There was no guarantee, no matter how much he'd fallen for Matt, that they'd stay together. He'd learned that lesson well from Lucky.

"Wow. That took a lot longer than I expected." Matt slid his phone across the bar. "If there was something that could go wrong today, it did. Aaron can't get the parts on the Caddy to fit right, Deighan put the wrong tires on the Lincoln and someone hit a rock or something that cracked the windshield of Aaron's car while it was parked at the shop."

"I'm sorry to hear that." Aiden tried to act nonchalant, but ignoring the images on the wall wasn't so easy.

"Want to order a pizza or Chinese? I don't feel like cooking." Matt untucked his shirt and stretched. "I don't feel like doing much of anything."

"Your shoulder is probably sore." Aiden left his stool long enough to check Matt's healing wound. The skin was still red along the line where the stitches had been, but it looked good. "How's it feel?"

"It feels normal. A little stiff, but I just spent forever on the phone." Matt rubbed Aiden's upper arms. "What's wrong? When we left the hospital, you were horny and ready to go. Now you seem withdrawn. What'd I do?"

"You didn't do anything." He eased out of Matt's embrace. "I'm tired. It's been a long day and the weight of what I've been through is on my mind."

"Makes sense." Matt grasped Aiden's hand, keeping him close. "But I'm guessing it's more than just being tired. You saw my collage."

He bowed his head. *Damn it.* He'd been caught. "It's yours and very colorful."

"Want to go with that? Or do you want to tell me the truth?" Matt hugged him from behind. "I'd be miffed if I saw the guy I was currently involved with in the arms of another guy—even if it was only in a picture."

"You're fine. I'm guessing each one of those images is something to symbolize what you've been through." Reminders of friends, good times, great places… The pictures told the story of Matt's life. They also showed the flaw—Matt hadn't let go of the past. He'd never match up to the others in Matt's life. Maybe it was irrational of him to think that, but he couldn't help himself.

Matt tensed. "Sort of."

"See?" Aiden wriggled free from Matt. "I should go. I wasn't lying when I said I had to work tomorrow. You sound like you've got your plate full too."

"Don't go."

"Matt." He faced his boyfriend. "This thing we're doing is new. We've just been through a trying event. I need time to comprehend it all. I don't want to leave, but I feel like I'm putting a lot of expectations on you because my life kind of went to shit overnight. This morning we were touching, kissing and getting to know each other. Then the crap with my father and Ross got in the way. I don't trust him, but I can't say anything because he's with my father and they seem happy. I'm not convinced. Then I made things worse when I went and admitted I'd fallen for you. It's too much." Besides, he should've seen something like this coming. He should've been prepared.

Matt leaned against the bar. "Yeah, it is, but it's ours to deal with. I didn't get into this situation with my eyes closed. I knew the kind of man I'd welcomed into my bed. You're special, and so you come with baggage. Like I don't? Your accident got us in the same room, but my being shot was the catalyst for me to ask you out." He tipped his head to the side. "See? Crap happens. We learn and lean on each other."

Aiden sighed. He'd done a lot of leaning in a short period of time. Most guys might not appreciate his clinginess, then being pushed away. He couldn't seem to make up his damn mind. *What is happening to me?* At the hospital, he knew what he wanted and how to do what was expected. Once he stepped out of the ER, he seemed to lose his mind. Was this how real love affected him? Making him second-guess his feelings? Why was he only confident at the hospital? *Damn.*

"I can't think of anyone else I'd rather be with right now." Matt smiled and crossed his ankles. "No one else."

Aiden stared at him. There were problems. He'd found faults in Matt—moving too fast, being a tad clingy and still holding on to his past. If Aiden went with his head, then walking out and putting some distance between them would be good. If he believed his heart, then he should run to Matt and throw his arms around him. He willed his feet to comply, but his limbs refused to cooperate. *Well, fuck.*

Chapter Nine

Matt gripped the edge of the countertop to keep his hands from shaking. Things had just gotten started with Aiden and already Aiden was tense. What else could he say to make Aiden understand? Sure, he had his issues, but he was there for Aiden. He wanted the doc to give him a chance and open up.

"What do you say, Doc Cedarwood?" Matt asked. He still wasn't sure Aiden even liked the nickname he'd given him. But the name seemed so perfect. The people in Cedarwood went to Aiden when they arrived at the ER. He was the one who cared for them. Was Matt being selfish to want some of Aiden's attention for himself?

"I say I'm tired. I'm overwhelmed." Aiden crept across the expanse to him and threaded his arms around Matt's waist. He rested his head on Matt's good shoulder. "I'm in over my head. It sounds goofy, but until now, my life was pretty well ordered."

"Aiden. When the hospital shouts, you run. That's not exactly order. That's controlled chaos." He petted Aiden's hair.

"But it's my chaos. I knew what to expect. They call, I go in and do my job." He splayed his hand over Matt's heart. "Then came the night of the wedding. I hate weddings. Hate watching the pageantry of it. I doubt I'll ever get married. But it brought us together."

"It did." He cupped Aiden's face in both hands. "I don't know how you do it. I bet you're so strong and collected when you're dealing with the relative pandemonium in the ER. I'm sure it seems so easy for you. Then you go out into the world beyond the hospital and that confidence melts. Babe, you're a brilliant doctor and a handsome man. I can feel you climbing into your own head to either hide or overthink this. Don't. I'm not going anywhere." Matt spotted the collage. He hadn't thought about the images in the various connected frames, but the moment he looked over the faces, he understood Aiden's shift in mood. Some of his reluctance probably had to do with the events of the day, but the rest no doubt revolved around Theo.

"I'll be all right." Aiden said the words, but he didn't pull away.

"Uh-huh." He couldn't stop himself once the words started pouring out. "I've known Farin since I moved here ten years ago. He knows I don't read all that much, but he's always trying to get me to try some of the newest books. He conned me into reading digital books. Colt and I tried to join the chamber of commerce together and were both turned down. Him because the powers that be claimed he'd submitted the wrong paperwork. Me? Because I was gay and unashamed to admit it. I've known Ashley as long as he's been with Colt. Nice guys, and they remind me I can be myself."

"I get it." Aiden's voice cracked and he didn't sound sure at all.

"Yeah, but I know who you keep looking at. I don't blame you. The guy in those pictures, the one who looks like he stepped out of a fashion magazine, that's Theo." Matt steadied himself. Talking about Theo wasn't fun, but he owed Aiden an explanation. "He looks hot and knows it."

"Matt." Aiden leaned back in Matt's embrace. "It's okay."

"No, it's not. Remember how you told me you kept trying to stay away from Lucky, but it took a lot longer to cut the final cord?" He curled his fingers under Aiden's chin. "Theo was that way for me. He's great to look at, but his attitude leaves a lot to be desired."

Aiden stared at him but said nothing. The worry in his eyes spoke volumes. *Is he looking for reasons to run?*

"Theo was the type of guy who knew what to say to get what he wanted. He'd charm anyone if it meant getting ahead or getting head." Matt let go of Aiden and eased onto the stool. "We met at a time when I thought I knew what I wanted." *Shit.* He had to word this just right. If he spilled the beans about his addictions, he'd drive Aiden away in moments. But so much of his past with Theo had everything to do with his addiction. "Theo liked me because I had the right look—tough and rugged. I was his bad boy."

"You're not a bad boy," Aiden whispered.

Not that Aiden knew…and not that he'd ever find out. Matt half shrugged. "I look like I'm bad. The ink, the piercings… For someone wanting a dangerous guy—at least in appearance—I fit the bill."

"You're human."

Maybe so, but he'd made his share of mistakes. "True. The difference is that Theo wanted the danger." And he'd given it to him. Matt held Aiden's hand. He needed Aiden's strength to get through this — at least the parts he was willing to share. "I thought I wanted to marry Theo. Like, I'd picked out rings and talked to a guy I knew who performed weddings. I had a life planned out for us. Theo seemed to be on the same wavelength. Then he wasn't." He remembered the instant things had changed — when he'd woken up face-down in the empty tub, with no recollection of how he'd gotten there. Blood had seeped from his nose, and the purple bags had been darker than normal under his eyes. Theo hadn't helped him or checked on him. No, Theo had been in the living room with another man.

"I'm sorry." Aiden stepped into the vee of Matt's legs and toyed with the wrinkles in Matt's shirt.

"I used to think I wanted someone I could read like a book. Someone who would do what I wanted and not challenge me. I wanted easy. Theo made me see that easy sucked. Easy meant settling." He clasped Aiden's wrists. "I don't expect what's starting between us to ever be easy."

"The sex is," Aiden murmured. "It's great."

"True, but I can't make you tell me what's bothering you. I can't force you to be honest with me. What I can do is ask that you level with me. If you're worried about Theo coming back into the picture, you're on the wrong path. I kept those pictures in the frame because it reminds me of what I had and what I thought was good. You're right — each image has a reason. Maybe you and I should take a few pictures together so we can write better memories for the frame."

"I'd like that." Aiden draped his arm around Matt's neck, careful not to put weight on Matt's healing shoulder. "You asked for honesty. I saw those and how handsome Theo is. I'd be drawn to him, but he's not you. I'm worried you want him back. I'm neurotic in my own way. I wouldn't blame you if you walked. But it scared me to think things weren't as good as I thought because of my fear. I look for the failings in everything. Relationships fall apart and I don't want to be there when they do."

"Nah. Not all of them." Matt tugged him close for a kiss. The moment his lips touched Aiden's, his own fears melted. He and Aiden were good for each other — better than Theo or any of his other exes had been. He bit Aiden's bottom lip and savored the taste of his kiss. A groan rumbled in his throat. "Come upstairs with me. Stay tonight." *Need me as much as I need you.*

Aiden nodded. He grasped Matt's hand and tucked his phone into his back pocket, then headed to the staircase.

Matt's heart skipped a beat. He grasped Aiden's hand. *Damn.* He wanted to stop and make love right there on the steps. Halfway up, he crashed into Aiden and collapsed on top of him. "Ever made love on a staircase?" he asked. Doing just that seemed like the sexiest thing in the world.

"I'll kill my back, and you'll mess up your shoulder." Aiden patted Matt's ass. "Keep going. We'll do whatever you want in your bedroom."

Matt moved off Aiden and tweaked his shoulder. *Fuck.* He ground his teeth. He didn't want Aiden to see him in pain, but he shouldn't have pushed away from the step with his bum arm.

"You did, didn't you?" Aiden didn't rush away from Matt. Instead, he stayed beside him.

Matt didn't say anything until he reached the top of the steps. "No." Liar. "I'm fine."

"Right." Aiden remained behind Matt and palmed Matt's butt. "If you hurt yourself…"

"You'll go home?" He stopped in the bedroom and faced Aiden. "Huh?" He wasn't mad. Truth be told, he deserved a little hell from Aiden. He'd done too much and his shoulder was letting him know.

"I should," Aiden said. "You'll mess up the work I did and the healing you've accomplished. Probably already set yourself back a bit."

"But I've got a personal doctor." Matt hugged Aiden to his chest. "If I mess up too much, then you're here to save me."

"I probably will, but don't push it." Aiden eased Matt out of his shirt. He tossed the garment onto the closest chair. He trailed his fingers down Matt's chest, stopping to tweak his nipples. "You've got slight bruising around the wound site. It's normal to have some, but you're trying to do too much."

"Sorry. I'm fine." Although he did like knowing Aiden was worried about him.

"Lie down." Aiden rested his hands on his hips. "No. Drop your pants first. I want you naked and to do it before you're wriggling on the bed too much. I don't want you to screw up your shoulder even more."

Matt stopped in his tracks. *What a switch.* He hadn't expected Aiden to be so assertive outside his job. He liked it and unbuckled. With Aiden's help, he shoved his pants and boxers down around his knees. He stumbled forward into Aiden's arms. "Sorry."

"You've said that already." Aiden maneuvered him onto the bed.

Matt collapsed on the mattress and grunted. He tried to kick his wadded-up clothing from his ankles but failed.

Aiden tugged Matt's shoes free. "You're unorthodox but effective." He removed Matt's socks then helped him out of the rest of his clothes.

Matt didn't fight Aiden as he took control. He rested on his back and sighed as the cool air in his bedroom wrapped around him. His nerve endings were on fire and his need for Aiden grew.

Aiden stood at the foot of the bed and shrugged out of his shirt. Only half-naked, he knelt between Matt's knees. He slid his hands over Matt's chest, arms, then down to his belly and over his thighs. He massaged Matt's calves and feet.

Matt shivered — not from the chill but the tenderness in Aiden's touch. He'd experienced Aiden the doctor and Aiden the lover, but this was Aiden the partner. A lover's caress. He arched his back as much as possible without straining his shoulder. A groan ripped from his throat. He hadn't expected having someone touching his feet would turn him on so much.

Aiden switched his attention to Matt's cock. He rubbed his face along Matt's inner thigh and blew warm air across the blunt head of Matt's dick.

"Oh shit." Matt spread his legs apart more. His thoughts blurred as he threaded his fingers into Aiden's hair. He loved the way Aiden touched him. The tenderness and compassion overwhelmed him. He felt cherished — like he was the only person in the world. Was that possible? No one had ever treated him like that before. He pushed lightly on Aiden's head. Allowing Aiden to take charge didn't bother him, but he couldn't hold back.

Aiden buried his nose in Matt's pubic hair, then pulled back and swallowed him to the hilt. He bobbed his head and planted his palms on Matt's thighs. The move allowed Matt to remain on his back without hurting himself but also gave him so much pleasure. He marveled at Aiden's concern for his condition. Other lovers wouldn't have been so worried.

Aiden hummed around Matt's shaft, then pulled back before plunging his mouth down onto Matt's dick. Matt closed his eyes. He balled his hands in the sheets and planted his heels on the mattress. The love and desire building in his heart grew. This wasn't the warm and fuzzy feeling he'd expected, but something more. He cared about Aiden and wanted him around. He'd pushed the romance fast at the beginning, but now that they were together and had gone through a few rough situations, he understood. His heart wasn't jumping the gun. He truly had fallen for Aiden too. He opened his eyes and stared at Aiden.

A grin spread across Aiden's lips. "Like that?"

"Yeah. I love it." He wasn't kidding. Everything Aiden did made him happy.

Aiden pulled up and flicked his tongue across the head. Matt tensed and curled forward. He'd missed too much and needed to see everything Aiden was doing. He flopped his good arm, hunting for the pillow. *Where is the damn thing?* He grunted. The change in position bothered his shoulder.

"Shit." Matt collapsed against the sheets. *Damn it.*

Aiden stopped and met Matt's glance. "You're hurting." A frown marred his face and the lines around his eyes deepened.

"Yeah, but I don't want you to stop." He wasn't stupid. The connection and desire were real. He'd been through a lot with Aiden and he wasn't about to turn back. He didn't want to. Right now, he wanted his head back in the game so he could better appreciate Aiden giving him head.

Aiden scurried off the bed and grabbed a pillow. "I'll kick your ass if you strain too much. Getting you off isn't a good idea. You'll tense again." He stuffed the pillow behind Matt's head. "I shouldn't have let you put those piercings back in, either."

"It's worth it. All of it. So are you." Matt reclined against the extra support. He loved the new vantage point and the reduced strain on his shoulder. "I'm very fond of you."

"I'm glad to hear that." Aiden's eyes sparkled. He resumed his position on the bed and sucked on Matt's dick. His hair slipped forward on his brow. The tresses tickled Matt's lower belly.

Within seconds, the heat returned to Matt's body. The passion resurfaced and he gasped. He threaded his fingers into Aiden's hair. He pushed his dick into Aiden's mouth and rocked his hips. A growl ripped from his throat as he fought the urge to lose control.

Aiden hummed, then groaned. At least Matt thought that was what he'd done. He wasn't sure. Heat flowed from his belly to his limbs. He trembled and closed his eyes as he tried to breathe. He yanked on Aiden's hair. He tensed and the muscles in his legs twitched.

Aiden bobbed his head faster and sucked Matt to the hilt each time.

"Holy…" The rest of the words were obliterated as he let go of Aiden's hair. His restraint melted away. A shudder racked his body as the orgasm washed over him. He moved his torso and fucked Aiden's mouth a couple more times, then sagged onto the bed. While he gathered his bearings, he opened his eyes. He sucked air into his lungs. Aiden had managed to blow his mind while blowing his cock. He couldn't wait for that rim job…once he healed enough to do it. He cupped the back of Aiden's head.

"Damn." He nudged Aiden. "Loved that. Thank you." The moment he said the words, he regretted them. *Thank you? What the hell?* Aiden wasn't providing a service.

Aiden sat back on his heels. "Thank you?" His brow furrowed. "Interesting."

"That's not what I meant." He blew out a long breath. "You knew how to do what I wanted and needed before I knew. I've never had a boyfriend who understood the way you do." The moment wasn't lost on him. Aiden was special. No way he'd let Aiden go. Aiden was in his blood. He wanted Aiden's name inked onto his body. Maybe the gesture was a tad drastic and way too permanent, but Aiden had already imprinted himself on Matt's heart.

Aiden laughed. "I know what you were trying to say." He wiped his mouth with the back of his hand. "I lost my head, though."

"You…what?" He stared at Aiden for a moment. "I don't understand."

"I swallowed. It's like my normal response – to keep germs at bay – it went out of the window. I forgot my fears," Aiden said. "My thinking on a lot of stuff has changed since I met you."

"Likewise." Matt sobered. He wanted to reassure Aiden but worried he'd made a mess of things. "I like you, too."

Aiden's eyes flashed. "I've had other boyfriends, but you're the first since Lucky to make me come out of my shell."

Matt opened his arms. "I want you to fuck me — but once I grab a nap. You wore me out."

"Did I?" Aiden chuckled and stretched out beside Matt. He'd kept his pants on.

"You did." He stretched out his bum shoulder. *Damn it.* Coming had fucked him up. But he wanted Aiden. How else could he show the man he craved that they were good together?

Aiden dragged a blanket over them and sighed. "I'm not fucking you tonight."

"Why?"

"Because you've done too much today. You need a break. If we have sex, it'll be in the morning and you can do me or we can get each other off in the shower. I don't want you straining." Aiden snuggled up on Matt's unhurt side. "I'm not going anywhere until the morning anyway."

Matt closed his eyes again. The sleepy, happy, post-sex glow overtook him. He'd leveled out his life. He had a great guy in his arms and he'd learned a hard lesson about the shop — it would survive without him. He wanted to go back, though. Just like Aiden, his automotive-repair business flowed in his veins. He wasn't ready to spill the rest of his secrets, but he was close. Once Aiden's dad was out of the hospital and settled enough that Matt could have Aiden's full attention, he'd have a talk with him. Until then, he'd bask in the love blossoming between him and his hot doctor.

* * * *

When Matt left the doctor's office the next afternoon, his emotions warred within him. Since he'd forgone the pain meds and was healing better than the specialist expected, he'd been given permission to resume driving. No riding his motorcycle or biking, but he didn't care. He wasn't in the mood to get the cycle out. Having the ability to drive was enough. What bothered him was the mess at the shop. He'd called Aaron before the doctor appointment and the place had sounded busy, but when he'd had Aiden drive past, nothing looked right.

He walked the short distance from the hospital complex to the body shop and bit back a growl. Candy wrappers littered the counter, the key box had been left wide open and when he peeked into the garage bays, he didn't see anyone within sight of the counter or register. Something clanged against the floor. *A dropped wrench?* He hoped so.

"Hello?" Matt closed the key box then stood in the doorway to the garage. "Aaron? Deighan?"

"Hey." Deighan stepped out from behind a lifted Chevy. "Hi." He wiped his hands. "Are you back or checking in?" He left the car and stepped in close to Matt.

"I'm back. I thought I'd finish out the day here. Is everything under control?" He made his way over to the counter and tossed the wrappers. "The place is a mess."

"That's Aaron." Deighan glanced over his shoulder then stuffed the rag into the front pocket of his coveralls. "I don't know what's gotten into him. He was fine until yesterday. When you called off, he flipped out."

He'd said he could handle the shop. Matt forced a smile. "I had to take my boyfriend to see his father."

"You did? I thought you couldn't drive?"

"He needed moral support. His father had a stroke—a mini one, I think." Matt shook his head. "He drove and I held his hand, so to speak."

"That's cool." Deighan looked back again then lowered his voice. "Just promise you're back, okay? Aaron got stuck on the Dodge and I had to bail him out. He screwed up the keys and gave the wrong one to Mr. Danvers, even though it clearly said who they belonged to. He keeps taking the candy out of the display and moaning about being left behind."

Shit. He should've seen this coming. Aaron tended to get mopey when he didn't get his way. But overeating and failing a job weren't his normal. Matt had to stop being the goofy man in love and focus on the shop. Letting Aaron steer the ship wasn't working. "Okay, well, I've got permission back to drive as of today, so I'm mobile again. I'm here to catch the paperwork up and get the lobby back into shape. I'll handle any incoming vehicles and when I see Aaron, I'll try to talk him down."

"Thank you," Deighan whispered. "I like working with him, but he has to get his head into the game. He almost ripped his arm off with that timing belt."

Aaron wasn't usually that sloppy. Matt sighed. "I'll do my best. Thanks. You should get your first paycheck on Friday."

"Nice." Deighan tugged the rag free from his pocket and tossed it into the bin. He turned on his heel then went back into the garage portion of the building.

Matt sagged onto the stool behind the counter. He busied himself with paperwork. Aaron hadn't kept up with the receipts. Money was in the register, but there were no corresponding work orders. When Matt checked his paperwork for the stock, he sighed. At least Aaron had the stock up to date in the last twenty-four hours. He scratched his head then resumed trying to figure out the discrepancies. If he had Aiden working with him, he doubted there would be such problems. Aiden's anal-retentiveness would've kept the ship righted.

"I hear you're looking for me." Aaron stomped into the lobby. "Well?" he snapped.

"You don't have to be combative." Matt tugged the work orders from the nail. "Which of these are done and which are still out? What did you complete? I see money but no idea of where it came from."

"Oh, so now you're Mr. Businessman?" Aaron shut the door to the garage. "It really pissed me off. We've been doing this thing for how long and you ditch me and your job for a guy?"

Matt dropped the pencil and moved the tablet out of the way. With no customers in sight, this was as good a time as any to deal with the problems. "I'm sorry. I dropped the ball. You're right. This is my business and I should be here."

"At least you get that," Aaron growled. He narrowed his eyes. "You get a piece of ass and forget your priorities."

"I thought you were happy for me. I thought you wanted me to get his number and go out." Matt didn't understand. "You and I are great friends and business partners. You're the rock. If I have a problem, I rely on you, but that's all we are. Business partners and friends. Not lovers."

"Give me the chance to prove we can be more than that. Owning the shop, running it together and being the way we used to be." Aaron flattened his palms on the counter. "Right?"

"You'll always be my closest friend and my best worker." He wasn't so sure about the best worker part, but if he could neutralize the problem with Aaron, he'd lie a little. "Aiden needed me and I've been here pretty much every day since we opened. I deserved a day off that didn't involve me being at the hospital. Yes, I went with him, but it wasn't like we fucked the day away. His father had a stroke. If I hadn't gone along, he would've made it, but he'd have been a mess. I know you needed me here, but he needed me too. This was one of the few times. This is still my business and my priority." He'd have to take a few days off here and there because life demanded it. If Aaron didn't like it, he'd have to deal. "Okay?"

"I'm sorry I got angry." Aaron stood beside him at the desk. "I'll get my head out of my ass so we can get the invoices and work orders figured out."

"Thanks." He appreciated Aaron coming clean to him, but two hours later he still wanted to throttle his employee. Matt waded through the paperwork until he found the bottom of the stack, but the entire time, Aaron stayed too close. Matt tensed and kept scooting away, but there was only so far he could go. If he moved much more away from the archaic computer, he'd have to sit on Aaron's lap in order to type.

Aaron kept watching him too. Not just glances or anything, but full-on staring. Matt's skin crawled. Aaron had never been this…clingy before. He wanted to ask Aaron a hundred questions, like why in the hell was he sitting so damn close, but he kept his inquiries to himself. He still had to work with Aaron.

Matt cracked his knuckles and wished for acetaminophen. Just a little something to dull the ache in his shoulder from sitting at the computer. "Whew. That took longer than I expected." He sent off the order for the next round of parts, then moved the tablet out of the way. "Orders up to date, paperwork crisis dealt with and I'm not totally broke." Tomorrow, he'd tackle properly cleaning the lobby.

"I'm a slob." Aaron stood beside Matt. "Between getting behind and just not feeling like myself, I let everything slip."

"I did see the disaster on the counter." He knocked on the acrylic sheet on top of the desk. "I threw the wrappers away and tossed the empty soda can."

"I eat when I'm depressed."

"I thought you worked out." He stared at the wastebasket full of wrappers. Confusion hit him hard. "Don't you?" Matt assumed Aaron was a gym junkie. Whenever he wasn't at the shop, Aaron claimed to be sweating it up hard at the fitness center.

"It's a vicious cycle." Aaron winked. "You should know. You think you're level, then it all goes to pot. You had your vices and mine's food." He shrugged. "I need to get back to the Chevy. Regaining my groove helped." He touched Matt's hand and lingered longer than Matt would've liked.

Matt stifled his groan. He knew exactly what Aaron was getting at—all the things he'd hinted at. He'd turned to painkillers and alcohol to dull his heartache and the aftereffects of knee surgery. But he'd overcome his addictions. Aaron appeared not to have, despite his beliefs. Then there was the hint about getting together. Aaron hadn't wanted him to date Aiden. Not a chance. He couldn't have known the shooting would occur, but even so, he'd probably assumed Aiden would be out of Matt's life by then.

Matt massaged his temples. He had too much stress in his life. Unfortunately, he'd created most of it.

The bell on the front door dinged. When Matt looked up, Jordan strolled into the lobby. Matt cringed. He'd forgotten all about the meeting he was supposed to have had with the officer. *Fuck.* "Hi."

"Hi yourself." Jordan closed the door. "You appear to be up to your eyeballs in God knows what. I'm guessing you haven't eaten lately or checked your phone."

Matt froze. He wasn't even sure where he'd left his phone last. He slapped the counter to no avail.

Jordan pointed to the potted plant by the candy display. "You put the phone over there beside the plant. Did you switch the setting to silent?" He offered up the phone. "Or was the workload that strenuous?"

"I forgot where I put it." Matt turned the sound back on and checked the status. Seven missed calls, six texts and two voice mails. He swiped to the missed calls—all from the police department. "Sorry. I see you called. A lot."

"I did. You didn't show up for our meeting and I was worried, so I came looking for you." Jordan folded his arms and widened his stance. If he was going for intimidating, he'd found the right look. He tilted his chin. "Everything okay?"

"I'm tired," Matt blurted. He hadn't realized just how much coming back to work would wear him out. Maybe it was dealing with Aaron and his shenanigans... He wasn't sure. "My coworker didn't keep the books like I would've preferred and he made a mess of the lobby-slash-office, so there's that. Since the robbery, I've changed my personal status to in a relationship." He refused to call the night of the robbery a shooting. *Screw that.* "Then Aiden's father had a stroke. We went to see him and reassure Aiden. Besides all that, my shoulder aches and I have no idea who wanted to rob me or why. I'd love to know what's going on and I missed the meeting because I got busy putting out fires. Would you like to know anything else?"

"You've summed it up nicely." Jordan leaned on the counter. "Aaron won't help? I heard you hired Molly Daniels' nephew. He's not working out?"

"Deighan? No, he's great. It's Aaron. I know half of what's gotten into him and I don't want to know about the other half." Matt pinched the bridge of his nose. "So yeah. I'm sorry." He wasn't sure what else to say.

"Is Aiden's father okay? Len's a good man. Forthright and opinionated, but his heart's in the right place." Jordan half smiled. "He's funny too."

"I didn't know you'd met him." He tried to hide the shock and the streak of jealousy. "Did you date Aiden?" He didn't want to think about it if Jordan had, but everyone had a past.

"No. His father visited the hospital right after Aiden was hired on...six or seven years ago. They'd finally opened the renovated pediatrics wing and the whole town had a party. Don't you remember? Maybe you weren't there. I thought you were." Jordan frowned.

"Anyway, there was a big bash and Len showed up with his partner. How's Keye handling the situation?"

"He's dead. Has been for five years." He hadn't meant to blurt that part out, but he seemed to have lost all tact.

"Oh." Jordan wobbled against the counter. "I'm sorry to hear that. Aiden mentioned he was sick, but I assumed it was a cold or something." He shook his head. "I guess that's why I hadn't seen him in forever. I should've said something before now."

Matt toyed with the pens in the chipped coffee cup. He didn't know all the details with Keye and didn't think he should be discussing someone he'd never met.

"Then you aren't kidding. You're dealing with a lot." Jordan stood tall. "Most of the time when people say they're stressed, it's just because I'm there. You've... Yeah."

"Yep." He tapped one of the pens against the blotter. "So, what did I miss in the meeting?" Part of him wanted to know, but the rest of him wanted the whole damn situation to disappear.

"We've got three people of interest on our radar but haven't brought anyone in yet," Jordan said. "They're not the easiest individuals to find. But we've matched the bullet from the wall to bullets used in another robbery. Oddly enough, the gun from that case was recovered—clean of any fingerprints—two days ago. The striations on the test bullets matched the ones from a robbery on Tenth Street and yours."

"Can you connect the crimes?"

"Nothing's impossible, but since we don't have anyone in custody and no leads, it's harder. I'm hoping we get a few tips and can bring at least one of the persons of interest in for questioning." Jordan tipped his head to the side. "If that happens, we'll bring you in to view a lineup."

"I'll do whatever you want," Matt said. "Anything to get this over with." He hated living with fear that whoever had robbed him might come back. He could replace vehicles, money and other objects, but not his life, and he had too much to live for. "What do you think they wanted? Why would someone target me?"

"The cash in the register, the credit card numbers on the receipts and the cars in the lot would be my guess. They could use the numbers to make charges or sell them. The car parts, even on the cars still, have value." Jordan rubbed his chin and sighed. "There haven't been a rash of robberies otherwise or complaints in this area. Trust me. This situation not getting solved has the chief stymied and pissed. It's crazy. How can the man from the video just disappear? You didn't know him, did you?"

He'd been asked that question a hundred times and he still didn't know the identity of the robber. "I've never seen him before, but I'd be able to pick him out of a lineup. I'll never forget his eyes. Blue, but dark and piercing. Unique." He paused. "No one's come forward? Really?" He would've thought someone would've seen something.

"Nope. No tips, false leads…anything. We put up a five-thousand-dollar reward for information on the case and it's brought in zip."

"Jeez." He would've assumed the offer of that kind of money would've brought in crank calls, cold leads and anyone else wanting what seemed to be easy cash.

"Well, I'm glad you're okay — as much as you can be. I'll keep you posted on our progress. Tell Aiden I said hi. Farin and Steve are back from their honeymoon, all tan and happy. I love them, but I hate them. I keep promising Colin we're next, but I can't seem to get a wedding organized."

Matt snorted. Weddings, honeymoons, cold cases... Jordan had a lot more on his mind than Matt. "If it's meant to happen, it will."

"You're right. I'm just glad the coalition crap has died down." Jordan rapped his knuckles on the counter. "Speaking of coalitions, we're going to have a single-parent mixer after Halloween. I know you're not a single parent, but you're welcome to come. Bring Aiden. Dance, party and eat. Oh, and if it tickles your fancy, Colin's having a special comic-book gathering the night before the next superhero movie comes out. I haven't been able to make the last two, but I hear they're a lot of fun."

"I'll see what I can do." He rounded the counter and followed Jordan out to the parking lot. The last vestiges of sunlight streaked through the trees and across the pavement. "Thank you."

"Remember, the invitations are always open. We deserve to go back to our regularly scheduled life." Jordan waved, then climbed behind the wheel of his cruiser.

Matt remained outside until Jordan's car disappeared around the corner in the direction the hospital. Everything seemed so chaotic but calm at the same time. He'd found a great man and had him in his life. The shop was getting back to normal, albeit slowly, and the person who'd robbed and turned his world upside down was still roaming around free. He wanted to be scared, but what would that do? Give him an ulcer and not much else. The only option was to keep his faith in the Cedarwood police as well as the sheriff's office. Until the person was rounded up, he had to live his life like nothing had happened. Not the easiest thing, but less of a challenge with Aiden around. *Good thing I found Aiden.*

Chapter Ten

Aiden parked in the staff lot and groaned. Matt had to work, and he needed to earn his paycheck too. He climbed out of the car and glanced into the back seat. *Well, crud.* The flowers from Matt were still there and now crispy. At least they were dried out. He'd put them in a vase at home once he went back to his place. But maybe his and Matt's conflicting schedules were what would doom the relationship. He had to think about that.

Aiden gathered his bag and locked the car then headed into the building. He waved at a few of the nurses. Being called in early wasn't his idea of fun, but he'd deal. He tossed his things into his locker. Based on the noise in the hospital, the place was already hopping. He changed and logged in.

He joined the nurses at the shift briefing. The sheer volume of patients never ceased to amaze him. Two gunshot-wound victims, a kid with a broken arm and a woman in labor, not to mention a man with Norovirus.

"Going to be exciting," Madison said. "Oh, I've got a surprise for you."

"You do?" *Is Matt here?* Having his man show up without a major wound would be nice. He headed into the main bank of ER bays.

"I don't know how he knew, but he's got timing." She yanked the curtain back. "He came in just at the moment you did too."

Aiden stared at the man in the bay. His excitement dimmed. *Not Matt.* "Lucky."

"Hi." Lucky held his ribs and chest. "Long time, no see."

"I guess so. What's wrong?" He moved Lucky's hospital gown out of the way. "No bruising at all. What did you do?"

"Nothing much." Lucky gave him a shit-eating grin. "I'll be fine."

"Right." Madison tugged Aiden over to the computer and closed the curtain. "He claims he was crushed while playing touch football. He was tackled and piled onto." She brought up the chart and lowered her voice. "Not so sure I buy that answer."

"I doubt that's what happened too." He pulled the stethoscope from around his neck. "I'll check him out."

"I'm sure you will." She elbowed him. "But what's your thought?"

"He hates sports," Aiden murmured.

"So the ex we heard about and never saw really exists and he's a liar?" She frowned. "No."

"Yes, that's him, and he's got a way with storytelling." He groaned. "He's got timing too."

"I thought that was him, but damn." She stepped between Aiden and the computer. "I'm jealous."

"What? Why?"

"The way you talked about him…I didn't think he looked like that." She grabbed his shoulder. "The way you look at him, I'd think you still have feelings for him. Didn't end well, did it?"

"It was fine. I'm with Matt." He wasn't sure why he had to say that so loudly. "I'm involved, remember?"

"Nothing surprises me about you any longer." She rested her hands on her hips. "I don't know if he really hurt himself playing football, but he needs you. Go to him."

Aiden rolled his eyes. Sure, there were doctors having affairs with other doctors on staff. Some of his colleagues were sleeping with anyone they could find to fill their bed. A few of the nurses were known for their prowess in the bedroom—not that he knew firsthand. He wasn't into carrying on with a bunch of people. Matt was enough. So why was he still reminding himself of that fact?

Aiden moved the curtain out of the way. Lucky sat on the exam bed. He'd shrugged out of his hospital gown, leaving him exposed from the waist up. His upper body was still defined. His muscles flexed as he breathed. Damn, the man was still model perfect. Bruising started on his ribs, but nowhere else.

Aiden's breath caught in his throat. He'd thought he was over Lucky, but the old feelings came rushing back. He'd walked away from him. They'd been horrible together. They were mismatched and the sex had been decent. He doubted any of their past could be good again. He wobbled on his feet. *Holy shit.* What was he doing? Was he considering another go-round with his ex? He had Matt now and thought he loved him. Why was he thinking about Lucky?

"Hi." Lucky straightened up. "Aiden?"

"Dr. Connor." Aiden forced himself into professional mode. He was here to do a job, not hook up. "How are you feeling? According to your chart, you were injured playing football. Correct?"

"That's what I told the girl." Lucky smiled. "Yep. Football accident."

I'll bet. Aiden looked over the lack of bruising. "I'm sending you to X-Ray. I want to check for broken bones and anything I might have missed." He typed the code into the computer, then logged out. He stared at Lucky. "Level with me. You hate sports."

"Hate is such a strong word," Lucky said, his voice smooth.

"Uh-huh." And he'd thought he was the doctor. Lucky sure knew how to operate. "It's also correct."

"So?" Lucky shrugged.

"Why were you playing football? It's raining." He folded his arms and tried his best to look authoritative. "Or was that a lie?"

Lucky squirmed. He didn't answer right away or look Aiden in the eye. "It started as football." He drew up into himself and hugged his waist. "He didn't like how I knew nothing about the sport. After the game, Ethan let me know he wasn't happy."

"With?" He wasn't sure he believed his ex, but he had little reason not to.

"His fists." Another shrug. "Couple of times."

"You can report it." He checked Lucky's ribs again. Getting so close, he smelled Lucky's cologne, and his skin prickled. Oh, shit, he was in trouble. "No one has the right to hurt you."

"Because you still care?" Lucky rested his hand on Aiden's. His breath hitched. "I never stopped caring about you."

"Lucky." He should've seen this coming. *Damn it.*

"We're good together," Lucky said. "Really good. Remember?"

"I do." He lowered his voice to a whisper. "You used to cut on me because I didn't make enough money and I was never home. All we had was sex. Is that what you're musing over?"

"I can handle your schedule." Lucky batted his eyelashes. "I'm not the same guy I was before."

"I'm seeing someone." The words came out more growly than he'd planned.

"See me too." Lucky held tight to Aiden's hand.

"I'm not that kind of guy." He pulled away from Lucky. He refused to divide his loyalties and be a total jerk to Matt. Besides, Lucky was a horrible choice for him. "I'm needed by my patients. I'll be back after you've been down to X-ray."

"Aiden?"

He turned around, despite his best intention to leave the bay.

"Think about what I said," Lucky said. "I meant every word."

Aiden forced a smile, then ducked out of the ER bay. He'd had enough of the craziness in his life. A break would be good. He read through the next chart, but his thoughts never ventured far from Matt and Lucky. He had to be nuts. He had a great guy in his life. Matt was sweet and charming. He'd been there when Aiden needed him most and didn't demand Aiden's time, but made the moments they were together special. The sex rocked and the connection made him happy. But there had to be some defect lurking that he hadn't considered. Something would go wrong. It always did.

Then there was Lucky. The relationship with his ex ran the gamut from white-hot to ice-cold. Good times to crap. They weren't great together. But Lucky embodied everything Aiden had thought he wanted physically in a man. Matt wasn't the guy he'd dreamed of being with when he'd thought about his perfect mate... He was hot but rougher around the edges. Did that matter?

Aiden managed to complete his rounds and finished out his shift. By the time he stepped outside for a break, morning sunshine stretched across the lot. *Damn.* He'd lost an entire night. *Where has the time gone?* He should grab a nap. Lord knew he was tired, but he doubted he'd be able to sleep.

He headed back into the building and changed in the locker room. He'd never be able to turn his brain off. Not now. Too many thoughts of Matt and Lucky filled his mind. Instead of going to the break room for a nap, he wandered down to the recreation wing. If he couldn't settle down, he'd get some exercise. A little sweat would make him forget his troubles. His father's old saying hadn't gotten any less corny over the years.

Aiden ran through his battery of stretches, then stepped onto the running track. He started along the outer lane and passed a couple of older women already walking. Some of the patrons he knew, but others were fresh faces. Thank goodness the few big talkers weren't there yet.

He broke into a longer stride and increased his speed. His muscles burned and his lungs ached, but he liked being able to think about nothing but running.

"Aiden?"

He slowed a bit and glanced over his shoulder. Lucky sprinted up to him. He hadn't expected to see his ex there, especially if he'd just been assaulted or hurt in a football game. "Hi." He slowed to a jog. He'd play along. "What's this? You're hurt."

"I thought about what you said and what I said." He kept in step with Aiden. "About reporting Ethan… I'm good. I can't do that."

Probably because he'd lied. Still, he'd keep up the charade until Lucky gave himself up. "If he did what you said…"

"It's not worth it."

Trust Lucky to make up a gigantic story. He should've known this was a lie. "You'd dismiss being abused? Why?" Why would he make Ethan, if he existed, into a monster? What the hell was wrong with Lucky?

"I left him, so why make it worse?"

Because you're lying. Damn it. Lucky had just minimized what others had been through — and all for his own gain, probably. "If he beat you…"

"I'll be okay." Lucky nudged Aiden off the track and cornered him. "But you being so worried makes me feel better."

"Domestic violence is never okay. Real or otherwise." He stopped talking and stared at Lucky. *How did I once love this man?* "Are you sure? I'll call the police. I'm not afraid of Ethan." He couldn't stand to see someone hurt if that was the truth.

"I knew you still cared about me." Lucky threw his arms around Aiden. "I knew it."

"I care when you're being abused." Why did he have the feeling he was being used instead?

Lucky crushed Aiden in his grasp and kissed him. "You have no idea. This makes everything better. I don't have to be in fear. You'll help."

"I don't…" *Shit, fuck and balls.* "Lucky."

"I knew I could count on you. Aiden, this isn't a fluke. You and me. Always." He kissed Aiden again. "I knew this was the time. If I had faith, believed and followed my heart." He held Aiden tighter. "Knew it."

"Lucky." He'd been conned. Had to have been. "What's Ethan's last name?"

"Doesn't matter. He's history."

"I'm with someone. I'm not a cheater, and this won't work." He shrugged out of Lucky's grasp. "Come on." He'd seen plenty of abuse victims during his time working in the ER and none of them walked away from their abusers that easily or changed their minds that fast. Lucky didn't seem fazed. Hell, he seemed cocksure about the situation. *The asshole.* Aiden gritted his teeth. People like Lucky gave the real victims a bad rap.

"You still want me. Dump him." Lucky flattened his palm on Aiden's chest. "You know you want to."

"I can't." He didn't want to and wasn't interested. "You're full of shit." *Damn it.* His frustration had gotten the better of him. He hated to swear in public, and Lucky brought the negative trait out.

"No, you won't. That's the truth. You're a nice guy and you won't dump him, but you're thinking about me, so that means I have a chance." Lucky wriggled his eyebrows. "I've always had a chance."

"I can't, I won't and I'm not thinking about you." Matt deserved better and he wasn't sure he wanted to throw what they'd created away. He hadn't been kidding about being in love with Matt.

"You'll change your mind. You always do," Lucky said.

"Lucky. What about Ethan? I thought you loved him." He wasn't entirely sure about the love part, but he had to catch Lucky in the lie. "You can't just turn your feelings on and off like a light switch."

"You're right." Lucky crowded against him again. "Some people are hard to forget. For me, it's always been you."

"And every other guy you've been with. Our problems are still the same. I'm working crazy hours and I'm not made of money. I don't have invitations to fancy parties or clubs and I'm not planning on leaving Cedarwood for what you call better chances." Aiden sidestepped Lucky. "I've got to go."

"Who says I want all that?" Lucky asked. He hurried back up to Aiden. "You're not understanding me. I don't need your money."

He knew that tone of voice. When Lucky used it, he wanted trouble. And what was this about not needing money? Lucky had always wanted a payday on someone else's dime. "What are you trying to do? Was there even an Ethan? Or did you make all this up? And what about your cash flow? What's this all about?"

"I want you. You want me. Why can't we just be together?" Lucky stuck out his bottom lip. "I'll pout. You always loved when I pouted."

"No, I didn't." He hadn't back then and the trait annoyed the hell out of him now. "I'm with someone. That's why we can't be together."

"For now." Lucky folded his arms. "Look, I need to go. The doctor in the ER released me. He says I'm bruised, but the X-rays are clear. Probably a muscle strain and deep-tissue damage, but nothing that won't heal. Nothing too serious."

"Answer my questions," Aiden snapped. He'd ask them one at a time. Maybe then Lucky would be straight with him. "What are you trying to do?"

"Get you back. Duh." Lucky rolled his eyes. "It might not be working now, but it will. I know you."

Jesus. "Was there even an Ethan?"

"Yes. I didn't make him up."

"What about your financial situation?" He had to know the answer to this one. "Come on."

"I came into some money. I don't need your cash, so there." Lucky stuck out his tongue. "Anything else?"

"No." He brushed past Lucky. He'd get answers. The asshat couldn't dodge the truth forever. "I need to go too."

"I'll walk you out." Lucky eased his arm around Aiden. At the doorway, he kissed Aiden on the cheek. "I'll call you." He winked. "Bye, Doctor."

Aiden stood rooted to the spot. *What the hell just happened?* Lucky liked to cause trouble and lie, but he'd never gone to such lengths before. Aiden watched Lucky disappear down the hallway. Was he really considering another go-round with Lucky? *Why? Holy shit.* He had Matt and they were happy together. He'd fallen for Matt.

So he had some old feelings for Lucky. So he missed the few good times they'd shared. Hindsight was twenty-twenty, wasn't it? What about all the cheating, the lies and the constant need for attention on Lucky's part? Lucky was a dead end.

"Fucking shit," Aiden murmured. He'd thought he had his life sorted out. Not now. His phone buzzed in his pocket. *Damn.* He glanced down at the screen. A text from Matt. His heart skipped a beat.

Meet for lunch?

Yeah, he wanted to see his man and know things would be all right.

I'd like that, he texted back. *I'm off for now. See you in twenty? Our usual spot?*

Matt's reply came within seconds.

Cool.

He sagged against the hallway wall. He'd see Matt and they'd share lunch. Christ, he needed a dose of Matt. He needed to be reminded in person that the feelings he'd developed for Matt were very real and very strong.

* * * *

Matt stretched and cracked the bones in his back. His muscles ached. He'd been stuck under the Dodge for most of the morning. Great for the owner, because he'd found the leak and fixed it, but horrible for his shoulder.

Deighan knelt down beside the car and peeked beneath the undercarriage. "Hey. You said to let you know when twenty minutes was up. It's up." He handed over Matt's phone. "The alarm went off, so I silenced it."

"Thanks." He tucked his phone back into his rear pocket. "How are you coming on the Caddy?" He shimmied out of the pit beneath the car and crawled up to ground level. "Okay? Any issues?"

"The Caddy is done and I called Mr. Goran. He'll be by to pick it up at two." Deighan widened his stance and folded his arms. "He had a dead mouse in the engine, which was why the thing stank, and one of the belts had been nearly chewed through. I replaced it, removed the mouse and checked his fluid levels. He needs a quart of oil, but I thought I'd mention that when he comes to pick it up in case he does his own oil changes."

"Thorough. Nice." He glanced around the shop while he wiped his hands clean. "Where is Aaron? We're caught up, but still. He didn't say anything about taking off."

"He told me he had an appointment and you knew about it." Deighan shrugged. "Sorry."

"It'll be fine." He'd have to hire another kid from the vocational school at this rate. That was probably a good thing, though. The students got to learn on the job, and he had cheaper labor.

"With Aaron gone, there aren't any tools flying across the garage." Deighan laughed. "He cracks me up, but man. When he gets pissed, he really gets pissed."

"He has a temper." He dusted himself off then washed his hands in the sink. "You haven't seen him after a few beers."

"Yeah, I did. I was at the diner and he showed up shitfaced," Deighan said. "Mr. Harrison tossed him out and one of the cops took him home — well, that's what Mr. Harrison said to the guy at the counter."

"You're good at eavesdropping?" Matt asked.

"Only when I'm sitting one stool over."

"Ah." He tossed the rag into the bin. "Close the garage doors. I'm going to shut down for lunch and walk over to the sub shop with Aiden. Want to tag along? I'll buy."

"As long as it's not hospital food, I'm good." Deighan pressed the buttons to shut the main doors. "I had my tonsils out when I was ten and the food sucked. I don't want surgery again just so I don't have to eat there."

"It's not so bad." He turned the sign around on the front door. "It's better than when I was a kid. At least this food has color."

"Ew." Deighan followed Matt outside and waited as he locked up.

Matt twisted in an attempt to relieve the tension in his back. No dice. He'd have to break down and take something when he returned to the shop. His stomach soured. Breaking down and giving in sucked.

Deighan's chain on his pants jangled as he walked. "You know. You're calm when Doc's around. I'm glad you paired up."

"I am too." Pride swelled in his heart. He loved telling anyone who'd listen that he'd found something great. "What about your girl? Quinn?" He started across the street with Deighan beside him.

"Sierra." Deighan stuffed his hands into his pockets. "Quinn got a date with a football player and dumped me, so I'm seeing Sierra."

"Can he fix Quinn's car when it breaks?" Matt asked.

"He'd buy her a new one. His dad owns the Lakeside dealership."

"Money isn't everything. He can't rely on his dad forever, either." He sounded like someone's dad — certainly not his own.

"Maybe, but it helps."

"It causes new problems," Matt said. "The old problems are still there and new ones come along too. Money exacerbates everything." He crossed the

190

parking lot but slowed down when he noticed Aiden by his car. Another man stood with him. Matt balled his hands. He wasn't jealous, but he wasn't fond of the way Aiden stood so close to the mystery man. Was the person someone Aiden knew? Another doctor or a nurse? Friend of the family?

"Who's that steppin' in on your man?" Deighan asked.

"Don't know." Matt wanted to rush up to Aiden but felt more like an interloper.

The man hugged Aiden and though Aiden didn't hug him back, he also didn't push him away. Maybe the guy was a former patient and thanking Aiden for a job well done. Whatever the reason, Matt didn't want to watch from a distance any longer.

"Hey, you. Break it up," Deighan shouted. He stormed up to Aiden. "Nothing to see here."

The kid had his heart in the right place, but no tact. "Deig." Part of him wished his employee would've kept his mouth shut, but the rest of him approved. He didn't like the way the man stayed so close to Aiden.

"Jesus." Deighan tapped the guy on the shoulder. "Excuse me. We'd like Doc now." He stepped between Aiden and the man. "Hiya, Doc. How the hell are you? Me and Matt are here for lunch."

The kid had a great handle on being suave. Matt scratched his forehead. He'd have to teach Deighan the fine art of knowing when to hold 'em and when to fold 'em.

Aiden put his hand up, keeping mystery man at bay. Was he doing that out of guilt? "Matt. Deighan. Hi, guys."

"I said I'd meet you." Matt couldn't keep the irritation from his voice. He bit the tip of his tongue to remind himself to go slow, but it didn't help. The fury welled within him. "I guess you couldn't wait." He swept his gaze over the mystery man. Thin, well kempt, preppy with his tailored clothes and casual shoes and designer-type sunglasses… The kind of guy Aiden claimed was his type. *Well, fuck me sideways.*

"Matt." Aiden didn't reach for him. His mouth opened and closed, but no sound came out.

"Don't let me bother you or interrupt." Matt brushed past Aiden and kept going toward the opposite end of the lot. He needed separation from Aiden and time to cool off.

"Matt," Aiden called.

Deighan touched Matt's arm but kept his mouth shut.

"Matt." The pleading in Aiden's voice got through to Matt, but he refused to turn around.

"I'll see you," mystery man said. "Later."

Matt froze. He recognized that voice, but from where? He wasn't sure. Although he wanted to keep going across the lot, he turned to face Aiden. Thank goodness mystery man had left. "Is he a doctor too?" He'd tried to sound nonchalant but failed.

"No." Aiden didn't bridge the gap between them. "He's a bad decision."

"Seemed good to me." He glanced around the general area for the guy. *How in the hell did he disappear so fast?* No screeching of tires or an engine sound to give away his location.

"I'm going to get us a table." Deighan nodded once, then hurried away.

Aiden massaged his forehead. "You weren't supposed to see that."

"Oh? What? My boyfriend with another guy?" Matt snapped. He'd thought he had his anger under control. He'd been wrong.

"No, me losing my nerve." Aiden bowed his head. "That was Lucky."

"I see." Aiden's ex, the dipshit, had come back and hugged him. *What else did the prick do?*

"I told you he comes sniffing around every so often. Today was his day." Aiden's shoulders sagged. The purplish cast under his eyes seemed deeper than usual.

"Did you indulge?"

"I thought about it. We have a history." Aiden met Matt's gaze. "It was stupid."

"We had a future, but not now." Matt swore if he gritted his teeth one more time, he'd crack every molar in half.

"I can explain." Aiden finally reached for him, but Matt stepped out of the way.

"I wish you would, but I'm not sure I want the answer." He didn't know if his heart could take the truth.

"Lucky was there when Keye died. He got me through. Okay? He and I are oil and water. It doesn't work, but I have a soft spot for him. I know he's wrong for me. Trust me. I should've learned my lesson the last time. I thought I had." Aiden stood in the middle of the lot where anyone could hear his conversation. If he was ashamed, he wasn't showing his hand.

"It sure looked cozy when you hugged him," Matt shot back.

Aiden groaned. "He hugged me. Not the other way around. I checked him over…"

"I'm sure you did," Matt said, interrupting Aiden.

"He was beaten up by his partner and came to the ER. I tried to get him to report the incident to the police, but he refused. I'm trying to get more information so I can. That's why he hugged me." Aiden raked his fingers through his hair. "I'm not sure if he was grateful I got involved or that I hadn't turned his partner in yet."

"You're shitting me. Him? He wasn't beaten up." Actually, he couldn't be sure of Aiden or Lucky's story, but the way Lucky carried himself, he wasn't acting like a man who'd been assaulted.

"You don't think so, either?"

"I don't know what to think." Matt toyed with the zipper on his overall pocket to keep his hands busy. "That guy didn't fit the mold for someone who's been assaulted, though."

"Right. He didn't." Aiden snorted. "You of all people should know that molds are meant to be broken. People lie and cheat. People make mistakes. They have weaknesses and imperfections."

Irrational anger filled his brain. He tried to keep himself in check, but the desire to unleash his frustration overwhelmed him. He didn't believe Aiden was so naive as to think Lucky was telling the truth. He saw right through the charade. The reason Lucky had gone to the ER was to find Aiden. He knew a good thing when he saw one, and Aiden was... Matt had once thought he was good. Now he wasn't so sure. "He lied to you." He had no proof but a strong hunch. "He knows who left him and he's desperate. He'll get beaten up to get your attention."

"You've lost your mind." Aiden's eyes widened. "I suspected him, but you're going overboard."

"I thought I had lost my mind, since you mentioned it. I'm crazy about you." Matt stood tall. "Now I see I'm just crazy." He needed to leave. The longer he stayed, the more he risked ruining any chance he might have with Aiden — if they could patch things up.

"You're being overly dramatic," Aiden replied. "You're shouting at me for no reason. I'm on your side — even if I can't help but look for the weaknesses."

"Are you? I can see it in your eyes and tense body language. You were considering more than just a hug with old Lucky. You were tossing around the idea of him or me." Matt's head ached and his shoulder throbbed. "You wondered if maybe you'd made the wrong decision."

"I had," Aiden whispered.

"What?" He sure as shit had to have heard Aiden wrong.

"I did. I debated. I ran the walking track three circuits trying to figure this out. I'm a goddamn mess." The blush on Aiden's cheeks went down his throat to beneath his collar. His chest heaved. The vein in his forehead popped out. "I debated my past and my future. Did I want decent sex with a guy who'd use me? Even though I knew it would be wrong, was I willing to go that route? Was I looking for safe-ish and familiar? Or did I want to stay in this crazy rollercoaster situation I've got with a guy I've fallen for and am getting to know? Having great sex and being happy again — even though it's not familiar and a little scary? That's what I've been trying to figure out. I'm scared there are weaknesses and shortcomings I'm not seeing. That's how I am — I worry and look for the faults."

"You're scared of me?" He'd heard what Aiden said but couldn't process it all. The part about fear stuck in his brain. "Aren't you?" He should've known this would happen. The tattoos and piercings were too much for Aiden.

"I am scared of you right now. You've flipped. What happened with Lucky was a hug. It was me being weak. It was him wanting something that wasn't available and me realizing what I wanted." Aiden reached for Matt. "It was me getting the swift kick in the ass that I needed."

"Right. You need a pretty boy who fits with your doctor persona." He wasn't sure where that had come from, but he'd showed his hand and had to play it out.

"Jesus Christ, Matt. You're so hung up on how everyone looks. I know you're insecure. I understand why and I even understand why you don't trust me. It makes sense. The thing is, I didn't run off with Lucky. I didn't fuck him here in the parking lot or make you watch. I just told him I'm not interested. I've got a man — well, I thought I did." Aiden shook his head. "I had one. Now it's all messed up."

Some of Matt's fury melted. *Shit.* "Aiden." He'd gone too far and pushed Aiden too much. Aiden had cut him to the marrow. He'd been right, even if Matt hadn't wanted to admit the truth.

"Just don't." Aiden put both hands up. "I'm not the other guys. Yeah, I'm weak, but I know my heart. I trust you." He backed away from Matt. "Right now, I don't like you, but I'm in love with you. Hoo-fucking-ray." He turned on his heel and walked straight to the hospital. He disappeared behind the sliding doors leading into the ER.

Matt didn't bother to chase him. He could follow and should, but didn't. He'd done too much damage for the moment and Aiden needed some space.

Deighan appeared beside him and held up a bag. "I had the feeling we'd want these to go."

"Yeah." He scrubbed the back of his hand across his mouth. "I'm sorry you saw that."

"And heard it." Deighan nudged Matt. "And I thought Aaron was the drama queen. He blubbers. You pitch a fit. Let's go back to the shop."

"Sorry." He shoved his hands into his pockets. "I owe you for lunch. I'll pay you back." He walked in silence until they reached the road. "For being eighteen, you're damn smart."

"I'm observant," Deighan said. "I'm not into dudes, but I see why you like Doc. He had a decision and stuck to it. He's strong and can fix you up if you cut your arm off. That's rad."

"Rad?" He hadn't heard someone use that word in ages.

"Yeah." Deighan stuck one of the sandwiches into the refrigerator. "I assume you'll want that later."

"Thanks." He wasn't hungry and was too damn embarrassed to eat anything.

"He stood up to you, Doc did." Deighan unwrapped his lunch on the counter and plunked onto the stool. "Aaron won't. His version of defending himself is to bitch and throw a fit."

"Aaron has his own issues." He sank onto the stool behind the counter. "I agree, Aiden is tough. Me? Not so much. I was shot. I don't like discussing that." *I'm ashamed I couldn't protect myself.*

Deighan shrugged. "A gun makes everyone tougher. Even if you can't aim, you'll most likely hit something and do damage." He rolled his eyes. "You're tough without a side piece — don't forget that."

"I feel like shit." He couldn't explain the ways he felt — embarrassed for losing his cool in front of Aiden, angry for allowing his emotions to get the better of him and for jumping to conclusions, frustrated that he'd screwed everything up with Aiden, and defeated.

"You look like shit too." Deighan half smiled. "Don't quit on Doc or yourself." He polished off the sandwich, then wiped his mouth with his napkin. "I'm going to text Sierra. I'll be right back." He ducked into the break room, leaving Matt alone behind the counter.

Matt drummed his fingers on the plastic sheet protecting the brochures on the counter. If he called Aiden right now, he'd most likely get his voice mail. An apology text was the cowardly way to deal with the situation. Besides, Aiden was probably working and being super doctor. He wouldn't get the message — vocal or text — right away anyway.

Matt groaned. Deighan was right. He'd overreacted, but he didn't trust Lucky. He'd been in Lucky's shoes — although not to such a degree — because he knew what it was like to be with Aiden. If there was a guy he wanted to keep around in his life, Aiden was the one. But what had he done? Shoved Aiden away.

What in the hell should I do? He couldn't badger Aiden, but he also couldn't focus. *Shit.* He brought up the text screen.

I'm sorry.

Matt hit Send before he second-guessed his decision.

I can explain too. When you're available and we've cooled down, I want to talk.

The additional text probably rambled, but oh well. The screen lit up with a reply from Aiden.

I am too.

If Aiden was sorry, then there was hope. He'd hold on to the hope that a second chance was possible.

Can we try again for food tonight? I'll buy and grovel. How about the next day you're off?

Matt sent the text and tapped his foot on the floor. The nervous energy would be the death of him.

Don't need to grovel. You made your feelings clear.

He read and reread Aiden's reply ten times before he figured out what he wanted to say in return. *Shit.*

No, I didn't.

Another message arrived, almost before he'd sent the last one.

Just stop. Okay? I'm not in the mood.

Damn, damn, damn. He had to say something.

What happened besides Hurricane Matt? Is your dad okay?

He wanted an answer—any answer—but got nothing. Aiden must've been called away. Matt sighed. He'd earned the silence. He shoved his phone next to the register and out of the way. Aiden deserved better and time to process what had happened. Although he wanted to bombard Aiden with messages, he refrained. He'd try again later.

Giving Aiden space and time were the right courses of action, but why did doing so feel so wrong? Because he'd messed up and wanted to make things right.

Letting his anger get the best of him hadn't been good. He'd probably lost Aiden because of his low self-esteem, outburst and the trust issues. God help him when Aiden learned about his past. Things were bad, but they could get a whole lot worse. He had to hope Aiden didn't find out from the wrong source and would be willing to give him a chance to fix everything.

Like that would happen the way I want...

Chapter Eleven

For the next two days, Matt kept his phone with him and checked it religiously. No replies from Aiden. No texts, no visits, no voice mails… Nothing.

The emptiness in his heart and the loneliness damn near killed him. He ached, and not just from his shoulder. Aiden had broken his heart.

Deighan knew the truth, but if he'd told Aaron, Aaron didn't seem to care. Or he hadn't noticed Matt's foul mood.

Aaron strode into the office. "Hey. We're going down to Aces High. Want to come?" He grinned and wiggled his fingers. "You love clubbing. The dancing, the men… It might take your mind off your troubles."

"It's not my thing." He liked his troubles, as Aaron called them. *Well, no.* He'd like to not have the problems in his life. He'd rather have Aiden there with him. Going to the club might be fun for half an hour, but it wouldn't fix anything. "Deighan can't go," he said. "Too young, and you can't get him in." Someone had to be the voice of reason.

"He's not going. He said something about a wrestling meet or match. I don't know. He left over a half hour ago." Aaron leaned against the door frame. "I meant, you and me go and meet up with Rex. You remember him."

"Bald, all muscle and sounds like he gargles with lug nuts? I remember." He wasn't interested in Rex or attracted to him, but that hadn't stopped Rex from trying.

"Yes." Aaron's smile widened. "So?"

"I'll pass."

"Are you sure? We'll have fun." Aaron patted the counter. "You always have a good time when we go out. Come with us."

"I'll be lousy company. Thanks, but no thanks." He wanted to be alone. Just him and his business…a place to wallow in his own Matt-ness.

"Which is why you need to go out." Aaron tugged Matt off the stool. "So you aren't grumpy. You need people and music and noise."

"I need a lot of things, but a crazy techno beat and throbbing bodies aren't on the list." He plopped back down. "Have fun. You deserve it."

The bell over the door dinged, and when Matt looked over Aaron's shoulder, Aiden strolled into the lobby. His heart skipped a beat. Aiden was there. He hadn't expected to see Doc—not tonight or for a while.

"Lookie who crawled over," Aaron snarled. "You'd be hotter if you weren't such an asshole." He laughed, then waved. "Hey, Matt, if you want another rim job, I'll be at the house waiting." He winked before he strolled out of the building.

Matt toyed with the tablet and wished he could've muted Aaron before he'd spoken. Things were messy between him and Aiden and Aaron only made it worse. Matt wasn't sure how to proceed. "Hi." He wanted to say more but didn't.

"Hi." Aiden stayed by the door. "Closing soon?"

"Yeah. I'll keep my phone on in case someone needs a tow or there's an emergency." He fumbled for more words. "Are you off or just on a break?"

"I'm done for the night. I can't go back for twelve hours." Aiden didn't come closer. He smiled, but the light didn't reach his eyes.

Damn it. Things were too tense between them. What was he supposed to do? Blurting sounded good to him. "Aiden, I'm sorry. You were right. I let my issues get in the way of what we have."

"Apology not needed," Aiden said. He cleared his throat and closed his eyes. "Really, it's not."

"Sure it is. I laid into you in public. I acted like a fool in front of the entire world and my employee. God only knows who at the hospital saw us. That's irresponsible." He rounded the counter. "Doc, I'm sorry. I am hung up on appearance. You're right. My tats are a shield. If people think I'm tough, then they won't try to get close. If they stay away, I stay safe. It's a sucky way to live."

"You do what you have to in order to survive." Aiden leaned on the door frame and folded his arms. "You were right about Lucky. He made the story up."

He hadn't wanted to be correct on that account. His heart ached. "Aiden."

"It's okay. I knew he was bad news. Has been the last however many times we tried to work it out. This one was no different. I reported the incident, then did some checking. The Ethan he's talking about doesn't exist. He's seeing a man named Chuck and was engaged. A mutual friend informed me that Chuck is a great man and a tax accountant. He owns a house. He's almost forty, but he looks younger. He's never laid a hand on Lucky." Aiden shook his head. "Lucky proved that he's not changed, even though he says so, and that he just wanted a quick fuck. I don't even understand. He has a man—probably a handsome one, but I wouldn't know since I've never seen Chuck—who will have sex with him. Why did he need me?"

"You had something together. He wasn't ready to let go." God knew he wasn't ready to give things up with Aiden.

"He wanted a quickie." Aiden met his gaze. "Cheap and easy."

"Did you?" He shouldn't have asked the question but couldn't help himself.

"What?"

"Fuck him?" Matt asked.

"No. He even told me he'd take care of me. Lies. I should've known. The only person he wants to pamper is himself. He was probably going to use Chuck's money to make me feel important." His brow crinkled and his shoulders sagged. "Matt."

Matt wound his fingers around Aiden's wrist and tugged him away from the door. "Come here." He clicked the lock into place, turned the sign around then headed for the office. "We can go in here." He ushered Aiden into the back room.

"You don't have to be nice to me. I was an asshole to you back in the parking lot." Aiden tensed in Matt's grasp.

"Stop it." He curled his fingers under Aiden's chin. "You said so yourself. Lucky was familiar territory. I'm new. He's predictable. I'm a wild card. The things you pointed out about my hang-ups were right too. We both said a lot of shit we shouldn't have, but now that it's out, I feel better."

"You deserve better than me. I can't seem to make up my mind," Aiden said. "I think I know who I want then I change my mind."

"Nah. I'm pretty damn lucky I've got you around. So you're confused." He threaded his arms around Aiden. "I'm not. We had a fight. Big deal. Christ. It could've been a worse argument. Yes, I lost my cool in public and it was stupid, but people fight. They have issues. I'm still overcoming my past." He crowded Aiden against the desk. "I'm not quitting on you that easily."

"You should," Aiden whispered.

"Nah. I like you too much." He cupped Aiden's face in both hands. "Touching you, being with you, listening to the sounds you make when you sleep… The way you look at me and aren't afraid. I don't want to lose what we have."

A tear slipped down Aiden's cheek. "You're determined to get me to fall harder for you, aren't you?"

"Is it working?" He wriggled his eyebrows. "Yeah, I am."

"You're doing a great job." Aiden sagged against Matt. "I'm sorry."

"How do we move forward from this?"

"No idea. Usually when I have a fight with a guy, one of us leaves and that's the end." Aiden half shrugged. "Normally, I'm the one left behind."

"How about neither of us is left and we both play with behinds?" He kissed Aiden hard on the mouth.

"My place? Make-up sex? A little dinner, more sex and just being together?"

Aiden finally smiled, and the sparkle returned to his eyes. "If you put things that way…how can I resist?"

"You can't." He kissed Aiden again. "Let me get my stuff and we'll go."

"I should retrieve my car." Aiden didn't pull away. "I don't want to leave it in the lot when I'm not there."

"Of course. I'll follow you." He let go of Aiden long enough to stuff his wallet into his back pocket, his phone into the breast pocket of his overalls and to snatch his keys from the desk. He set the main alarm and checked the video feed to the security system. Once satisfied everything was fine, he followed Aiden into the lobby and picked up the tablet. "All I need to do is lock the lot fence, then we can go. I'll drive you to your car."

"You're too good for words." Aiden twined his fingers with Matt's. "But I'm glad you're mine."

"I'm just me. Thickheaded, oddball, but what you see is what you get." Matt tugged the front door of the shop closed and engaged the lock. He set the security code through his phone, then strode over to the newly installed keypad and locking mechanism on the gate. Once satisfied his business was secure, Matt glanced back at Aiden. He shrugged. "Probably overkill, but after the shooting, I'm taking nothing for granted." He swatted Aiden's ass. "Ready?"

"I am." Aiden fell into step beside Matt. "You're a unique man—my unique man." He climbed into the passenger seat. When Matt joined him in the car, he held Matt's hand.

Matt's heart swelled. He hadn't figured they'd get beyond the argument this fast. Aiden had shown Matt a side of himself he hadn't thought still existed. Matt did have low self-esteem, and this had been his moment of weakness. He'd have to sort himself out if he wanted to stay good enough for Aiden.

"Are we leaving, or are you going to stay in your head?" Aiden asked.

"Sorry." Matt shifted into gear. "I'm not used to being with a guy who gives me a hard time only to help me be a better man." He drove out of the lot and headed to the center of town on the way to his house.

"You're already better." Aiden leaned over and kissed Matt on the cheek when Matt stopped at the first traffic light. "You don't need me."

"Want to bet?" He kissed Aiden back, wishing he could have a longer taste of him before the light changed. He then hurried the rest of the way to Oakdale Avenue. He couldn't get home fast enough. Once he turned into his drive, he pressed the button to open the gate. He parked and turned the engine off. Technically, they were home. But he'd forgotten to take Aiden to get his car. *Shit.* He tugged Aiden across the console and rained kisses over his face. Maybe Aiden would forget about needing his car.

"You didn't take me to retrieve my car." Aiden laughed and didn't let go of Matt. "How am I supposed to go when I have to get back to work?"

"You're not?" He nibbled on Aiden's earlobe. The more he tasted Aiden, the more he delighted in his lover and fell head over heels for him. Aiden could laugh at him and keep him in check while still being firm with him and making him feel like they belonged together.

Aiden groaned. "Uh-huh."

Matt sighed and sucked on Aiden's tongue, deepening the kiss. He palmed the bulge in Aiden's jeans too. Holy shit, the tingles in his body overwhelmed him. He couldn't breathe. He wanted to crawl across the console and tug Aiden onto his lap. He wished his shoulder wasn't still messed up, or he'd probably have Aiden naked in the back seat already.

Aiden pulled away and panted. "Whoa. We should go inside." He sagged against the seat. "We will definitely have sex. Just not here in the car. It's not good for your back and I'd rather be on the bed anyway."

"Nice." He scrambled out of the car and hurried after Aiden to the house. He crushed Aiden against the door and mashed his mouth on his lover's neck as he stuffed the key into the lock. He groaned. Heat and immediacy filled his brain. Once he got the door open, he and Aiden tumbled into the house. He managed to stay on his feet.

"Good thing we didn't collide with the floor." Aiden clutched his belly and laughed.

"I've got a doctor. We'd be fine." He wound his arms around Aiden. "I want to strip you down right here and kiss every inch of you. But I stink like the shop."

"I smell like disinfectant." Aiden shrugged. "Shower, then we hit the bedroom?"

"Yes." He had to slow down, or he'd combust from his need for Aiden.

Aiden bounded up the steps first and stripped along the way. He shrugged out of his shirt and left the garment on the floor. In the hallway, he shoved his jeans to the floor and managed to kick out of the pants and his boxer briefs without falling over. He wriggled his ass.

"Tease." Matt reached for Aiden but didn't connect.

Megan Slayer

"Of course." Aiden marched into the bedroom like he owned the place and took charge. He didn't stop until he reached the bathroom. He turned on the water and removed his socks, then placed the towels on the closed toilet seat.

Matt marveled at Aiden's ability to do what needed to be done without seeming to think about it. Aiden could give him shit, but he cared. He did the little things like starting the shower, putting out towels, holding hands and kissing him when he least expected it. He could see him and Aiden being domestic together on a more permanent basis, and while the thought was heady, he loved it.

Matt removed his shirt and tossed the soiled garment into the hamper. He should join Aiden, but the sight in the tub was more than he could handle.

Aiden tipped his head back and water sluiced over his body. The lighting accentuated the muscles in his slim frame. When he parted his lips, he reminded Matt of a model. *Fuck the shit about me being the handsome one.* Aiden had him beat in all the right ways. He didn't need ink or anything else to make him sexy. He was perfect.

"Are you joining me or watching?" Aiden asked. Water slid down his face and his hair stuck fast to his forehead. "I don't mind showering alone if you want a show, but together is better."

"Sounds like a cheeseball come-on." He shoved his briefs and work pants to the floor, then nudged the pile out of the way. "Yeah, I'm coming."

"Not yet." Aiden grinned and scooted to the back of the tub. "You will be."

"Christ. This is why I like you." He cupped Aiden's jaw and feathered a kiss over his lips. "You're a smart-ass and a hot-ass too."

"I try." Aiden lathered the washcloth until suds dripped down his arms. "I already washed up since you gawked for too long."

"I wanted to make you work." Not really. He'd enjoyed the show. "And I like you this way."

"Me too. I don't want to stick my face in anywhere I might regret, so I make sure everything's squeaky clean." Aiden scrubbed Matt's chest, taking extra time around his nipple piercings.

"That's why I made sure and watched you. I don't like leaving that stuff to chance." He groaned as Aiden turned him around. Aiden massaged the cloth over Matt's back. He worked down his legs and into the crack of Matt's ass then sank to his knees. "Turn around again."

Matt faced him and bit back a moan. "You're so hot down there."

"I know." Aiden cleaned Matt's dick and balls. He stroked Matt, drawing another sigh from Matt's lips. Aiden met his gaze. "Did your piercings hurt?"

Water prickled Matt's shoulders. "Kind of. Which ones do you mean?"

"This one." Aiden stood and trailed his fingertips over the barbell in Matt's nipple. "I've seen a lot of them. You'd be surprised how many people come to the ER because they let a piercing get infected, and never in places I want to look." He flattened his palm over Matt's heart. "I had my ear pierced—the right one—for a week. It hurt like hell and I was never sure if it was the right one, so I took it out. I figured, why do something if it doesn't feel right? You know?"

Matt paused. The moment couldn't have been more pressing. Aiden didn't blurt out information like that often. He could see the scar from the hole, faint but visible. "Have you ever told anyone that? About the piercing?"

"Nope. Not even Dad. Keye knew because he caught me playing with it." Red infused Aiden's cheeks. "Seems so silly now. But back then it was a huge thing."

He cherished Aiden's honesty and desire to disclose the story. "What'd he say?" He embraced Aiden. He didn't want to leave the shower.

Aiden balled his hand on Matt's chest. "Do what I needed to. He said that and at least I'd picked something that would close if I changed my mind. He never judged, but he did remind me I was going to be a doctor and most doctors he knew were uptight assholes."

"Um…nice?" *What a guy.*

"It was Keye's way of saying I wasn't the right type to act out a lot. I'm good at following orders and doing things according to specs. He was right. Now, Dad would've killed me. Body modification was a huge no-no."

"Yeah?" He let go of Aiden long enough to dump shampoo onto his hand. He worked the suds through Aiden's hair. The man smelled and felt good. "I thought he'd be more permissive."

"On anyone else, yes. I'm his kid. He wanted me to stay perfect forever."

"He wanted you to stay respectable. Rinse." He moved out of the way as Aiden ducked under the water.

"I guess," Aiden said. Shampoo bubbles and water slid down his back. He shook his head and his hair stuck out at crazy angles around his face.

Matt bit back a laugh. Only Aiden could be sexy, boyish and charming while getting shampoo out of his hair. He dumped product onto his hand and washed the gel out of his own hair. "You wouldn't like being inked. It's not you. You either get into it or you don't. There's not much halfway about tattooing. If you do, then you're all-in. If not, there's nothing wrong with it. I like you as you are—just you."

"Thanks?" Aiden's eyebrows furrowed. "I think?"

"I mean it. You're beautiful the way you are." He leaned forward and rinsed the suds from his head. Some of the shampoo ended up in his eyes, but he didn't care. The burn didn't bother him. "Are you done?"

"I am."

Matt turned the water off and nudged Aiden onto the mat first. "Dry off and stretch out on the bed."

"Pushy." Aiden worked the towel over his body. "I might get the idea you like telling me what to do."

"A little." He winked and accepted the damp towel. "I really like watching your ass wiggle when you're walking around naked."

"Nice." Aiden patted his own butt and headed into the bedroom.

"On your hands and knees," Matt called. He dried off then hung the towel up. Before he left the bathroom, he grabbed condoms and a bottle of lube from the cabinet. He checked his look in the mirror, then snorted. What did it matter what he looked like? Aiden was there and wasn't leaving because he hadn't styled his hair or put on cologne. He strolled into the bedroom, stopping only when Aiden whistled. Matt frowned. "You're not in position."

"How can I be? When I look at you, I don't want to look away." Aiden chuckled. "Even when you don't spike it, your hair stands on end. What's worse is that it looks like you meant to do that."

"I didn't, but why fight nature?" He dropped the supplies onto the bed and ran his fingers through his tresses. "Now getting it to stand up all in the same direction is the hard part. If I didn't tame it, once my hair dried it'd look like I stuck my fingers in a light socket."

"It works for you." Aiden flopped onto the bed. "My hair just looks like a mess."

"I like your hair." He crawled on top of Aiden. His dick rested against Aiden's and heat rushed through his body again.

"I've always wanted a dark color like yours. Mine's a cross between boring and bland." Aiden shrugged. "Kind of like me."

"You've never been boring or bland and your hair is sexy." Why were they arguing about hair color? "Not everyone is meant to be…exciting. Me? I'm never going back to glitter and eyeliner."

"Why? I bet it works for you." Aiden grabbed Matt's ass. "I can see it, and I think it would be hot."

"Nah. I did my glam phase after high school and it's not happening again." He eased off Aiden, stood and rolled his shoulders. Putting his weight on his arm hadn't been smart. The pain wasn't bad, but he should've thought twice before he crawled onto Aiden.

"Are you okay?" Aiden sat up. "Tweaked something?"

"I pushed myself a little too far. I'll be okay." Matt grunted and stretched. *Damn.* "How about you make me forget I'm hurting and show me your ass?"

Aiden didn't move right away. Was he toying with Matt? Trying to gauge if Matt really had overdone it? Matt stroked himself.

"I'm fine," Matt said. "I told you I wasn't at one hundred percent. I'll rest while you flop over and show me your ass." He squeezed his own dick, then toyed with his balls. "Doc?"

"You're a harsh man." Aiden rolled onto his belly then rose up on his hands and knees. He wiggled his butt. "Better?" He spread his legs and his erection bobbed between his thighs. When he arched his back, his asshole flexed.

"Damn." Matt dropped to his knees at the foot of the bed. He loved giving oral sex and learning his partner. He opened Aiden's ass cheeks. "Such a pretty pink asshole." He dragged his tongue along the puckered skin, then dragged his nose over Aiden's rump. The scent of his soap and Aiden's cologne filled his senses. His heart hammered again. The excitement threatened to overwhelm him, but it relaxed him too. Pleasing Aiden was easy but scary-hard. He wanted this moment to be right. No pressure or anything. He wasn't just in lust with Aiden. Not horny as hell, either. He'd fallen for Aiden.

"Oh wow." Aiden arched his back and ground his ass into Matt's face.

"Like that?" Matt grasped Aiden's hips and flattened his tongue over Aiden's hole. All the pieces were falling into place. This was the right time, circumstances and a great guy... He could have everything he wanted if he just accepted his feelings for

Megan Slayer

Aiden. No more denying himself. Aiden was more than he'd thought he wanted and everything he needed. He curled his fingers around Aiden's dick while he speared his tongue into Aiden's asshole.

"Matt." Aiden shivered. "You're dangerous."

Matt patted the bed for the lube. He wanted to be sure he prepped Aiden right. If something went wrong, he'd hate himself forever. He squirted the clear fluid onto his fingers, then returned his attention to Aiden's dick. He alternated between strokes and taps on Aiden's asshole.

Aiden moaned. "Do it."

He would. In a moment. "Breathe. You're so tense."

"I want you in me." Aiden sighed and arched his back again. He relaxed a little, but not much. When he exhaled, he backed into Matt.

"Better." He eased his middle finger into Aiden's hole, one, then two knuckles deep. God, Aiden was so tight. Matt stroked him from within and snugged his grasp on Aiden's cock. He wanted Aiden to come apart.

"Matt." Aiden jerked. He backed onto Matt's digit. "Fucking hell."

Nice. He pressed his thumb on the head of Aiden's erection. When Aiden grunted, Matt added another finger to his ass. *Time to blow Aiden's mind.* He tilted his head and sucked on Aiden's balls while moving his fingers and stroking Aiden.

Aiden made a sound that could've been a grunt or actual words—but if he'd said something, Matt wasn't sure what it was. He tensed, then rode Matt's fingers. "Oh my fuck." Aiden curled forward and shuddered. "I'm…" Instead of finishing his sentence, he moaned. Cum spurted onto the bed and he shivered.

Matt hummed on Aiden's sac. He moved his digits in and out of Aiden's ass until the aftershocks wore off.

Aiden collapsed on the bed. "Wicked man. Whoa."

"You say that a lot." He eased his fingers free from Aiden's rump. "Flip over." He wasn't sure how much longer he could wait to be inside Aiden.

"I don't know if I can." Aiden managed to roll onto his back. Cum sparkled on his belly and side. The look worked for him — so natural and sexy.

"God. You're... I don't believe you." The words weren't right, but he couldn't manage to come up with anything better. He stroked his dick. Just looking at Aiden got him hard. He tore open the condom wrapper with his teeth.

Aiden folded his arms over his chest and drew his knees together. "What did I do? I made a stupid face, didn't I?"

"No." Yep, he'd stepped into it up to his eyeballs. He grabbed the lube. "Doc, don't be so self-conscious. I meant I can't believe you're here. You're mine." He lubed his dick and parted Aiden's thighs. "You make me want to be better."

"Me?" Aiden unclenched a little. "Matt."

Matt nudged Aiden back onto the bed. The move wasn't smart for his shoulder, but Aiden gave him an assist and didn't fight him.

"You'll hurt yourself." Aiden opened his legs. "Then I won't be a nice doctor when you need rehab."

"You can't be mean." He wouldn't allow Aiden to act that way. He preferred Aiden happy and sweet.

"I can, but you haven't seen that side," Aiden said.

Matt lined his dick up with Aiden's hole and pushed, slow and steady, until he filled his lover to the hilt. Aiden gasped. He relaxed beneath Matt. Matt groaned. Being there with Aiden was perfect. Aiden held him tight, but the snug feel reminded him of being protected. The love in his heart grew. More than love, he cherished Aiden. He couldn't see life without him. This man was made for him.

"Matt," Aiden said, drawing his name out. "You need to move. Feels good, but...damn." He groaned. "Please?"

Matt moved his hips. He hadn't given Aiden much time to recover after his orgasm and he hadn't even offered to clean him off. But seeing Aiden in cum was so hot and Aiden didn't seem to mind.

Aiden reached for him and wrapped his hands around Matt's wrists as Matt worked up a steady rhythm. The sound of skin slapping skin echoed in the room. Fever rushed through his veins.

"Oh, fucking balls," Matt bit out. He teetered on the edge of control. He pushed deeper into Aiden. They connected on a level he barely understood. He trembled and his thoughts blurred with each thrust.

"Yeah, come, Matty." Aiden squeezed Matt's wrists. "Do it."

He hated being called Matty, but when Aiden said it he didn't mind. He shook his head. He wasn't coming apart this fast. No way. He wanted to make this special for Aiden and show him just how much he cared. Climaxing now wouldn't help the matter. Still, his resistance shattered. No amount of holding back would keep the orgasm at bay. He grunted and his thrusts turned feral. *No going back now.* "Jesus."

"Yeah, Matty. Do it. Feels so good in me. Fuck me. Christ, I could come again." Aiden wriggled his hips. "Need you."

Between Aiden's encouragement and the heat swarming his body, he stopped fighting the orgasm. His knees buckled. "Fuck."

When Matt curled forward over him, Aiden embraced him. "Pretty boy."

He rested his forehead on Aiden's. He wanted to speak, but the words didn't come. The weight of the moment hit him hard, though. He hadn't just fallen for Aiden. He loved the man down to his soul. He could see forever in Aiden's eyes.

Aiden laced his hands together around Matt's neck. "You'll hurt yourself if you don't get up. Now, I'll take care of you, but as your physician, I encourage you to take the stress off your arm."

He laughed. *Of all the times for Aiden to be in the role of doctor but not...* "Of course, Doc Cedarwood." He kissed Aiden. He'd never get enough of his lover. Aiden owned his soul. He eased his dick from Aiden's ass and missed his warmth immediately. When he stood, he wobbled.

"Are you okay?" Aiden sat up. He'd been in the post-orgasm glow moments before, but now focus filled his eyes. "I was joking about being mean. If you need..."

Matt placed his un-lubed finger over Aiden's lips. "I'm fine."

"You're sure?"

"Don't tell me your knees aren't a little weak after sex." Matt removed the condom and headed into the bathroom to throw the rubber away. He retrieved a towel. "You do that to me." He strode back into the bedroom. "I'd like to think I do that to you too."

"Oh, well…when you're this awesome, those kinds of things happen." Aiden laughed. "I'm even trying to sound confident and it doesn't work."

"You sounded fine." He wiped the dried cum from Aiden's belly, then his ass. "I like your humble side."

"It's easier than trying to remember something cocky." Aiden stopped Matt's hands and pulled Matt onto his lap. "I'm not going to be the most perfect boyfriend. I don't know how, but I do know how to have a stable relationship. Dad and Keye were a great example for me. We can do this."

"I know." He tossed the towel onto the floor. "I don't want perfect. A little jealousy isn't bad — at least I know you care. As for arguments…they'll happen. We'll get through them and fuck like crazy afterward. Right?"

Aiden nodded.

It was time to pour out his heart. He drew in a long breath and exhaled. "I don't want you to be perfect. Just be my Doc Cedarwood. If you get a little too doctor preachy, I'll adjust. I like you — your weird edges, your lack of ink and all." He paused. "I could see putting your name on my body. I've never done that for anyone else."

"Matt." Aiden's eyes widened and his lips parted.

"Call it one final tat." He cupped Aiden's jaw. "I don't need to hide from the pain when I have someone to help me deal."

"I will, but you need to be sure." Aiden's voice came out low and fire lit in his eyes. "What if I let you down?"

Matt wasn't sure what else to say. He'd offered up his heart and Aiden held it in his hands, but Aiden wasn't acting as confident as he'd expected. "Stay. I want you beside me when I sleep." He left Aiden's lap and yanked the blankets free. "Please?"

"I can't go. I don't have wheels. Remember?" Aiden crawled between the sheets, and when Matt stretched out beside him, he snuggled up to him. "I'm assuming you forgetting to take me to the car is payback for me driving you around and being pushy."

"Nah." He turned off the light. "That was all overenthusiasm on my part. You can drive me around whenever you want, and in the morning, we'll get your car." He held Aiden against his chest and closed his eyes. Everything felt right—even the argument. Life was finally balanced and healthy. He wished he hadn't needed to look for so long to find Aiden, but his Doc was definitely worth the wait. Now he'd never let go.

Chapter Twelve

Aiden stared at himself in the mirror. In the last week, he and Matt had shared so many experiences. When they weren't at work, they spent time together. He cooked for Matt at his townhome and helped Matt pick out additional furniture. Despite their wacky schedules, he loved how they managed to make the relationship work. He finished shaving and rinsed the razor. Being with Matt made him happy, like they were meant to be together. Things could still go sideways, but he wasn't looking for every potential problem.

"Are you about ready?" Matt stood in the bathroom doorway. "I haven't been to Rods in forever."

"I've never been there." He toweled his face off and drained the sink. Part of him wanted to visit the club, but the rest of him wasn't sure. Loud noises and crowds weren't his idea of fun.

"You should like it." Matt snagged Aiden in his arms. "Besides, I'm sticking to you like glue. I'm not sharing."

"Really?" He appreciated Matt's possessive streak.

"Uh-huh." Matt patted Aiden's ass. "Let's go."

Aiden shrugged into the tight T-shirt, then followed Matt through the living room. "You're driving?"

"Thought I would since I can." Matt twirled his keys around his fingers. "You don't mind, right?"

"Nope." He stepped into his boots. "It's nice to let someone take control for a change."

"So that's why you love to bottom for me." Matt grinned. "Here I thought you were worried about my injury."

"That's the biggest reason." He went outside and locked up, then fell into step behind Matt as he walked over to the car. "I don't want you to get hurt just so we can have sex."

"You're a smart man." Matt held the door for Aiden and closed it once Aiden eased onto the passenger seat. He rounded the trunk and climbed behind the wheel. Matt said nothing as he drove across town to the club, but he did hold Aiden's hand.

Aiden closed his eyes and listened to the music on the radio. He couldn't remember the last time he'd gone out to a club. But he'd be with Matt, so he'd be fine.

The car stopped and Aiden opened his eyes. "We're here."

"Yeah. I thought you were sleeping." Matt parked. "I'm that boring, huh?"

"Nope. Just listening to the radio." He left the vehicle. Bright blue light shone down onto the parking lot from the neon RODS sign. "Are you sure about this?" He hated to admit having second thoughts, but the worries wouldn't go away.

"I'm positive. We need to go more public. I want everyone to know you're mine." Matt draped his arm around Aiden's shoulders. "It'll be cool." He pressed the fob on his keys and nudged Aiden forward. "You'll have fun."

"Sure." He ventured into the club with Matt and recoiled at the throbbing music. *Holy shit*, the bass thundered. He clung to Matt's side.

"I'm getting a water. You want anything?" Matt asked.

"Same." Aiden folded his arms and waited by one of the thick columns near the dance floor. He surveyed the crowd. *How many of these people have visited the emergency room? Did I work on any of them?*

Moments later, Matt returned with two bottles. "Here you go." He downed half of the water in one gulp. "I forgot how hot it gets in here."

"Yeah." He polished off some of the water. "It's nice to be out with someone who doesn't want to get drunk—or are you planning on doing that later?"

"I don't drink." Matt tucked his bottle in his front pocket. "Want to dance?"

"Sure." He finished the water and left the empty bottle on the closest tray. Although he wanted to hide in the shadows, Aiden allowed Matt to tug him into the throng of people. He didn't know the music and wasn't up on the current songs, but he did his best to not look silly as he danced. Once the tune switched to something slower, he curled his arms around Matt. He could move to this.

"Hot." Matt nipped Aiden's earlobe. "Sexy." He ground his crotch into Aiden's, making sure Aiden felt his erection straining against the denim.

Aiden groaned. He wanted to go—not because he hated the club but because he wanted to fuck.

"Shit." Matt held Aiden tight. "What the hell?"

"What? I'm horny. Can't you tell?"

"I can." Matt leaned back in Aiden's arms. "My ex is here."

"So?" Aiden shrugged. He trusted Matt. He continued to dance but realized Matt wasn't moving. "Ignore him."

"I'd love to, but he's coming over." Matt tensed. "Why now?"

"Don't know." Aiden noticed someone out of the corner of his eye. He looked in the direction of the person and bit back a groan. *Go figure. Lucky's here too. Jesus.* Should he introduce Matt and get it over with? He'd wanted to when they'd run into each other at the parking lot but had never gotten the chance. Was tonight the night? Or should he just keep his mouth shut? He sighed. Keeping his mouth shut sounded like the best option.

"Here he comes." Matt kept his arm around Aiden and squeezed Aiden's side. "Damn it."

"Why don't I go to the bathroom? I need to and you can talk to him in private?" Aiden wriggled free from Matt. "It'll be cool."

"You're taking it well." Matt narrowed his eyes. "I like it."

"Thought you might." He winked and wandered around the crowd to the red neon sign advertising the restrooms. He wandered into the room, then stepped up to the urinals. Another man joined him, but he finished before he could get a good look at the guy.

Aiden left the bathroom but ran into a solid wall of muscle. "Ooof!" He pushed away from the person he'd collided with and his eyes widened. "Sorry."

"No need." The man gave him a wolfish grin. "You must be Aiden."

"I am. You are?" He knew but wanted the man to introduce himself.

"Theo. I was with Matt before you." Theo nudged Aiden into a corner near the bathroom. "Did he tell you?"

"About the two of you? He mentioned you." Aiden held his ground. He wasn't about to argue with Theo.

"Right. Then he didn't." He nudged Aiden out of one of the doors to the smokers' lounge outside.

The chill wrapped around Aiden and the scent of the cigarettes choked him. He wasn't used to the scent and had never picked up the habit. Being in the clouds of smoke churned his stomach. He coughed and turned away.

"You're taking it well," Theo said. He folded his arms and cocked his hip. "Better than I would've thought."

"Him having an ex? Sure. We all have those, so there's nothing to take wrong." He wasn't about to back down. People had pasts and Matt wasn't any different.

"Right. Then he didn't tell you."

Good God. "Tell me what? Your half sentences and riddles make no sense." Aiden sighed. "Just spit it out."

"About his past," Theo said. "He hasn't talked about it. If he had, then you probably wouldn't be here."

"I know about the tattoos and piercings. They're not an issue." Aiden shifted his weight from his left foot to his right.

"You're a doctor, right? Did he mention his pain fetish?" Theo asked.

"Yes. It's been discussed and, again, not an issue."

"Uh-huh. He also used something else to deal with his pain. Did he tell you he had an addiction to pain pills? Has he asked you for some since the shooting?

You do know he dated a doctor in order to get pills from him too? The relationship lasted a week, but he found another source." Theo notched his chin in the air. "Yeah, bet you knew none of that."

He didn't, but didn't think Theo had the right to talk about any of it. Part of him was angry he'd been kept in the dark. The rest of him was let down. Why would he keep that a secret? Shame? Did he think Aiden would leave him?

"He'll probably demand you become his new supplier. He's very persuasive. Don't say you didn't know. Everyone does." Theo's grin widened.

Supplier? Good Lord. Matt wasn't that way. Matt wasn't a user. "Sure, I did. So?" He'd lied through his teeth. He wanted the facts from Matt before he rushed to judgment.

"Then are you okay with being with a guy who fakes injuries to get pills?" Theo asked. "Please. No one is that gullible."

Aiden bit his tongue to keep from snapping at Theo. He didn't know what to do or say. Theo had to be lying. Had to be.

"He'll use you like he's used everyone else." Theo rested his hand on Aiden's shoulder. "Don't believe me? Ask him. I need to go. My date looks lonely and my cousin looks just as sad." He darted away from Aiden, leaving him alone by the bathroom.

Aiden leaned against the wall. His brain buzzed with the new information. Shocked and stunned were the tip of the iceberg. *What the hell?* Matt seemed rough around the edges, but he was also almost too good to be true. *He can't be an addict or former addict, right?* But could Aiden honestly trust Theo? After all, Theo could be making the whole thing up. Matt hadn't begged him for pills. No, he'd refused them. That didn't mean he wasn't taking anything, but still.

"There you are." Matt laughed. "Damn, it's thick out here. I haven't had a cigarette in years. I remember now why I quit, though. The smoke stinks." He swept his gaze over Aiden. "What's wrong? Do you want to go?"

"I do." He couldn't quite meet Matt's gaze.

"Are you okay?"

"Fine."

Matt paused. "No, you're not. Fine is an avoidance answer." He curled his fingers under Aiden's chin. "Talk to me."

"Are you using me?" he blurted.

"What? Where'd that come from?" Matt's eyes widened. "Aiden?"

"Tell me." Aiden stood tall. "Please? Are you?"

"No."

"Not for drugs? Pain pills, maybe?"

"What makes you think that?" Matt shook his head. "I've never done anything to you to make you believe any of that."

Matt had a point. He hadn't stolen the script pads — not that he had any of them lying around — and he had no real proof, but still. He felt like he'd missed something.

"I'm serious, Aiden. What has gotten into you? Why did you bring up the pills thing?" Matt asked.

Aiden shook his head. "I want out. I've been used enough." He darted into the club and through the people to the main doors. *Time to go.* He strode out to the parking lot. Embarrassment washed over him. He should've known something like this would happen. Things were going too well.

"Aiden." Matt caught up to him by his car. "Hey. You can't go. I drove. Let me take you home."

"I'll call a taxi or that ride service. I don't care." He pulled his phone from his pocket and inputted the info on the app. "The driver will be here in five minutes."

"Enough," Matt thundered. "What is the matter with you?"

"I was told about your addiction," he snapped. "Now lower your voice."

"Theo." Matt glared at Aiden. "Of course. That asshole couldn't keep a secret if I paid him."

"So it needed to stay a secret?" Aiden waved his hands. "Whatever. Yeah, he told me. The question is, why didn't you?"

"I needed the right time."

"When was that?"

"I don't know." Matt paused. "You don't understand."

"Then help me to."

Matt's shoulders sagged. He lowered his voice. "I was addicted to pain pills. I did stuff I'm not proud of, but I beat it. I did the rehab and got my life in order. I did my time. Whatever Theo said…he probably made it all up."

"Right. I'm a doctor. I deserve to know if the guy I'm involved with is going to steal my scripts to get drugs." He'd been too harsh. He had no proof and he'd gone off, but still.

"Have I?"

"Not that I know of."

"You don't trust me."

"It's kind of hard. I've told you everything — Lucky, my reluctance with guys, my being used and broke.

228

Nothing held back. But you? That's pretty big. I'm not sure what to believe." Aiden's heart sank. "I'm lost."

"How about you believe me? Yes, the temptation is there. It's always there, but my being clean and sober is more important. You are more important." Matt reached for him. "That's the honest-iest honest I've got."

"I don't know what to think." Aiden's skin itched and his stomach churned. He needed space. He hadn't anticipated this problem. Matt was pretty darn great, but he wasn't perfect.

"Aiden."

"I need a lot of trust. Okay? You didn't think enough of me to be honest to begin with." He paced beside Matt's car. "I would've understood. I'd have been more cautious, sure, but I know people overcome addiction. They do it all the time. Keye kicked meth. It's possible." He bowed his head. "But I need time." *I need to know I can handle this.*

"You do? My fucking ex spilled my secret," Matt snapped. "Good God."

"Then we both do. Look, there's my ride. I'm leaving. I'll get my car later." He wandered away. He shouldn't go but couldn't stay. His heart ached. What Matt had held back wasn't a horrible secret — especially if he'd overcome it — but he still felt betrayed. It was like he'd been told once more that he wasn't good enough. He settled in the back seat of the car and spoke to the driver. "I need to go to the Briar Estates."

"You got it," the driver replied.

Aiden hated retreating, but he couldn't be around Matt right now. He couldn't be rejected again. He hadn't seen the weaknesses or found all the faults — except in himself. He'd fallen hard for the wrong man.

Matt watched Aiden leave. He should've argued and begged. But why? Aiden was gone. He'd made up his mind.

He didn't blame Aiden. Not really. If Matt had relapsed and lost his mind then he'd have put Aiden at risk. He refused to jeopardize Aiden's career.

But that was just it — he didn't want to relapse. He liked his life and being clean and sober. He had his own business, steady-ish work and a great man. Okay, he wasn't sure Aiden was still his, but that didn't make him anything less than a good man.

He tensed when he heard footsteps crunching on the gravel. *Fuck.* He didn't feel like talking to anyone right then.

"Hey, you," Theo said.

Matt didn't turn around. 'Disgusted' was putting his emotions mildly.

"Where'd the new guy go?" Theo asked. "Aiden, right?"

"You mean Dr. Connor." Matt kept his back to Theo. He preferred to call Aiden by his name or Doc Cedarwood, but still. He wouldn't reveal that tidbit to Theo.

"So? Where'd he go?"

"Home," Matt growled.

"Home? Without you? Or is he getting things ready?" Theo stood right beside Matt. "I know how you like men who prep."

Theo's cologne made Matt gag. "What do you care?" *And why do you need to know?*

"I care lots. If you're attached, then I'm out of luck. If you're not, then I'm making a play." Theo bumped shoulders with Matt. "So?"

"I'm not interested." He hadn't fully lost Aiden — not yet, anyway.

"Come on. We had fun." Theo stood in front of him. "Has he seen your back tat? The one inspired by me?"

"You suggested the design, not inspired." He'd been smart enough not to do the exact design Theo had wanted. He refused to put Theo's name anywhere on his body. Theo might have been his longest relationship, but certainly not the healthiest.

"Whatever. If he can't handle your ink, then he's not a good match."

"Who said he couldn't?"

"I assumed Mr. Uptight Doctor wouldn't lower himself to being with an inked man."

His disgust morphed into rage. "What he couldn't handle was you telling him about my past. That wasn't your business to discuss."

Theo rolled his eyes. "He had to know, and based on him not being here, he must not have been able to handle your truth."

"You blurted it all out."

"Because you couldn't tell him." Theo rested his hands on his hips and shrugged. "Someone had to. You didn't care about him that much. If you had, then you would've opened your damn mouth."

"Oh my God. You live to fucking ruin my life." He wanted to go. They shouldn't be having the conversation in the parking lot. He should be begging Aiden for another try.

Theo groaned. "You're always blaming me. I didn't love you the way you wanted and I wasn't willing to give you more pills."

"Christ, you were the reason I drank," Matt thundered. "You drove me crazy."

"I was good to you," Theo challenged.

"You cheated on me, plied me with booze and told me over and over how you liked me best when I was out of it." Looking back, he knew he'd fucked up. He'd allowed the wrong person to have too much power and the right one to get too far away.

"You were nicer."

"I was high and drunk." *How in the hell did I know what I was doing?*

"Still, you were nicer."

"I'm done. Don't call, text, talk to me or remember my name. I'm dead to you." He needed to go. *Fuck it.* He moved Theo out of the way and opened his car door. "Go."

"And here I needed my car fixed," Theo said. He grabbed the doorframe. "Only you can work on it."

"Liar." He'd wasted enough time. *Screw space.* He needed Aiden.

"Uh-huh. I saw your boy here in the club talking to someone else. Lucky's pushy, but I'd fuck him — well, I would if I wasn't related to him." Theo shrugged. "I do have standards."

"Aiden isn't like that." As much as Aiden might not believe him, Matt did trust him.

"Talk to Lucky yourself. He'll tell you." Theo cocked his hip. "My cousin wouldn't lie."

"Your cousin?" He had to be joking.

"Lucky is my first cousin. That's the main reason I can't get with him. That, and he's still with Aiden."

"Whatever. We're done." He hit the button to lock the car other than the open door and groaned. "I'm out."

"Nice. Then take me with you." Theo rounded the car and yanked on the passenger door. "Open up."

"I didn't invite you," Matt pressed the button to lock the doors, despite them already being secured.

"Why not?"

A shiver ran the length of Matt's spine. He knew that voice and it wasn't Theo. The robber-slash-shooter spoke just like that. He forced himself to look the speaker in the eye. The moment he saw the man's steely blue-eyed gaze and lack of warmth in his smile, Matt knew. *Oh fuck.*

"Well?" Theo snapped. He yanked on the locked handle. "Why not? We're good together."

"You," Matt growled. "You robbed my shop." The longer he looked at the man beside the driver's side of his car, the more Matt knew. "You shot me."

"Lucky? Are you kidding?" Theo laughed. "Oh my God. That's a riot."

Lucky's smile widened but was still ice cold. "Right, because I go around robbing auto garages and shooting the owners."

Matt pressed his lips together. What Lucky had said were details he could've seen in the paper.

"Next, you'll say I stole the cars too." Lucky shook his head. "Christ."

Was Lucky that stupid? The news station hadn't mentioned anything about stolen cars. They'd focused on the shooting and monetary theft. "I remember your voice," Matt managed. "I can't forget it."

"You didn't seem to know me when I visited Aiden." Lucky snorted. "So it sounds like your memory is faulty."

"Things change." His confidence grew. He might not have been sure when he'd seen Lucky with Aiden, but he knew now. No questions.

"Maybe you should step out of that car." Lucky inched toward Matt's car. "I'd hate for you to have another accident."

"Yeah, and I'd hate for your precious doctor to see the asshole side of you," Theo added.

Fuckety fuck. Matt noticed the guard in the lot. He'd have a witness if they decided to do something stupid. "Better not threaten me. The rent-a-cop will see you and I'm not above turning your ass in right now." He'd do that once he talked to Aiden. The name Lucky, a description and his suspicions probably weren't enough.

"He won't... Shit." Lucky nodded to Theo. "Scatter."

When the pair started away, Matt yanked the door shut. He locked the driver's-side door and gunned the engine. *Fucking hell.* He needed to get out of the locked vehicle. His mind spun more than his tires as he left the club. The more distance he put between himself and Lucky, the better.

Matt drove straight across town to Aiden's townhouse. He might not be on the best of terms with Aiden, but Aiden would understand. He should call Jordan too. He nodded. Calling the police would have to wait until he wasn't driving. His heart hammered and he drummed his hands on the steering wheel. Nervous energy zinged through his veins. *Dear God.* He couldn't contain the worry or fear—worry Lucky would try to hurt him again and fear Aiden would push him away for good.

Despite his hesitation, Matt parked outside Aiden's townhome and rushed to the front door. He pressed the bell and tapped his foot while he waited. *Shit.* He couldn't hold still. "Come on, Aiden," he growled. Damn. He sounded angrier than he'd meant to.

The door opened, and Aiden stared, wide-eyed, at him. He parted his lips but didn't speak.

"I need to talk to you. No fighting. Please?" Matt barged into Aiden's place. "I'm serious."

"Matt." Aiden stumbled against the door. "What's going on?"

"I know who robbed me." His chest heaved and ached. "I remembered the voice." Matt grabbed his phone. "Holy fuck."

"You… Who? I don't understand." Aiden closed the door and clicked the lock. "Explain."

"I need to call Jordan, but I needed to be safe first." Matt tucked the phone to his ear. He could do this. He could talk to the cops and turn in the man who'd shot him.

Aiden sank onto the arm of the couch and reeled from Matt's declaration. He didn't want to listen to Matt's end of the telephone call, but he had little choice. Matt spoke so loud Aiden heard everything Matt said as he gave a statement. Aiden caught bits and pieces, despite Matt speaking so fast. Lucky and Theo had been in the parking lot, Lucky said something to cause trouble and Theo tried to barge into the car. He shook his head. *Lucky?* Sure, the guy was pushy and could talk a lot, but Aiden didn't understand the connection. Did they know something about the robbery? Aiden hadn't gone back to the police department since giving his initial statement. Maybe he should've inquired about the case.

Once he finished, Matt stopped pacing the length of Aiden's living room and stared at Aiden. "Sorry," Matt said. "Thanks."

"About what?" Aiden rested his hands on his lap. "What happened? I'm confused."

Matt recounted the incident with Theo and Lucky. The lines around his eyes deepened. He seemed defeated. "I'm sorry."

"You've said that. I still don't understand why Lucky would do that, but you don't have to apologize for it." Aiden tipped his head to meet Matt's gaze. "Sit and take a break. You're wound tight."

Matt sank onto the cushion beside Aiden. "I'm sorry I ever lied to you. Even if it was by omission, it was bad."

Oh, so Matt wanted to deal with their relationship issues. *Okay…* "Matt."

"No, I need to say this." Matt shifted in his seat and faced Aiden. "I'm not proud of everything in my life. Trust me. I don't think I'd like to go back to being a kid whose father hated me for being gay, but I learned from it. I don't want to go back to cruising bars for guys because I don't think I'm good enough for anyone to love me. But I figured out I'm worth more than I ever thought. Would I relapse and become an addict again? Not a chance. I hated myself back then. When I think about who I was, I wonder how I'm still alive. I loathed myself, but I learned from that too. I know bottom and I'm never going back. I will never drop that low again."

Aiden didn't say anything. He wasn't sure what to say and hadn't gotten over his shock. He'd heard the words and understood, but the gravity of Matt's past hadn't really hit until now. He might have been damaged, but Matt had been in spades. He understood why Matt wouldn't come out and boast about pulling himself up by his bootstraps. If he could get beyond the shortcomings of his past, then Aiden could do the same. Matt was pretty darn important to him.

"I'm sorry. I should've been honest, but I thought if I ignored what I needed to say that we'd never have to deal with it." Matt rested his head in his hands. "Just…shit. Everything is out of control."

Aiden rubbed Matt's back. No matter what Matt had held back, he'd come clean now. Besides, he had bigger problems. "We'll get through it."

"I don't know."

"I do." He had confidence.

"I feel so helpless."

"But where did you turn when you thought you had nowhere else to go? You came to me. Did I tell you to go? No. When it's all said and done, I'm still here and I didn't balk when you barged past me. You're still here too. I thought I'd look for the flaws—and I did—but I also looked for the bright spots. If you hadn't come to me, I was on my way to you—eventually." Aiden petted the back of Matt's head. "We'll get through this."

"Aiden."

"Right here." He scooted onto the couch and sat next to Matt. He rested his arm around Matt. "I'm not going anywhere."

"It helps that it's your place." Matt sighed and met Aiden's gaze. "You don't have anywhere to go."

"I could retreat to the hospital, but I don't want to." Aiden shrugged. "Call me living here convenient." He embraced Matt and kissed Matt's temple. "So, Lucky admitted…he shot you?"

"He basically said I'd made it up when I said he'd shot me. I knew his voice. When he said things about the incident, like the stolen cars, I knew." Matt's voice caught. "No doubts."

"What'd Jordan say?" Aiden asked.

"He'd handle it. He called my information a tip, which is probably police speak for he'll bring Lucky in or something. I don't know how he'd know exactly. I don't even know Lucky's last name."

"Emmett Luck, aka Lucky," Aiden said. "Trust Jordan. He and the other cops are smart. They'll get to the bottom of this." Meanwhile, he wished he hadn't gotten involved with Lucky ever.

"Aiden."

"What about us?" Aiden asked. Time to redirect the conversation to keep Matt from losing his cool again. "We're going to get through this. I've got to work in the morning, but until then I'm yours. If you'll take me to the hospital before my shift starts, we'll sort out the car situation later. I'd rather you be here than alone. Besides, I love having you next to me when I sleep. I'm rather fond of you."

"Just fond?" Tears slipped down Matt's cheeks.

"Maybe a little more." Aiden rested his forehead against Matt's. "I'm in love with you, Matt Phillips."

"You are?"

"Uh-huh." He brushed his nose on Matt's and smoothed his palm around the back of Matt's neck. "I'm irritated that you didn't tell me about your full past, but I'm not quitting. The shock's still there, and it'll take time to get over it, but not forever. Part of me doesn't want to believe addiction was part of your past, but the rest of me understands and it's not that earth-shattering. It doesn't make me love you any less. I'm proud you overcame it."

"Aiden." Another tear slipped down Matt's cheek. He wiped the wetness away and averted his gaze. "I don't deserve you."

"I disagree." Aiden toyed with the tiny hairs at the base of Matt's skull. "I hate secrets. Christmas is a bitch because I want to tell everyone what I got them and know what I'm getting in return. Drives my father crazy. But I understand. You did what you had to do. That doesn't mean I'm not a little irritated, but I'll get over it. I've got you and that's more important." How else could he make Matt see his truth?

"Are you sure?"

"I've got a good man in my life and I love him. I never thought I'd fall for anyone after the way Lucky trashed my pride. Yeah, I'm a hopeless romantic and I've got lots of faith—in the right people. I'm positive I love you."

"I love you too." Matt finally looked him in the eye. "I never thought I'd say that, either. I didn't think I was allowed to love anyone."

"See? We'll get through this because we've got each other. Fuck Theo and Lucky." If he never heard their names again, he'd be happy.

Matt managed to smile. "You see so much more in me than I ever did. Thank you."

"You're welcome." Although being thanked wasn't his goal. Matt was hard not to love. He held Matt tight and breathed in his scent. Being so close comforted him. Blood rushed through his body and heat settled low in his belly. He shifted his hips as his cock pressed against the zipper of his jeans.

"I want to go to your room and fuck, but I want the thing with our exes done. Let's go to the police department. Maybe Jordan needs an in-person statement from me." Matt started to get up, but Aiden stopped him. "Doc, I feel so helpless."

"I understand that too." He sighed. "Jordan said to sit tight. He'd call if there was anything to do, right?"

Matt stood and hauled Aide to his feet. "Then fuck it is."

Aiden tipped his head back and laughed. "Last one to the bedroom gets fucked." He loved how he could be himself and free with Matt.

"What if I want you to?" Matt asked. He stayed behind Aiden as they raced to the bedroom.

"Be last? Sure." He didn't care as long as they both came.

"No." Matt turned Aiden around in the hallway. "Fuck me."

Aiden paused. Every instinct hit him to barrel onto the bed with Matt in his arms, but he stayed still. He couldn't have heard Matt right. "Are you sure?"

"Positive," Matt said. "I haven't bottomed in a long time, but I want to with you. I trust you... Just be gentle."

Aiden nodded. "I'll do whatever you want."

Chapter Thirteen

Aiden nodded. "Then let's go to bed." He led Matt into the bedroom. The gravity of the moment wasn't lost on him. Matt wasn't one to give over power and he certainly wasn't the type to bottom. If he was giving himself up to Aiden, then he wanted to make this moment perfect for Matt.

Matt removed his shirt and shucked his pants. He left the clothing in a wad on the floor. "What do you want me to do?"

"Stretch out on the bed." Aiden yanked his shirt over his head and tossed the garment onto the pile of clothes. He noticed Matt on the bed and gasped. *Damn.* Matt lay on the mattress with his legs dangling over the edge. The pull of muscle on Matt's body, along with the tattoos, made him look strong and tough, but sexy as hell. He leaned over Matt and kissed his way down Matt's chest to his abs and lower belly. He'd never get enough of tasting Matt.

"Nice." Matt threaded his fingers into Aiden's hair. "You're making my skin tingle."

"Good," he said against Matt's lower abs. He slid his hand between Matt's legs and curled his fingers around his lover's dick.

"Oh shit." Matt blew out a whistle. "I didn't realize I was on this much of a hair-trigger." He let go of Aiden's hair. "You're dangerous."

He chuckled, then knelt between Matt's knees. If he wanted to please Matt, he had to move with caution. He nuzzled Matt's inner thigh and continued to stroke Matt's erection. With his free hand, he pinched Matt's nipple.

"Aiden." Matt curled forward and tucked the pillow behind his head. "I want to watch you." He slipped his right hand behind his head. "I'm enjoying the view."

Aiden looked into Matt's eyes. Now that they'd said they loved each other, he saw that passion and a new fire in his lover. He knew how special this moment was and wanted to make it even more perfect.

Matt groaned and spread his legs. He reached for Aiden again. "Please?"

Aiden smiled then palmed Matt's thighs. He licked his way up and down Matt's erection, memorizing every nuance of him. Pride swelled within him and his own cock throbbed. He couldn't wait to be inside Matt. He breathed in the scent of Matt's cologne. He needed lube.

A moan rumbled in Aiden's throat. He couldn't hold back his craving for Matt. He plunged his mouth down on his lover's cock. He bobbed his head, licking and sucking all along Matt's shaft. He embraced his passion for Matt. No matter what, he wanted to make him happy. He toyed with Matt's asshole.

Matt tensed, then relaxed. "God, yeah."

Aiden released his hold on Matt. "Like that?" He grinned. "Give me a moment." He left Matt long enough to retrieve the bottle of lube. When he searched through the nightstand, he couldn't find any condoms.

"What?" Matt rolled onto his side and propped himself up on his elbow. "What're you looking for?"

"I'm out of rubbers."

Matt shrugged. "You're clean. I'm clean. We're not planning on splitting up. I don't see why we can't go bare. I want you to."

Aiden stared at Matt. He knew what he'd heard, but he didn't believe it.

"I mean it." Matt shut the drawer. "I've never gone bare with anyone—no one else. Just you."

"I love you." Aiden didn't think twice. He grabbed the bottle and returned to his place between Matt's legs. He sat on his heels and left the lube on his lap. Power resonated within him. He parted Matt's ass cheeks and nuzzled his asshole.

"Wow." Matt's sharp intake of breath echoed in the room. He planted his feet on the edge of the bed and parted his legs more. He stroked his dick. "I like it."

Aiden hoped so. He liked having Matt so turned on. He licked along the seam of Matt's ass. Each moan and whimper from Matt encouraged him. He hadn't forgotten how special this moment was. He flicked his tongue over the wrinkled skin, then traced his fingertip down Matt's rump.

"Aiden." Matt tensed again. "Don't make me wait."

"I can't rush." He dumped lube onto his fingers, then resumed playing with Matt's asshole.

"Don't care." Matt rocked his hips. "Please?"

Aiden tapped the tight ring of Matt's ass. He eased his middle finger into his lover and twisted. Matt whimpered again and bore down on him. The sound of the bed creaking resonated in Aiden's head. He focused on his lover and the rhythm of his finger in and out of Matt's hole. After a few strokes, he added his index finger. He needed to stretch and prep Matt. God, the man was tight. He wasn't sure this would work, no matter what he did to get Matt ready.

"Fucking hell." Matt grinned. He curled his fingers around his shaft. "So good."

He'd make it better. Aiden flicked his tongue over the blunt head of Matt's erection while he pumped his digits in Matt's ass. The combination of his tongue and his fingers must've pushed Matt to the edge.

Matt jerked and pre-cum shimmered on the head of his dick. He rolled his torso and grunted. "Damn."

He loved having Matt reduced to one-word sentences. He moved his fingers in and out faster, pushing Matt closer to coming. Matt moaned. Aiden slowed down again and eased his digits from Matt's body.

"Yes." Matt nodded. He stretched back on the bed and stared at Aiden. "I want this. Want you."

"I'm right here." He picked up the bottle and stood. Aiden dumped more lube onto his hand, then stroked his dick. Just the few touches on his body had him as horny as Matt. The groan erupted from deep in his chest. He lined his cock up with Matt's hole and pushed. He kept his gaze fixed on Matt's as he sank into his lover's ass.

Matt tipped his head back and his lips parted. He whimpered again.

"You're doing well. So pretty and tight. I'm protected when I'm in you." He grasped Matt's hips. "Breathe and focus on me. You're doing great."

"I'm trying to..." Matt grabbed two handfuls of the sheets. "I'm too full."

Aiden shifted his hips, moving in a slow rhythm at first. He added extra lube between thrusts. "You're so beautiful. I love this. Love you." He continued to push into Matt until he sank balls-deep into him. He eased all the way to the hilt, then pulled most of the way out before going in again. "How do you feel?"

"Nervous, but damn." A lazy smile curled on Matt's lips. "I forgot how good this can be."

"Better than good." Aiden rolled his hips and increased his pace. His heart overflowed with love for Matt. The tightness of Matt made the action of lovemaking a tad harder but worth it. The power overwhelmed him, but he embraced the tenderness of being together with Matt.

He hooked his elbows under Matt's knees and worked himself into a frenzy. No matter how much he wanted to go slow to protect Matt, the need and desire won out. He held tight to Matt's legs. The sound of skin slapping skin thundered through the room. His growls echoed in his mind. He met Matt's gaze again.

Matt stared up at him. "Damn," he murmured. His brows crinkled and he flexed his asshole. "Do it. I need you. Fuck." He drew out the last word, and his eyes rolled back.

Withholding wasn't an option. Aiden's restraint clung by a thread.

"Please?" Matt's eyes widened. "I need to come." He let go of the bedding and stroked his dick. His movements turned frantic. He grunted. "Need. To. Come."

The headboard clunked against the wall and Aiden knocked his knees on the edge of the mattress, but he didn't care. Any sense of delicacy was gone. Aiden pushed into Matt's body at a frantic pace. A moan escaped his lips.

"Matt," Aiden bit out. "Oh my God." He trembled as the orgasm hit. Everything around him blurred. Only Matt and the moment existed. He pistoned into Matt until his resistance shattered. The climax washed over him and weakened his knees. He slumped forward over Matt and braced himself on his hands to keep from putting too much weight on his lover. Aiden kissed him.

"Fucking hell, yeah." Matt grunted and kept stroking his cock. He squeezed his eyes shut and tensed beneath Aiden. His breath warmed Aiden's face.

Aiden leaned back enough for Matt to finish jerking himself off. "Yeah, babe. Let go. Christ, you're beautiful. Come for me. Do it."

Matt dug his feet into the mattress and bucked against Aiden. His mouth formed an O and his brows knotted again. He jerked forward and sticky cum shot across his chest. Another ribbon landed on Aiden's lower belly. He didn't open his eyes right away but instead panted and slumped on the bed. He whistled and the smile returned.

"Good?" Aiden kissed him and smeared the cum between them. "It was for me. I love your O face. So sexy."

Matt chuckled. "I probably looked dorky."

"You? Never." He kissed Matt again, then backed up enough to pull out of him. Aiden stood and the energy drained from him. "You blew my mind."

"You're pretty special too." Matt patted the bed. "Come here."

"I need to get a towel." Aiden retreated long enough to grab something to wipe the jizz from his chest, then Matt's. Once dry, he stretched out on the bed and snuggled up to Matt. "I love you."

"Love you too." Matt sighed and closed his eyes. "You wore this old man out."

"You wouldn't have it any other way." Aiden draped his arm across Matt's belly and nuzzled his neck. He couldn't imagine being anywhere else and thanked God they'd found their way back to each other. Matt was the only man for him and he wasn't about to let go.

* * * *

Aiden surfaced from sleep and blinked as the room came into focus. He heard the thumping on the front door. *What the hell? Where's the noise coming from?* His front door? He patted Matt's ass. "Do you hear that?"

Matt grunted, then rolled over. "Hear what?"

"Thumping." He crawled out of bed and snatched a pair of sleep pants from the floor. When he stopped moving, he listened for the noise. Voices filtered through to him. *Voices? Who in the name of God is outside?*

Aiden grabbed a shirt from the dresser, then poked his head out into the hallway. Shadows darkened the front windows of his townhome.

"I hear you fucking in there," someone screamed.

Aiden froze. He knew that voice. Lucky. He waved at Matt. "Stay in the bedroom," he whispered. "Don't turn the lights on, but call nine-one-one."

"Don't go out there." Matt grabbed Aiden's arm. "Please?"

"I'll be fine." He wasn't sure what in the hell to do, but *Jesus*. He eased out into the living room and ducked behind the sofa. The hulking piece of furniture wasn't the best hiding spot, but it worked for the time being. "Don't do this," he said. Maybe he'd be able to defuse the situation.

"Why?" Theo pressed against the window. He tapped something on the glass. *A gun?* His eyes widened and his lips curled in a sneer. "Where are you, pissant?"

"This isn't you." Aiden curled up tight. Keep them talking. He blew out a long breath and tried to keep calm. "You're smart. Both of you are." He hoped Matt had gotten through to the cops.

"I know he's in there," Lucky snarled. "You can't miss his car."

His must mean Matt's. Shit. "So?" Aiden asked.

"You're my boyfriend. I told you I have money," Lucky said. "You won't give me another chance. I can handle myself."

"You stole that money from the auto body shop. Lucky, you aren't that kind of guy. Tell me it wasn't you. Please?" Aiden knew the truth but wished Lucky hadn't been that underhanded. *Strike one.*

"You can't prove anything," Theo said. "Can't."

"Jesus. Let me shoot them. He's fucking my boyfriend." Lucky clunked another gun on the window. "Turn a light on so we can see you. I want to shoot the fucker who's with my boyfriend."

"And Theo will shoot me? No." Aiden balled his hands.

"I'm going to break down the goddamn door." Lucky thumped against the security door. "I'll shoot the both of you. I don't care."

The deadbolt and chain mechanism held, but damn… Lucky was stronger than Aiden remembered. "Don't do this. You're a good man. You're smart and funny. Don't screw it up," Aiden pleaded. With Theo and Lucky both having guns, the glass wouldn't be a match. He and Matt were so screwed.

"You didn't give me another chance," Lucky shouted. "I hurt myself for you."

"The dangerous ex wasn't real?" Aiden pounded his fist into the carpet. He knew the truth but kept hoping Lucky would prove him wrong. *Strike two.*

"No. Jesus. I refuse to let anyone do that to me." Lucky laughed, and the evil sound echoed in Aiden's brain.

"Lucky," Aiden said.

"Let me in." This time, Lucky's voice turned sweet and soft. "We can work this out. You love me."

Dear God, where are the police? "Lucky, Theo…put the guns down. You don't want to do this."

"I want you back," Lucky pleaded.

The blood thumped in Aiden's ears and his fingers ached from keeping his fists clenched. He swallowed against the dryness in his throat. He almost answered *oh hell no* but thought better of the idea. "Okay."

"Okay…what?" Lucky asked.

"I made a mistake." Aiden stayed behind the couch. No way he was leaving his hiding spot—except if the cops ordered him to. Lucky didn't need to know that truth. "I'll go with you if you put the gun down."

"Not until you're outside," Lucky answered. "I want proof."

"We don't want to kill you," Theo said. "But…" He didn't speak, and neither did Lucky. Blue lights flooded the townhome. "Motherfucker," Theo screamed. "You called the damn cops."

The loudest noise Aiden had ever heard filled the room. Glass shattered and the mirror on the far wall splintered into a thousand pieces. Debris rained down on Aiden. He bit his arm to muffle the sound of his screaming. Something boomed and more glass broke. He cowered behind the sofa. No matter how hard he tried, he couldn't curl up tight enough. *Jesus.* The fear overwhelmed him, and he covered his ears. He didn't want to die behind his couch, but what in the hell was he going to do?

Although he was scared to move, he inched forward enough to peek around the edge of the sofa and listened for Theo or Lucky. The silence paralyzed him. Something beside him crackled and he pressed himself back into his hiding spot.

"Aiden." Matt touched Aiden's arm. "Hey."

Aiden managed to glance up, but he couldn't speak. The words weren't there. Tears burned in his eyes. *Why is Matt with me behind the couch? It isn't safe. They could shoot him. Where's the noise? What's going on?* He wanted answers, but he also wanted everything to stop — the nightmare needed to go away so he could have his life back.

Matt gathered Aiden in his arms and petted his hair. There wasn't much he could do until Lucky and Theo stopped shooting up the townhouse. He and Aiden were stuck, but he'd shelter Aiden. If they were going down, at least they were together. He noticed a bright light and footsteps. Shadows moved just beyond the couch. Matt tipped his head. He'd thought he heard Jordan's voice and another one that didn't sound like

Theo or Lucky. The longer he listened, the better he could tell who was with Jordan. Detective Lutz. He'd talked to the older man during the robbery investigation.

"I found them." Jordan knelt next to Matt. "Bring the EMTs in. I can't tell if anyone else is hurt."

"I'm fine." Matt eased away from Aiden. "Babe."

"I'm…" Aiden wouldn't uncurl. "I'm fine. Are we safe?"

"Yes," Lutz said. "Both individuals have been apprehended."

Matt moved out of the way as the EMTs took charge. He heard them talking to Aiden, but he paid them little attention. He followed Jordan out of the townhouse. A sheet had been spread out on the lawn.

"I'd like to get a statement," Lutz said. He pointed toward the closest squad car. "We'll get you something to put on your feet."

Jordan appeared with a pair of shoes. "These might not fit. They're my spares in case…just in case." He draped a blanket around Matt's shoulders. "Once Aiden's free, I'll bring him over."

"Thanks." Matt sat on the bumper of the patrol car. "You wanted my statement. We were sleeping then someone pounded on the door. Aiden tried to de-escalate the situation, and I called the cops. I heard shooting and kept my phone with me when I went to be with him. I don't know who fired, but both said they had guns."

"Who said it?" Lutz asked.

He groaned. Just talking about the situation sucked. "Theo Bartelone and Lucky… I don't know his last name, or his real first one for that matter." He'd been told, but he couldn't remember. "Theo was my ex-boyfriend and Lucky was Aiden's ex."

Lutz nodded. "We've dealt with Bartelone before."

Jesus. He had a talent for finding men with issues. Thank God Aiden didn't have tons of them. "Can I see Aiden?"

Jordan and Aiden walked over to Matt and Detective Lutz.

Matt didn't think twice. He threw his arms around Aiden. He had to see the man he loved and know he was safe. "Aiden."

"I just needed a rim job," Aiden mumbled. He met Matt's gaze and sobbed softly. "If I hadn't hit the curb, then would this have happened?"

"I don't know." He held Aiden tight and kissed his lover's temple. "They were going to do something no matter what."

Jordan put one hand on Aiden and the other on Matt. "I'm glad you're both okay."

Matt nodded. He had Aiden. The rest would work out and nothing else mattered. "I'll take him to the hospital to be examined."

"I'm fine," Aiden whispered. "They didn't hurt me."

Jordan rested his hands on his hips. "Tell me about Bartelone. Was there a history of violence?"

"Yeah." He refused to let go of Aiden. "Nothing major, though. He broke plates and liked to shoot guns, but he never abused me. He swore he'd do anything to get me back, but I ignored him because he left me first."

"You were using when you were with him, weren't you?" Jordan asked. "I'm trying to get a better picture of what happened."

Aiden tensed but didn't pull away.

He hadn't wanted to discuss this, but fuck it. "I was. When I went to rehab, I dropped him. We had very little contact until last night at the club." A shiver ran the length of his spine as he thought about his ex and the white sheet on the grass. "What happened to them?"

Jordan didn't speak at first. He rubbed his forehead. "Emmett Luck was transported, but Bartelone wasn't." He averted his gaze. "Both have gunshot wounds."

Matt wobbled again. The sheet covered Theo. Had to. "Oh my God." He clutched Aiden tighter. He'd thought he'd been in love with Theo long ago, and knowing he was dead bothered Matt, but not as much as the possibility of losing Aiden.

"Luck wasn't in the system, oddly enough. We matched Luck's fingerprints with the ones lifted from your desk and the lock box as well as the recovered keys to the cars from the lot." Jordan folded his arms. "I'm sorry."

He'd been right. Lucky—Emmett Luck had been the one who'd robbed him. *Holy shit.* He frowned. "Wait. Lucky's name is Emmett?" He hadn't pictured Lucky as being an Emmett. Maybe an Oliver or a Jon, but not Emmett.

"Yeah," Aiden said. "Emmett Earl Luck. The name didn't fit him, and he hated it."

"Matt...that bothered you?" Jordan asked. "Really?"

"No, it just struck me as odd." He shook his head. "Why would he do it? What'd I do to him? What'd Aiden do?" He wriggled his frozen toes. Putting on the shoes would've been a lot smarter than standing there freezing. The air wasn't bad for late October, but chilly enough.

"I'm not sure. I would've liked to have asked him." Jordan widened his stance. "Andrew said he'd slipped out of consciousness and it didn't look good. The initial findings show that Luck shot Bartelone. We couldn't get a clean shot to stop them, and I'm sorry."

Matt's blood ran cold and he gripped Aiden. If he wasn't careful, he'd really hurt him. "Holy fucking balls."

Aiden shivered and buried his face against Matt's neck.

Jordan rubbed Aiden's shoulders. "I'm sorry. Really."

"Thanks." Matt kissed Aiden's temple. Holy shit, they'd been through so much. "I want to take Aiden home."

"Sure, I'll have them released. I'll give you a ride to your place?" Jordan nodded once, then held up his hand. "Or where?"

"The hospital to get Aiden's car, then my place. Long story." Matt debated not telling the truth but did anyway. He didn't want to look like he'd held anything back.

"Okay," Jordan said. "Give me a few minutes." He strode away, leaving Aiden and Matt in silence.

"We're going home," Matt declared. *Yeah, home to a warm shower and time together in bed.* They didn't have to fuck. He mostly wanted to hold Aiden to prove they were okay and the danger was gone.

"Where?" Aiden asked. "Mine's in splinters. Yours is yours."

"Babe." He cupped Aiden's jaw. "The house is mine, but I'm sharing. If I've learned anything from this, it's that nothing is guaranteed. I love you and I'm not willing to let you go. I want to protect you, love you and everything else. You're a strong man, but I want to be strong together. I want to be your support."

"Matt." Aiden didn't seem convinced.

He'd have to work harder to explain. Fine. He didn't care. "I've never been more sure of anything in my life. Between me kicking my addictions, coming back after the shooting, your father's health issues and now this, I don't want to waste another minute. Live with me." He rested his forehead against Aiden's and enfolded Aiden in his arms. "I see the wheels turning in your mind. You're scared. I am too, but we can do this. It's right."

"But Theo is dead and Lucky's all messed up...because of us," Aiden whispered. "He might as well be dead too."

"Don't think like that." He caressed the hairs at the base of Aiden's skull. "What happened would've happened with or without us. Those two had the idea already. Theo could be dangerous. He liked guns and threatening people. If it wasn't us, then someone else would've been the reason. You did nothing wrong. I'm sure."

Aiden sobbed against Matt's shoulder again. He shivered and clutched Matt's shirt.

Matt held him and wished he could take Aiden's hurt away. They'd been through so much, but none of the past mattered. As long as he had his Doc, he'd be fine and Matt would be the support Aiden needed.

"I'll give you a ride. Here are your phones and keys." Jordan stopped beside Matt. "I'm so sorry." When Aiden turned around but stayed in Matt's arms, Jordan continued. He spoke to Aiden. "Your home will be secured once it's processed."

"Thanks." Aiden sighed. He wiped his cheeks. "I appreciate it."

"Yes, thank you." Matt kept Aiden beside him. "Let's go home."

Aiden nodded.

Matt wasn't reassured by Aiden's responses, but he wasn't about to tell him otherwise. With a little separation from the scene, Aiden could understand. No matter what, Matt would be beside him so they could heal together.

* * * *

Forty minutes later, Aiden stepped into the bedroom and collapsed naked onto Matt's bed. He had too much to figure out. *Holy shit.* His brain hurt. His townhome, one of the few things he'd put money into, was in shambles. Lucky, the man he'd once thought he'd loved was in the hospital, dealing with gunshot wounds. He knew the truth—Lucky hadn't loved anyone but himself. He suffered from misplaced devotion and other issues Aiden didn't understand.

He couldn't comprehend what had gone wrong between Matt and Theo, but Theo was gone. The guy had seemed to delight in causing problems, but trying to kill people? *Jesus.*

Then there was Matt. Matt loved him and wanted him to live at his house. He should be thankful and thrilled. Part of him was, but the rest of him was scared. He hadn't wrapped his head around anything that had happened in the last few hours, but he knew he held Matt's heart in his hands. Until a few hours ago, he'd had the perfect life with Matt. Now? Things were…messy.

He sighed. He'd called his father and reassured Len he was fine. Everyone at the hospital had been told about the incident and the phone had dinged so many times it was nearly dead. He turned the ringer off. Yes, his friends wanted to check on him, but he needed silence and time to decompress.

"Hey." Matt stretched out beside him. "How are you holding up?"

"I'm alive." He faced Matt. "That's something." Hell, it was everything.

"It is."

Aiden grasped Matt's hand. "I'm scared." He wasn't sure he'd be able to vocalize his feelings, but Matt made confessing easier.

"About?"

"I've always faced stuff head-on. Give me a problem, and I'll find a solution." Aiden sucked in a ragged breath, then exhaled. "I can't fix this. I can't go back and save them or talk them out of what happened."

"I don't think anything or anyone could've convinced them to take another path." Matt scooted closer and draped his arm across Aiden's hip. His flaccid cock brushed against Aiden's, sending a quick shimmer of heat through Aiden's body. Matt bumped noses with Aiden. "What you can do is learn from the situation. Don't take people for granted. Don't expect to get your way. Speak the words in your heart and love without thinking."

He sounded like a greeting card or motivational poster, but Aiden didn't mind. "You still love me? Even though I come with baggage?"

"Of course."

No hesitation on Matt's part.

"Even after everything?" He had to be sure.

"An argument and stress is nothing. As for baggage, I'm packing my own and it's not small, either. The thing with…Theo and Lucky wasn't your fault or yours to control." Matt flattened his palm on Aiden's hip. "I love you more than anything. No regrets. I'm here for you. You make me a better man and I can't see the future without you in it."

Aiden stared at him. Everything Matt said made sense and he'd waited so long to hear those words, but he still wasn't sure he could believe his ears. "It's going to take some time to get beyond this."

"I'd imagine so. I haven't wrapped my head around what happened, either. Christ, I still don't believe it and I was there," Matt said. "But it's over. No one will hurt you. I promise."

"You can't promise that." He knew better. Matt couldn't be everywhere he was and stand guard all the time. But he appreciated the sentiment in Matt's words. "If you're where I am, then you'll never get your work done." He slid his hand along Matt's chest. "But I love knowing I'm not alone and you've got my back. You're very special to me."

"I love you." Matt kissed him and draped the blankets over their bodies. "So much."

For the first time since the shooting, he felt normal. Aiden wiggled tight to Matt's chest. "Do you still mean what you said about me living here?" He couldn't see any reason they shouldn't be together. They'd been through the fire in so many ways. If Matt could stand beside him this long, then they could go the distance.

"I do."

Then there was no point in arguing against fate. "Then I'm all yours. I love you, Matt Phillips."

"Love you, Doc Cedarwood."

Aiden closed his eyes. Life wasn't guaranteed. Things could change tomorrow, but he had right now with Matt. They shared a love he'd never thought was possible but had always wanted. He'd embrace everything coming their way and keep moving forward because he had Matt beside him. It wasn't how he'd envisioned the day starting, but it was a good way to continue.

Chapter Fourteen

Six weeks later

Matt shrugged into the long-sleeved shirt and checked his look in the rearview mirror. He needed a haircut. The spikes were longer than he preferred and brushed against the roof of the vehicle. He wasn't thrilled with the style, but Aiden said it was hot, so he'd leave it alone. Three or four silver strands shimmered in among the black. *Well, fuck.* He hoped Aiden wasn't against being with a salt-and-pepper man.

He turned his attention to the community center. Not long ago, he'd gone there on his and Aiden's unofficial first date. He'd been so unsure back then and worried. Now? He and Aiden were very much together and the uncertainty had evaporated. The weeks after the shooting and closing of the robbery case had helped him and Aiden heal. He thanked God they'd gone through all of it together.

Before, he would've dealt with his anger and frustration over the situation by getting yet another tattoo or having something else pierced. The urge to do so wasn't as strong. It overcame him from time to time, but he had Aiden there. Sure, Aiden still worked long hours, but he'd scaled back a bit. He also made sure the hours he spent with Matt were quality. They argued every so often and had moments when they didn't like each other much, but the love never left. When he looked into Aiden's eyes, he saw and felt love—something he'd never felt so deeply before.

He shifted in his seat and tugged the keys from the ignition. The pre-Christmas party should've started by now. Aiden had said he'd be late since his shift wasn't over until five-thirty. Matt hoped Aiden would show up in his scrubs. Aiden looked so cute in the awful green garb and sweet when he apologized for things he couldn't control.

Matt left the car and pressed the fob to engage the locks. He shut the door and, when he turned around, Colt was waiting in front of the community center.

"You made it," Colt said. "And mostly on time."

"I try." He stuffed his keys into his pants pocket and ambled up to Colt. "I'm glad you're here. I haven't seen you in a while."

"It's been busy. Speaking of seeing, I haven't seen you in forever, either. I have been so worried." Colt offered his hand. "In all seriousness, how are you? Ashley asked me about you the other day. You look good. There's color in your cheeks and you've got that irritating tan going on. I've always been jealous of your ability to have a tan in the winter. Have you been working out?"

"I'm running again." *Good Lord.* He shook hands with his friend. Does Colt have a hundred questions or what? Matt shook his head. At least he could keep up.

"Aiden and I run out at the metro park. We've met up with Bobby, Remy and the kids a few times. His boy looks good on the track. Is he winning at the cross-country meets?"

"Chris? Yeah, he made it to state this year." Colt tipped his head. "You dodged my unspoken question. Are you still clean? Sober?"

"I'm not using and I haven't had a drink in years. I did visit Bix at Tattooz, but not for the reason you think. I'm in a good place. Aiden makes me happy." He beamed. "We moved in together. It happened a tad quicker than we'd planned, but it was out of necessity. I'm glad. Having him at the house has been great in so many ways. He balances me out."

"I'm impressed. I didn't think you'd pull yourself up."

"No?" He wouldn't hide his mild irritation. Colt hadn't believed in him as much as he'd thought? *What an ass.*

"You were low and after Theo's… I just wasn't sure you'd come back from it." Colt folded his arms and widened his stance. "Some people wouldn't have."

"I've got a good reason to be where I am." He chuckled. He understood Colt's line of reasoning and couldn't blame him for it. "I probably wouldn't be in the depths of addiction without Aiden, but he helps. Like I said. He's my balance. We've even discussed getting a dog. There's this adorable mixed breed down at the shelter. We're supposed to go down there tomorrow to check him out, but I know we're taking him home."

"I believe it." Colt laughed and the sound bounced off the façade of the center. "Congrats. You're still evolving, but you've made tons of progress. Great job."

"Thanks." Matt shook his head. Colt had such a unique way of giving compliments. He hadn't thought Colt would be proud of him...not ever. Colt never showed his pride. He only displayed irritation. "Why were you so angry with me? No matter how many steps forward I took, you always seemed to disapprove."

Colt crooked his eyebrow. He didn't speak.

So he'd been right. No matter what, Colt wasn't thrilled with him. "Okay. Never mind." One of these days he'd measure up.

"Tough love." Colt sighed. "I knew you had it in you to pull yourself up, but I wasn't sure you'd do it. I figured if I kept on your ass, you'd either crack and start using again or follow through with your sobriety."

"Right, because riding my ass worked so well." He had to hand it to Colt for sticking with him, though. "But why weren't you available more often? You'd ghost me." Talk about annoying. He'd need his sponsor and Colt would be harder than hell to find.

"Not by choice, but I'm still sorry for it. Life got in the way. The incident with the Coalition, meeting Ash and starting a life with him and Wyatt... I fell down on the job. I'm a horrible sponsor, but I never didn't think about you."

"You did the best you could with what you had." He understood that saying so well now. What was someone's best was considered another man's subpar performance. Everyone had to be measured on their own merit. "If you'd been on me every day, I probably would've started drinking to escape. My coping mechanisms weren't always the greatest."

"I believe it. When I'm hardcore...I'm rough," Colt said.

"But you care. I appreciate it. Thank you." He clapped Colt's shoulder. "We should go in. If Aiden made it, he'll wonder where I'm at."

"He knows. I told him I wanted to talk to you." Colt relaxed a little and unfolded his arms. "I owe you a couple of coins. You earned them. You're up to, what…three years sober?"

"I am, but I'm not worried about the coins or getting to meetings right now. I know I can stay clean." He had once needed the sobriety coins to remind himself of what he'd accomplished. Now? He could live without them. He knew the road he'd been on and how he wanted to conduct himself.

"Fair enough." Colt nodded to the doors. "Let's go in."

"Good job stalling." Matt twisted the knob. If Colt wanted to speak with him and chattered for so long, then there must be something else going on. "What's the surprise?"

"Wow. Gee. I'm not that shady," Colt said. "I don't lie well."

"Uh-huh. I remember the surprise wedding in your backyard. You telegraphed pretty much everything. The only one who didn't know was Ashley." He went into the community center first. He'd thought he was the one with the surprise… The farther into the room he ventured, the more he realized there wasn't a shock involved. Nothing seemed out of the ordinary for a Christmas party.

Colored lights had been strung across the drop ceiling. Ropes of tinsel were draped around the door frames. Foot-tall Christmas trees decorated each of the round tables and a gigantic inflatable Santa stood in the corner of the main room. Boxes had been heaped under a lopsided Christmas tree next to Santa. Kids sat happily eating at the tables and some of the adults milled about. Aiden stood with Colin and Jordan by the serving tables. He still wore his green scrubs. When Aiden glanced back in Matt's direction, Matt noticed the dark circles under Aiden's eyes. The poor guy looked tired, but Matt didn't care. To him, Aiden was sexy as fuck. He'd just seen Aiden that morning before they'd left for their respective jobs, but still.

He rushed across the room to Aiden. When he reached his lover, he wound his arms around Aiden from behind.

"Hi, you." Aiden tipped his head back and rested it against Matt's shoulder. "I thought you'd gotten lost."

"Nah, I was just held up." The moment he'd said the words, he realized how wrong he'd sounded.

"What?" Aiden whipped around. His eyes widened. "What happened?"

"Matt?" Jordan stared at him. "I haven't heard anything."

"I…I meant I was talking to Colt. He stalled me." He tapped Aiden's jaw, causing him to close his mouth. "Have you eaten?"

"No." Aiden sighed. "You had me worried."

"I know and I'm sorry." He grasped Aiden's hand. Part of him wanted to spill his surprise now, but the rest of him decided to wait until the right time. He turned his attention to Jordan and Colin. "Sorry. Word choice isn't my forte."

"Hey, we all mess up." Colin put both hands up. "Excuse me. I need to peel Gage away from the girls. That boy will be the death of me."

Jordan snorted. "Yes, because you weren't hormonal at thirteen or anything." He rolled his eyes then followed Colin as he walked away.

Matt chuckled again. That was what he'd wanted from the start—a love like Jordan and Colin shared. Give and take. Push and pull, but always coming together at the end because love won out. He had such a thing with Aiden and he regretted nothing.

"I'm whipped. We had two car accidents, three kids from the school. Each one had fallen off the jungle gym. I've sewn up three chins today." Aiden rubbed his forehead. "One poor kid busted his front teeth too."

Matt rubbed the top of Aiden's hand with his thumb. "Sounds rough. Why don't we find a table? So you can get off your feet."

"Thanks." Aiden led him over to the closest empty chairs. "I'm not hungry. The nurses had cake brought in for someone's birthday. I'm not sure whose, because I didn't see the lettering before they hacked off pieces. Just seeing the gobs of frosting and smelling the sweetness churned my stomach."

"You're not pregnant, are you?" Matt asked. He snorted. "I'm kidding. I'm not much of a cake guy, either."

"I like cake, but there was so much." Aiden leaned against Matt and rested his head on Matt's shoulder. "I wanted to change, too, but I was running so late."

"Why? Did you have a last-minute patient?"

"No. Dad called around noon. He wanted to visit, so I invited him to the party. I was late because I had to talk him down. I guess he and Ross had a falling out. Ross went to Pittsburg, and Dad's coming here." Aiden patted Matt's thigh. "Don't ask. I don't understand it

Megan Slayer

all, but I'm guessing we'll get an earful once we go home."

"He's probably dying to see the house," Matt said. "He hasn't come over since we moved in together."

"True."

Matt sucked in a ragged breath, then exhaled. There was no time like the present to spill his guts. "Sit up. I want to talk to you."

"Am I in trouble?" Aiden did as asked and faced Matt. "If I did it, I'm sorry. If not, I'll do it later."

"No." He shrugged the long-sleeved shirt down a little, then paused. "Remember how I told you I wasn't getting any more tattoos?"

"You got another one?" Aiden's eyebrows knotted together. "A skull? Dagger?"

"Your name." He turned around and lowered his shirt. "See?" He held his breath. The tattoo wasn't going away, but he wanted Aiden to appreciate his gesture. He gasped and tried to settle. "What do you think?"

"You've got my name on the back of your neck," Aiden said. "Like a 'property of' tag."

He nodded. That hadn't been the idea, but it worked. "My shirt will hide the tat, so if we go out, I'll still look polished." He faced Aiden again and adjusted the garment. "I'm your property, though."

"No. You're your own man." Aiden grasped both of Matt's hands. "I've never seen my name in calligraphic letters on someone's skin."

"I hope I'm the only one who has that ink." He scooted closer to Aiden. "I belong to you. My heart, soul and now body. It's all yours and I wanted the world to know."

"They do." Aiden toyed with the wrinkles in Matt's shirt. "I didn't think you'd actually do it—put my name on your body—but I can't say I'm upset. It's sexy."

"I was worried you'd be angry." He sounded silly, and now that he'd said the words out loud, he couldn't take them back. "It's very permanent and official." *Not helping my case much.*

"Very true," Aiden said. "I'm not sure why you didn't think I'd be happy. First, it's your body. You can do whatever you want with it. Second, it's a pretty tattoo. Bix did a great job—I assume he's the one who did it. The ink looks like I wrote it on your skin."

"That's the idea." He'd only seen the reverse image in the mirror, but the tattoo looked right.

"It's cool. Which leads me to my third point. If you care about me enough to have me live with you, to get a dog—which we are, because I can't let that pup stay at the shelter for much longer—and to put my name on your body, then this love must be real and special. I'm glad I'm not the only one who feels the way I do."

"So you're saying you like it?" He sounded redundant, but he needed to know this was real. *Goddamn low self-esteem.* He'd thought he'd gotten beyond this.

"I do." Aiden laughed. "Remember what I just said. Dad's here."

Confusion clouded his thoughts. *What do the words 'I do' have to do with Len?* When Aiden stood, Matt did as well. He offered his hand to Aiden's father. Aiden hugged him.

"I'm so glad you made it." Aiden hugged Len again. "How is Ross?"

"Leaving." Len threw his arms around Matt. "Nice to see you."

"Wait, he's gone?" Aiden asked. "This wasn't just a fight?"

Len grabbed a chair and sat with Aiden and Matt. "No, I found the messages he sent you and your responses. Nothing you said was bad. I don't know where he made the leap from being cordial to acting like an ass, but I would've been pissed if I were you. I'm sorry, kid. He had no right to say and text those things."

"We all have to learn on our own." Aiden shrugged, but Matt noticed the relief in his eyes.

"I didn't have the use of my phone when I got out of the hospital. He took it. I was so mad. I looked forward to our weekly phone calls and he knew that." Len shook his head. "He expected me to choose him over you. I'm sorry, but I can't—not after he'd been so underhanded."

Matt rested his hands on his knees. He wasn't sure what to say or add to the conversation. He felt like he'd intruded on a private moment.

"It's fine. I'm happier since he left. I'm not worrying about what I've missed or if I'm not going to be told about you." Len leaned back in his chair. "So what's this big news?"

Big news? Matt wished he knew what it was too. "Doc?" His hands shook. "What's your news?" He'd tried to sound nonchalant but failed.

Aiden scooted his chair back and sat up straighter. The smile lit up his face. "My rotation in the ER is up. I've been asked to stay in the ER, but I've also been invited to join a private practice as a family physician. The new job would be better hours and steadier."

Matt stared at him. *Not an ER doc? Family practice...* He should be excited. He wanted better for Aiden.

Easier hours and more time together should be exactly what would be best. But he had virtually no say in the situation. He didn't have a right to add his two cents, but still. He wished Aiden would've said something before now.

"That's fantastic, kid." Len clapped Aiden on the shoulder. "You've been talking about leaving the ER for a while."

How come I didn't know that?

"What are you going to do?" Len asked. "Where's the practice?"

"In Liverpool." Aiden's grin widened.

An hour away? Matt's heart dropped along with his spirits. His stomach hurt. The hours were going to get shorter. Aiden would probably want to move. Matt wasn't considering moving. He loved his house. He gripped the edge of the table to settle himself down. For all he knew, he'd mentally flipped out for no reason.

"Matt?" Aiden slid Matt's hand into his. "You look a little flushed."

"I'm processing," Matt admitted. He couldn't wrap his head around what he'd just been told.

"I thought you might be." Aiden rested his arm on the back of Matt's chair. "Here's the thing. Liverpool is a great place. I'd be one of six doctors in the building and able to make my own hours."

"Sounds great." He couldn't hide his disappointment. He'd thought they had a good life in Cedarwood. Aiden seemed so happy and ready to go elsewhere. Could they make a long-distance relationship work? *Jesus.* He'd tattooed Aiden's name onto his body. How foolish could he be? What was the old joke — get a tattoo with your partner's name and you're asking for a break-up. He'd practically guaranteed Aiden would go.

"Well." Aiden faced Matt. "Babe?"

"Yeah." He sighed. "So when do you start?" He might as well know. "Are you staying in Cedarwood or going to get a place closer?"

"You've got me all but moved out, don't you?" Aiden chuckled. "Wow."

"It's coming," Matt said. *Time to level with him.* "I feel it. I've told you. Good things in my life don't last. Call it negativity or pessimism...I don't care. I know how this will play out. I'm not leaving Cedarwood. I've got my business here and a nice house. You'll want to go closer to your job." He shook his head and fought the urge to hop to his feet. "We'll start out as a long-distance situation then you'll spend more time there than here. After a while, you'll be there so much you'll get lonely. It's human nature to want company around and you'll figure out you're happier with the company than with me. I'll be a problem. You'll dump me and ride off into the sunset with Mr. Doctor Wonderful." He'd overthought the whole situation, but after coming clean with everything else, he believed in being up front with his feelings and worries.

"Wow. Okay." Aiden fully faced Matt, and their knees bumped. "Before you make any more snap decisions, hear me out. I mean really hear me. I'd love to have my own practice. I'd love to set my own hours and know what's on the schedule for the day. I'd love it more than I can say." He placed his hand over Matt's mouth. "But...I love the ER. There's an excitement in not knowing who or what will come through the door. Yes, it weighs on me. I'm ragged and tired, but I love it—not the ragged part, but the ER one."

Matt's heart beat overtime. He didn't understand. "Then what do you want to do?" He could hope all day long, but reality had a way of kicking his ass.

"I had this ten-year goal. Dad knows all about it. I'd do my time in the ER, move to a different wing and go back to geriatric medicine like I'd done in med school. I'd meet a guy, settle down in Cedarwood and adopt a kid. Then Liverpool General called." Aiden squeezed Matt's fingers. "It's a lot to take in."

The surprise was killing him. Matt balled his hands. He couldn't speak—not when he thought his life was falling apart again.

"My plan changed," Aiden said, his voice low.

That was the big news, then. Aiden would be going to Liverpool. Matt gritted his teeth. He should've known.

"You're not listening." Aiden grabbed both of Matt's curled-up hands. "You see, I met this great guy. He helped me to see this world in a more colorful way. He fixes things and gives the best rim jobs ever. He's solid and trustworthy. Did I mention sexy? He's that too. He came and saved me when I didn't know I needed rescuing. He showed me how to open my heart again."

He couldn't be hearing Aiden right. Things sounded too good. "But?"

"But what?" Aiden frowned. "I'm lost."

He'd had enough of the suspense. "What are you going to do? What are these big plans?"

Aiden chuckled. "I'm going to stay in the ER until a position up in the geriatric wing is free. I want to get back to what I went to med school for."

"So you're not leaving?" A lump formed in Matt's throat. "Right?"

"How can we rescue a dog if I'm leaving? I thought when I said we were getting Louis, that pretty much said I'm staying." Aiden laughed and shook his head. "You're a silly man."

"But you said you loved private practice." He didn't understand.

"I would have done, but not now," Aiden said.

"I'm confused." Nothing made sense to Matt.

"I'm not," Len said. "He's staying put."

"Exactly. The big news I told Dad about was us moving in together, getting a dog and this." Aiden pulled a small box from his pocket. He dropped to one knee in front of Matt. "I know it's quick, but I can't see my life without you. You make me so happy, want to rip my hair out, and feel so safe. You've even got my name on your body. I want to make an honest man out of you. Will you marry me?"

"Aiden?" This couldn't be real.

"What do you think?" Aiden asked. "We don't have to have the wedding right away. But I do want everyone to know I've got the special-est mechanic in the whole world." He held up the ring. "Yes? No? Matt?"

His mouth refused to cooperate with the words he wanted to say. Matt squeezed Aiden's leg. Man, he wished he had a mental link with Aiden.

Aiden grinned and leaned forward. "I'm so glad I didn't get everyone's attention first. I might be let down and I don't want a room full of people seeing that." He toyed with the ring, then closed the box. "The offer is good for the duration."

"Yes." Thank God he'd found his voice. "Doc? Yes." He kissed Aiden hard on the lips. "You stunned me." Shocked, flummoxed and blew his mind. His hands trembled, he wanted to run around the room whooping and hollering, and the lump dissipated in his throat.

"Me? I did that?" Aiden's eyebrows rose.

"Yeah, I thought I had the big news." *Married...* The word sounded so sweet. Matt blew out a long breath to calm himself. "It's not all about me, but I thought this was huge."

"It's a big damn deal." Len stood. His laugh rang out around the room. "I'm getting pie. This moment needs pie." He strolled away, leaving Matt and Aiden alone.

"That's my dad." Aiden smoothed his palm across the back of Matt's head, just above the ink. "A tattoo is a huge deal. It's a pretty big leap of faith and I like it."

"It's your handwriting," he said.

"I know."

"I did it so you'd know I'm not going to change my mind." He offered his left hand. "I will marry you." Now he understood why Aiden wanted him to remember the words 'I do'. God, he was so messed up. "I'll marry you today, tomorrow or whenever."

"Perfect." Aiden slid the ring onto Matt's finger. "I mean, Louis does need both parents and maybe a brother or sister."

"You weren't kidding about adopting — but another dog or a kid?" Now that he thought about the idea of not only getting a dog, but also becoming a parent with Aiden to a child, he liked it.

"I'd feel a little more credibility being part of the support group if I had a kid, yes. Maybe not right now, but I'd like to adopt." Aiden shrugged. "It's not something I'd go into lightly."

"I agree — with everything." He kissed Aiden again. The word *husband* sounded so nice and perfect. "I love it and you."

Aiden curled his fingers under Matt's chin. "I love you too." He sighed. "Dad is staying over tonight, so any celebrations you and I might do will have to wait until tomorrow, but when we can, we're hitting it hard."

"Nice." Matt bumped noses with Aiden. "Why don't you get your dad and we'll head home? We can have a movie night and order pizza. Maybe binge on Christmas movies or something corny like that? Then tomorrow morning, we bust Louis out."

"And see if he's got a best friend?" Aiden nodded. "I'm not due back to the hospital until Sunday afternoon."

Matt laughed until his chest ached. His heart lightened and his soul was at ease. Nothing could be better except for maybe having a night of sex with Aiden, but he'd wait until the next evening for that. They'd fuck until they couldn't walk straight. "I can't tell you no. Yeah, we bring him and a friend home."

"Then let's go, fiancé."

Matt loved how that word sounded and that it now applied to him and Aiden. "Best idea ever." He held Aiden's hand as they strolled through the community center. Colin winked and Jordan applauded. Matt's cheeks burned, but not out of embarrassment. Pride welled in his heart and mind. He loved being in public with Aiden. He noticed Colt. His sponsor nodded once then gave him the thumbs-up. Was he in on the story too? Matt wondered, but he also couldn't believe what he'd seen. He'd finally made Colt proud. *Nice.*

Matt stared at the ring while he waited for Aiden and Len. He'd never thought he'd be so lucky to get the guy. Now he had Aiden and so much more. *Thank God for the ridiculously high curb.* He'd fixed plenty of bent rims in his time, but every time he thought of rim jobs, he'd think of Aiden. The wrecked car had been the most unexpected but oddly perfect way to meet his very own Doc Cedarwood, and now they had forever to be together. *Best wreck ever.*

Want to see more from this author? Here's a taster for you to enjoy!

Cedarwood Pride: Finding Forever in Cedarwood
Megan Slayer

Excerpt

"You want me to do what?" Liam Blackwell rolled his eyes and squeezed his phone. "Pat, I don't know the first thing about small towns." *Christ.* How could his agent think he'd be right for the part of a farmer in Ohio or that he knew a damn thing about farming? He'd never been on a farm. If she were there in the same room, rather than on the phone, he could explain better.

"I knew when you did that audition for the superhero movie that you were a candidate for this film. I sent the producers and talent scout that audition and that's what got you the job. The director asked for you by name," Patricia Michaels said. "Just do it. It's a starring role, great pay and you get a percentage of the residuals. Why turn that down? You can get experience with this director."

"How?" He tamped down his irritation. He needed the money. He had a lifestyle to maintain. He was still trying to get his last girlfriend to keep quiet about his sexuality. He wasn't ready to come out. How was he supposed to play convincing leading roles in rom-coms if no one believed he was attracted to the heroine and not the other hero?

"Don't you have a ballplayer friend? Tanner Fox, right? He lives in Cedarwood, Ohio. The last time I checked, it's a sweet little town. They have quirks, but you might get the experience you need if you live there for six months. Call Tanner and get info about the town, then accept the damn role."

Well, fuck. "I'll call Tanner." He groaned. "And I'll take the role." He massaged his temple. He had few options. The last time he'd worked had been over a year before. "I read the script. It's not the kind of role I like. It's simple."

"Of course it is. He's a farmer. He's not a tortured artist or playwright. Jesus. You need a winner and this film is it," Pat said. "I've never steered you wrong before. The studio and the director want you. No one else."

"I'll do my best." He sank onto the bar stool. "You'll send me the extra details, right? Like anything about Cedarwood?"

"On the way. Call Tanner." She hung up, leaving him in silence.

Liam tossed his phone onto the bar and grumbled. *A freaking small-town movie. God help me to not bomb.*

His phone rang. *Patricia.* He should answer, but she'd hung up on him. He wasn't in the mood to have his ass chewed again. He hated to be pushed, even if he deserved it. He waited until the ringing stopped before he retrieved the device.

A notification appeared on the screen. One voicemail.

He tapped the screen and retrieved the message from his agent. "Get your butt in gear. I sent the details in an email and I've got the contracts on my desk. You'll report to the set in Washington in November. Now call Tanner and stop dicking around."

He frowned. She wasn't about to let up. November. He had until November…that was barely enough time to prepare for the role, let alone understand the small-town situation. He dialed Tanner's number. There was no guarantee Tanner would answer. He'd seen a press release saying Tanner had married a doctor. There might have been a kid involved, but he wasn't sure and didn't remember.

After four rings, the call connected. "Hello, Liam. How are you?"

"Tanner," Liam said. "I'm good. How's life treating you?"

"Fantastic. I'll resume my role with the local team as the assistant coach. Our son is starting the first grade and Dane and I are solid. I'm living the dream. What about you?"

"You have no regrets that you're not in the major league?" He'd have been crushed to not be a star. He loved the spotlight. *Doesn't Tanner love it, too?*

"I thought I would, but I'm good where I am. It's funny. I never thought I'd like Cedarwood. It's a small town. It's quiet — save for the Coalition — but even they've slowed down their assaults. Why? Are you thinking of leaving show business?"

"Not really. I love the excitement."

"Understandable. You love attention."

"I do." He chuckled. "I live for the spotlight."

"I know," Tanner said. "So what? We haven't talked in ages. I'd ask you want you want because you never call just to talk. Look, I can't set you up with anyone because I don't know who to ask."

"Huh? No." His irritation showed up again. Why couldn't Pat get him in with the right people in Cedarwood? She liked to convince people to fall into line. "I'm interested in visiting Cedarwood."

"You are? Who is she?"

"No one," Liam said. "I'm researching a role. I'm playing a guy who has a farm. A girl ends up stranded on the road in front of my farm and walks back to the house to get help. I take her in since it's a stormy night. I think it involves snow. Anyway, it's sweet and schlocky, but it's a job. It should lead to something meatier the next time around." *I hope.* "I called because I wanted to know if you knew the right place to stay when I come to town. Like a house for rent or something?"

"I do. We have a friend who has a duplex. You could rent half of the house. It's in town, but it'll give you a feel for Cedarwood," Tanner said.

"Fine. When I fly in, I'll find you."

"How about I send you the information? You can set it all up and do what you want, rather than depending on me," Tanner said. "I've got a house, man and child to worry about. You're not on that list."

"I know."

"Are you jealous?"

"Maybe a little." Or a lot. He wanted a lover who cared about him, not his movie persona.

"You bastard. You are. Why don't you just come out? You'll be happier."

"No, I won't." He couldn't risk his marketability.

"Why? Because you'll lose out on roles? You know that's shit. If you're half the actor you think you are, then you can play any role, no matter if the character is gay or straight."

He'd once thought that, but not now. "You don't know the business."

"Why not play gay characters? They're in the movies and part of the culture. We're not invisible any longer."

"Visibility is a relative thing." God, he sounded like an asshole.

"I call bullshit."

"Call it all day long, but I'm not asked to play gay characters. I'm a pinup." He rolled his eyes. He hated posing for the cheesecake-type shots, but women wanted to see him in as few clothes as possible. "Do you know my best download is that picture of me stretched out across the hood of that Jeep?"

"Gag."

"Shut up."

"I've seen you at your worst. You're not a pinup, but you're right. You've got a body women want. Hell, I bet men want it, too."

"The fans think I'm hot and I'm not going to argue," he said.

"Fine. I'll send you the info and get you hooked up with the rental car place, but I'm not your guide. You need to experience and figure out Cedarwood for yourself — like everyone else."

Fair enough. "You're an asshole." He didn't have to play the jackass role he'd perfected for the public. He could be nicer.

"No, I'm not letting you walk all over me," Tanner said. "I remember the last time we chatted and you tried to use me."

He hadn't wanted to admit he could be such a jerk, but Tanner was right. "Okay."

"Good." Tanner paused. "You're going to be fine. Be yourself. Most people won't know who the hell you are and that's a good thing. Don't be the movie-star jackass.

Be the nice guy that's buried deep inside you. They'll like you. It'll take a little bit, but they'll come around."

"Thanks, Mr. Greeting Card-slash-Motivational Poster Man. I'll be in touch."

"Just don't be an asshole." Tanner hung up.

Liam stared at the bar top and sighed. Tanner had a point. He could be a self-serving, greedy, needy pain in the ass. He'd let Hollywood and the business run his life. *Ruin my life, more like it.* He doubted he'd be happy in Cedarwood, but if no one knew him, he could be the guy beneath the veneer, like Tanner suggested. He might not be thrilled, but he'd make his time in Cedarwood work. If nothing else, he'd do his best.

PUBLISHING

Sign up for our newsletter and find out about all our
romance book releases, eBook sales and promotions,
sneak peeks and FREE romance books!

About the Author

Megan Slayer, aka Wendi Zwaduk, is a multi-published, award-winning author of more than one-hundred short stories and novels. She's been writing since 2008 and published since 2009. Her stories range from the contemporary and paranormal to LGBTQ and BDSM themes. No matter what the length, her works are always hot, but with a lot of heart. She enjoys giving her characters a second chance at love, no matter what the form. She's been the runner up in the Kink Category at Love Romances Café as well as nominated at the LRC for best author, best contemporary, best ménage and best anthology. Her books have made it to the bestseller lists on Amazon.com.

When she's not writing, Megan spends time with her husband and son as well as three dogs and three cats. She enjoys art, music and racing, but football is her sport of choice.

Megan loves to hear from readers. You can find her contact information, website details and author profile page at https://www.pride-publishing.com